Select Few

BOOK TWO

Select Few

BOOK TWO of THE SELECT

MARIT WEISENBERG

For Astrid and Margot—M.W.

Published by Charlesbridge
85 Main Street
Watertown, MA 02472
(617) 926-0329
www.charlesbridgeteen.com

Library of Congress Cataloging-in-Publication Data available on request
ISBN 9781580898294 (reinforced for library use)
ISBN 9781632897640 (ebook)

Printed in the United States of America
(hc) 10 9 8 7 6 5 4 3 2 1

Display type set in Freeland by Trial by Cupcakes
Text type set in Adobe Garamond Pro
Printed by Berryville Graphics in Berryville, Virginia, USA
Production supervision by Brian G. Walker
Text designed by Susan Mallory Sherman

Nothing in life is to be feared.
It is only to be understood.

—Marie Curie

JUNE

Chapter One

Ten, nine, eight . . .

I focused on the elevator doors, counting down, tapping my foot, impatient to be out of the small space but always afraid of what I might find on the other side.

Three, two, one . . .

The silver doors parted.

Go.

It was a race to see how quickly I could blend in outside my hotel room. I strode through the lobby of the W Austin Hotel, eyes zeroed in on the glass and wood door in the distance.

Keep moving, always keep moving.

It was when I stood still in public that someone might recognize me.

"Have a good afternoon, Miss," the residence concierge called as I passed by. I nodded, then put in my earbuds.

Before I saw them, I sensed the two paparazzi who lay in wait like sentries. An older man and a much younger woman, both of whom I'd seen before. I knew the exact moment they jolted to life at the sight of me. I could feel the intensity of their desire as they followed in my wake, ten feet behind me.

I knew I shouldn't, but I wanted to prevent their interference on today of all days. I swung the heavy exit door open with one hand and let it fall closed behind me, brushing it with the tips of my fingers and sending enough energy through to make a hairline fracture. A spiderweb of cracks slowly spread through the glass. I was out the door, two strides away, when one of my stalkers touched the handle to exit and the glass shattered, sending shards cascading to the floor and leaving the two paparazzi to deal with the debris and attention inside the lobby.

Outside, the muggy, summer city smell hit me, and I started my run. Head down, I cleared the hotel and moved through the downtown streets, feeling my shoulders relax by the second. If there were any photographers, hopefully all they would see was a girl wearing dark running clothes, a baseball hat, and sunglasses.

Suddenly I realized I was happy. I'd really been looking forward to today.

At a stoplight I continued running through the yellow even as pedestrians behind me slowed, not wanting to take chances in the busy traffic. Soon enough I crossed the First Street Bridge to run on the shaded trail that snaked around Lady Bird Lake, its banks lined by thick, green overgrowth. It was cool for mid-June but humid. Since it was midafternoon, the runners had thinned on the trail, but a crowd was on the lake in full sun, paddleboarding and canoeing, the din of their talking and laughing echoing off the water. A few dogs off their leashes splashed at the edges of the lake while their owners stood nearby, chatting.

The very last stretch was so sparsely populated, I let myself go, running uphill in a sudden burst. The faster I ran, the sooner I'd arrive at the house. The cypress and sycamore trees flew past, the muddy ground blurring beneath my feet, the music pounding in my ears. I kept going, running away from all of it. From all the eyes on me. From the ghosts.

I saw someone up ahead with two pit bulls straining on leashes, and I immediately slowed my pace before he noticed my ridiculously fast speed. I leaned my head back, taking in the fresh air and the heat and life outside the walls of my sterile, white apartment. It was Saturday. I hadn't been outside for three days.

Entering the Zilker neighborhood from the trail beneath Barton Springs Road, I passed Barton Springs pool on my right and kept my eyes straight ahead. It had been almost a year since I'd risked exposing my family's secrets to save my sister from drowning in that very pool. My stomach tightened, and I tried not to think about her, my dad, stepmother, and the rest of those radiant, inexplicable creatures that were my extended family.

When I entered the neighborhood, marked by the ranch houses and bungalows, election signs in front yards, and cracked sidewalks I knew well, I slowed to a walk. Only a block away from my destination, I didn't want anyone to see I'd been running in June heat but didn't have a drop of sweat on me. I slowed even more when I noticed the large number of cars parked on both sides of the narrow street. Upon arrival at the curb in front of the Ford house, I was met with a "Happy Graduation" banner that hung on the red-painted front.

The door opened and three girls my age, still in their dresses for their graduation, exited onto the walkway, phones in hand. I could hear sounds of a party coming from the backyard. This wasn't the small family gathering I'd assumed it would be.

The girls glanced in my direction.

"Is that who I think it is?" Though there was distance between us, I could easily hear the brunette with the floral sundress and messy bun murmur incredulously to the other two.

"What, are they back together?"

"No. The world would know."

"Then why is she here?"

This was the reason I hadn't gone to the graduation ceremony earlier in the day. I hated the scrutiny. But I'd reached the mailbox of the Ford's house and turning away would be even worse.

The girls parted in front of the door to make more room for me.

"Hi. Excuse me," I said, trying not to let my self-consciousness show.

I entered the house and carefully removed my sunglasses, tentatively stepping into the small living room. The sectional was piled with boys and a couple of men watching basketball playoffs on the TV. They all glanced up at once. I gave them a tight smile and averted my eyes.

French doors connected the living room to the small kitchen. Beyond it, smoke from the grill billowed past the open back door. From the sound of it, most of the party was outside. Cautiously, trying not to draw extra attention, I walked past the partygoers stationed in the kitchen and took the single stair down into the backyard.

At least forty people were scattered across the rectangular lawn—a collection of teens, their middle-aged parents, and some younger children playing horseshoes under the live oaks near the back fence, likely getting eaten by mosquitos in the damp grass.

My heartbeat picked up when I finally laid eyes on John. He stood on the grass in a group that included his younger brother, Alex, two other friends, and someone's dad in a tie. John briefly turned to kick an errant soccer ball back to the little girls who played behind him. I smiled inadvertently and quickly stepped off to one side of the patio, under the scant shady cover of the eaves so I could watch for a moment unseen.

When we first met, I couldn't acknowledge it, but now I saw that John was beautiful. He wore his almost black hair on the shaggy, sexy side. The brothers looked a lot alike, but John took after their father, more of his Asian heritage apparent with his much darker hair and eyes. Alex was a couple of inches shorter, and I guessed he would have killed to have John's height since they both played tennis. John had the ideal build for the sport he had come to resent: tall, lean, but still muscular.

The graduation ceremony ended hours ago, but John still wore a white button-down, only now with the sleeves rolled and paired with shorts and flip-flops. I recognized the shirt as the one I'd borrowed the first night I ever came to his house. That was the night I told him the truth about my uniquely evolved family, when we ended the night pressed up against each other and the wall of his bedroom, unable to keep our distance.

I was glad John didn't know I was studying him. I was always studying him, making sure nothing had changed—that he hadn't changed—since the last time I'd seen him. Six months ago, John scared me when he told me about a vision he had of where my family was hiding. Visions were something only Novak, my father, could experience.

The night I ran away from home, the same night our entire clan seemingly disappeared off the face of the earth, Novak told me about a prophecy. He said that we would be able to read the mind of an outsider and that person would be essential to our survival. Up until that point, I'd had an idea that he wanted to prove there were more of us—genetically advanced humans—or at least that there were people who might be able to shift to become more like us. But I hadn't known the details.

Novak had no idea that I'd been reading John's mind for months already, ever since I'd been banished to a different school and told not to even think about using any of my abilities. At first, I had been embarrassed by my strange connection to an outsider. Then I found I was strangely and overwhelmingly drawn to John the more I listened in on his thoughts. When I left my family, I took my secret with me.

But nothing out of the ordinary had happened during the time I'd been with John and since the day my family disappeared from Austin. Now I sometimes wondered if John had had a vision at all. He seemed completely himself, a typical eighteen-year-old, and different from the perfect, unearthly kids I'd grown up with. That was part of why I was in love with him.

I saw the soccer ball right before it hit the shoulder of the man in the tie standing next to John. The force of the ball knocked the glass out of the man's hand, and it flew through the air, projecting wine in one long, red arc. John extended his foot toward the flying glass, catching it on top of his flip-flop and shifting its descent from impact with the concrete of the walkway to a soft landing in the grass.

A quick, incredulous cheer erupted from the crowd.

"Nice reflexes," the man in the tie said.

Alex shook his head at his brother. "What are you *doing*? Way to risk your tennis career to save a wine glass."

Was this reaction something for me to worry about?

No, the man was right. It was just good reflexes.

The group still laughed, all except John, whose eyes were now on his father, Taro, who stood at one edge of the party, while another parent stood beside him tapping his glass with a utensil. The people in the yard quieted as they gave their attention to Taro.

In his strong, smooth voice, Taro said, "Thanks, everyone, for coming." He cleared his throat. "They say time flies, but it moves even faster than you think. Suddenly I'm watching my oldest son and his friends graduate from high school. We've known many of you kids for years, and it's been a privilege watching you grow up."

I looked at John, who hated being the center of attention. He tensed in anticipation of what was coming next, a trickle of sweat traveling from his temple down his cheek.

"We also wanted to say—since we don't say it enough—how proud we are of you, John. You've always surprised us. Kathleen and I will never forget when you were eight years old and we thought you and your brother were playing in the backyard. Being the most responsible parents in the world, we didn't foresee that you'd just leave the yard. Much less that you'd lead your brother to the park across the street to watch the kids at a tennis camp. Suddenly we heard a knock on the door, and there was a man holding a racket, with you by his side, asking me if I'd ever seen you hit a tennis ball."

Everyone laughed.

Taro smiled, but then his tone changed and he seemed to speak directly to John. "It hasn't been easy having the schedule you've had. We worried because you always said yes to more practice and more tournaments and never complained. It's taken incredible discipline to keep playing tennis hour after hour the way you have and when there were so many other things you said you wanted to try. When you came home early from Florida, we knew you were ready to quit."

I glanced at John. His face betrayed nothing, which was how I knew Taro's mention of being cut from the tennis academy got under his skin.

"Then, out of nowhere," Taro continued, "it was like you became a different person."

I stood up straighter and adjusted the brim of my hat.

"You got so focused. And that made the difference. You earned your scholarship, and now you're going to college halfway across the country. We'll miss you, but we couldn't be prouder. Happy graduation."

While everyone clapped, John's mother, Kathleen, walked

over to her son and put her arm around him. Taro joined them and pulled John's head close to plant a quick kiss on top.

John must have felt someone watching him and looked up. Our eyes met, and our gazes held. Whenever he turned his full attention on me, my stomach still did a somersault. Alex noticed and gave John a small shove and said, "Go."

"Excuse me," John murmured to his friends and family. *My girlfriend's here.*

I was surprised for a second—I hadn't been able to read his thoughts in months.

He must have remembered that I could read his mind because it went instantly blank, like he erected a wall to block me. John put that defense in place whenever he was with me now. It seemed like a long time since his thoughts had been an open book.

His dad put a hand on John's shoulder, stopping him from escaping. I heard Taro say, "Can you find a chair for your grandmother?" He gestured to the opposite end of the crowded yard.

John gave me a look that said, "I'll be right back." *Damn. More waiting.*

All I wanted was to be with him and now I needed to say good-bye in public while pretending to be just friends. He should have warned me the party was going to be so big.

The clouds had passed in front of the sun and the air felt heavy. While I waited for him, I watched the partying. I'd seen many of the kids from school. I never forgot a face; each one was cataloged in my brain. I kept myself mildly entertained observing a boy and girl who had their backs to one another but whose slight tilt of their heads and the angling of their shoulders gave away the attraction between them.

Still, slowly, as if I were on stage and they were my audience, all eyes began to find me. No matter how I dressed, no matter how I tried to avoid eye contact, I'd learned over time that there was something about me and my family that always attracted people's attention.

Time to move.

"You're Julia Jaynes, right?" A man in a checkered shirt with a heap of straw-colored hair practically jumped in front of me.

"Hi," I said with practiced politeness.

"I recognized you! I'm Louie. I just moved in down the street."

"Ah," was all I could think of to say.

"Any leads on your father?"

"Not that I'm aware of." I tried to take a step back, but the wall of the house was already at my heels.

"What about that kid with the super strength? The one they've tried to explain away. Where's he hiding?" Louie joked, wiping his brow.

When I didn't answer, he said, "I like how you have a watchfulness about you. Do people think you're superhuman too?" Louie laughed.

"That's funny," I said, deflecting.

I searched over Louie's shoulder for John. He was close but blocked by a couple I knew were the Ford's best family friends, visiting from Chicago. They were much like the Ford family—one white parent and one Asian parent. They were extending their congratulations and taking a photo of their daughter, Allie, with John. I was well aware that Allie had been the first girl John had ever had sex with.

"Pardon me," I said brusquely to the neighbor.

"What? Hard to mingle with us plebs? Once there was a time when the rich gave a shit—the Rockefellers, the Carnegies."

Wow. I moved farther away from the guy.

"Here, let me give you my card." Louie had his card at the ready and held it out for me. "I have a real estate venture I know you'd be interested in."

To avoid a scene, I quickly took the card, but he held on to it, pulling it back. I looked up, focusing on him anew.

"You need to put all that money somewhere," he said, almost leering. Then he let go.

In my mind, I shoved him away from me, hard. He stumbled a foot backward onto the grass, almost losing his balance. The look on his face was startled surprise at first. Half a second later, it changed to wariness as he realized that he hadn't felt anyone actually touch him.

I had been ready to intrude on Allie and John, but now I had to move. I walked with my eyes downcast, headed anywhere that was away from this man and the party. Now on a roll, I mentally gave a push to the boy who was clearly thinking about the girl behind him. He bumped into her, and from the corner of my eye, I saw them spin around to face one another as he apologized.

I made my way to the side yard where the lawnmower and trash cans were kept and drew up short when I saw that Alex's boyfriend, August, had had the same idea.

"Augustine," I said by way of greeting.

"Julia Jaynes," he drawled, smiling and giving a nod of his head in acknowledgment. Besides John's family, he was one of the few people who knew that John and I were together. August started to put out the cigarette.

"Don't on my account."

August pulled the pack out of his back pocket and offered one to me. I looked around and then reluctantly took it. The last cigarette I'd smoked had been months ago with the Lost Kids, my private name for the group of boys from my extended family who, like me, had been told not to use their abilities. We'd been a close group, crushed by the rules, banded together out of desperation and rebelliousness. We had all believed Novak's promise that once we moved on to a permanent home, once the Puris' last Relocation was over, we'd all be taught how to use our full abilities. In the meantime, I had been told to tamp down my distinctive traits: my powerfully acute senses, my off-the-charts aptitude in school and sports, the always-right premonitions, the telekinesis. Only the chosen kids, like my sister, had been tutored by the adults without interruption.

Most of us had found ways to cheat. I had most of all. I bowed my head to hover over the lighter that August held for me.

"Or shouldn't I call you that anymore?" he said.

"What?" I straightened and took a big inhale, leaning all my weight against the wall of the house behind me.

August flicked a piece of tobacco from the tip of his tongue. "Alex said you were thinking of changing your name once you moved to California."

"Alex talks a lot."

August laughed. "Well, that's for sure."

"I'm thinking about it." I realized I didn't need to justify myself to August and explain that all I wanted was a fresh start. To fly under the radar and blend in, to be able to go to a party like this one and act my age.

I changed the subject. "You should stop smoking," I said, meaning it and then realizing how obnoxious that sounded.

"What about you?"

How to explain it didn't do anything to me? I was immune to the side effects.

"I should too," was all I said, tugging at the hem of my shorts.

"Nice spread in *Vogue*."

"Ha. *Teen Vogue*, right? Someone showed it to John. Paparazzi photos of me walking down the street?"

"You didn't see it?" August asked, amazed.

"No, I stopped reading all news and magazines," I said more vehemently than I had intended.

August tried to smooth over the moment. "I didn't see it, but I heard about it. 'Street-style icon.' Nice."

"Yeah, since then I've stopped wearing nice clothes as you can see." I gestured to my running clothes.

"Why?"

"The less attention the better, I think." I tipped my chin to the greater beyond where John's parents were hosting his graduation party.

"They're just worried you're going to break his heart again," August said.

I'd meant to be light. I didn't want to know what John's parents really thought of me in case it would hurt.

"There's a better chance he'll break mine," I said seriously. I'd promised myself I would never hurt him again.

"Do you have security here?"

"No. I really didn't want Stuart to come."

"Why?"

"The Fords would think it was weird. They don't like the whole circus."

"I think they get it that you're the richest girl in the world and you need security."

"I'm not the richest girl in the world." I didn't like to talk about it.

"Do you worry about getting kidnapped?" August asked.

"No. Besides, it wouldn't be worth it for any kidnapper. There isn't anyone left to pay my ransom," I joked. It was a little too dark of a thing to say. For a second, August was taken aback. But what was the point of hinting around about it? Everyone at this party knew I was the daughter of a world-famous fugitive.

"Are you glad you stayed behind?" August asked.

No one had asked me that in the six months since my family—an entire group of sixty people—had disappeared off the face of the earth.

"Yes," I finally said. It was the truth. But it had been more difficult than I had thought it would be. I missed my sister, Liv, so much. It was as if she had died.

August kicked at a fire ant pile with the toe of his white tennis shoe. "I can't believe the whole family is leaving for the summer. Do you think Kathleen and Taro planned to be teachers just in case they had tennis prodigies for children? Then they'd be free to take Alex and John to the big tournaments across the United States all summer? It kind of seems too perfect."

"Seriously. It all worked out like it was according to some master plan. Why are you hiding over here by the way?"

"Eh. Their grandma isn't so into me. The black boyfriend."

"I haven't met her yet," I said. "Are you sure she even cares?"

"Maybe, who knows? But Kathleen and Taro and John are all going out of their way to make me feel comfortable. Alex keeps trying to put his arm around me in front of her."

I started laughing. It felt good to socialize. August was my ally since he was also an outsider dating a Ford son.

"It's going to rain," I said, looking up at the sky. I was thinking it would be a good time to leave, before it poured, when I heard the heavy breathing of the neighbor's dog as he barreled up to the fence opposite August and me. He began barking maniacally, sensing I was different, and hurled himself against the weathered wood.

Just then John's mom rounded the corner. August furiously stamped out his cigarette but was still busted. A beat ahead, I made sure my cigarette was already out of sight.

"August, honey. Really?" Kathleen chastised and gave him a quick one-arm hug to take away the sting. "I just came to investigate why this dumb dog is barking. You two are agitating him by standing here, I hate to say it. And I don't especially want our guests hanging out by the trash cans. Come back to the party."

"Yes, ma'am," August said politely.

"Seriously, August, if you smoke, that's on you—you know better. But I don't want my kids smoking."

August glanced at me, confused because Kathleen was singling him out.

God, I didn't even smoke anymore and I'd almost been caught by John's mom the one time I did. I hadn't even felt her coming until the very last second. I'd been working on dulling my hypersensitivities. It had felt necessary during these past few months of intense scrutiny and speculation, but now I was close to making stupid mistakes.

Kathleen left us to return to her guests.

"Damn," August said. "What is it about the Fords that makes me always want to please them?"

"Because they actually care," I said.

I walked partway back to the party with August.

"Group photo!" someone called. "Quick! Before it rains!"

I stopped in my tracks. I had no choice but to leave now.

"Not your thing?" August said.

"No, I'm trying to keep a low profile. You know, stay off social media." I knew how that sounded. Annoying. Self-involved. I wished I could tell him it was John I wanted to keep off the radar. I didn't want *them* to find him.

I hung back as August rejoined the party. From my vantage point, I watched everyone begin to arrange themselves for the photo. I saw a John I wasn't used to seeing—one who had a life completely apart from me. He was surrounded by people who loved him and had helped raise him. Teammates, coaches, friends. From across the yard, our eyes locked.

He had no idea how much I wished I could stay.

I heard one woman whisper to another, "Is that her?"

The rain started coming down hard, and people scrambled

to move inside. In the chaos, it would take a few minutes for John to realize I'd left.

I slipped out of the gate and began jogging home in the rain. When I was far enough away, I texted John: Got a little camera shy—heading home.

I wasn't in any hurry to shut myself back inside the W so I ran lightly, slowly, only half-seeing the lake now emptied of boats.

Thirty minutes later, discouraged and dripping from the rain, I woodenly walked down the long, empty hallway of my floor at the W. Nearing the door to my apartment, I sensed heat behind it. I couldn't help it—a huge smile broke out over my face.

I deftly punched in the lengthy security code that must have been entered just moments before.

Closing the door behind me, I leaned against it, wishing I wasn't so obviously blushing with pleasure.

John stood patiently in the middle of my living room, his phone at his side, looking like he had all the time in the world, like he hadn't just left his own party. The Ford's new dog, Spirit, pranced excitedly by his side.

"Hey," I said, trying for nonchalant, which was impossible because I couldn't stop smiling.

He smiled gently, his voice gravelly when he spoke. "Hey."

Then he cleared his throat and broke eye contact. John looked around the room, cocking his head to one side. "So I heard about a graduation party? At some rich girl's apartment?"

I pushed myself off the door, already holding my arms out. "You came to the right place."

JOHN

I'm just going to silently talk to you for a while so I don't go crazy. I have to take my mind off what's going on. I hope you can hear me, but I don't want you to hear me because it would mean you're nearby. And I want you close, but I don't want you anywhere near this mess.

Thinking back to the beginning of summer, I wish we'd just stayed in your apartment at the W. Why was I always rushing around? I should have appreciated every moment . . .

Chapter Two

"I guess the rain stopped," I said. At the top of this high rise, my sunlit bedroom lived in the clouds. And I was floating, languorously lying with John on my king-size bed, the cool, white sheets half kicked off, forming shadowed hills and valleys.

"It sucks. Sneaking around, rushing." John kissed the side of my neck, just beneath my earlobe.

"It's almost over." I smiled and watched the ceiling fan whir lazily above us. We were so close to making it out of the fishbowl called Austin. He just had his summer competitive tour to get through, and then we'd finally be together in California, where there would be no parents, and I'd be farther from the place that held so many memories of my missing family. California felt like the promised land.

John rolled on his back to button his shirt and then moved onto his side, propped his head on his palm, and looked down at me. We always did this—push the limits of our time together. One minute became five, five became ten, and thirty minutes meant he'd be late to tennis practice or family dinner. Recently, he missed an entire match. John bore the brunt of any consequences, but it didn't ingratiate me to the Fords. He began grazing his fingers over my collarbone, absentmindedly drifting down my arm. I held my breath as he lowered his hand to the hem of my T-shirt. Suddenly his fingers slid underneath and ran up to the side of my ribcage where he knew I was ticklish.

"Stop!" I jerked away, laughing. The white duvet at the foot of the bed slithered like a giant octopus to the floor.

I tried to stop laughing and catch my breath, daring to come near him again. I rested my wrist on his shoulder. "I'm sorry about the party. I was just kind of blindsided by the crowd. I shouldn't have left without saying good-bye. So thank you for coming to me."

"Thank you for having me," John said softly.

We both smiled, still staring at each other after all these months like we couldn't believe that we got to be with the other person.

"I wanted to tell you," I said. "I got an email from Stanford last week that I didn't open. Then, this morning, I got something in the mail. I haven't opened it either. It's next to you in the bedside table. Will you?"

John turned quickly and my arm fell away. He opened the drawer.

"It's big. That's good." He sat up higher in bed, leaned against the headboard, and extracted the first page with the official Stanford letterhead. Watching him closely, I knew when he had read for one second too long and the chance for good news had passed.

John handed me the letter. "It's not no. They just want to meet you face-to-face."

I read it and tried not to display my surprising disappointment that more steps to admittance were required. I'd assumed it was an acceptance packet. Still, I should have been immensely relieved it wasn't a done deal. "Look when it's scheduled. That's Nationals."

"Promise me, you'll at least go to this interview. It's only at the start of Nationals. You can be there for the later rounds."

"I don't know. Stanford or not, I'm still moving to California."

"That's not the same as going to college. With me."

I paused and then decided to be honest. Pulling my knees to my chest, pretending to be concerned with the chipped nail polish on one toe, I admitted, "I'd be scared all the time."

I glanced up to meet John's eyes, and I could see I'd surprised him.

"Haven't you gotten used to the pointing and whispering?" he asked.

"No." I shook my head. "That sucks. It's more than that though. It's too hard to be trying not to . . . to have to always be self-aware if I'm doing or saying something I shouldn't. I know there would be a lot I could learn, but I would spend more of my time hiding myself and my abilities. In addition to everyone knowing I'm loaded."

I thought John wouldn't know what to say and would see my point.

"You already made it through senior year at Austin High. You'll fit in a lot better at a big school where there's more freedom." He grabbed the tall, skinny bottle of water on the bedside table next to him and handed it to me. I'd just been about to ask him for it.

I took the water and unscrewed the plastic cap. "There's more scrutiny now. I've stopped using all my abilities, but I could mess up and do something telekinetic in public, or anticipate something I shouldn't be able to. There's the small stuff that adds up to make people suspicious or it could be one big thing. Some of the Puri tribe went to business school or med school to learn something for the benefit of the whole group, but I don't know how they made it through and now there's no one left to ask. And I seem to have more abilities than the average person in my . . . "

I stopped talking when he gave me a look. With those incredible eyes, he looked deep into mine, making me pay close attention to what he was about to say.

"Don't give up your abilities just because you stayed behind. I know you're scared, but you are the strongest person I know. You broke away from an entire way of life when that was all you knew. You've managed completely on your own. Have faith in yourself."

I smiled, but looked down, blowing off his compliment. "That is such a Ford thing to say. You sound just like your dad giving his toast."

My eye glimpsed something in the open drawer.

John saw it too. After a pause, he reached out and extracted the delicate necklace.

He held it high for both of us to see. A nugget of rough gold hung from a fragile chain.

"You kept it."

"I didn't know what to do with it." I cleared my throat,

wanting to tell him to put it away, but was spellbound. It was original gold carried by my ancestors who'd fled their home in Peru after a genocide. Through all the years of wandering, of hiding their differences, of relocating every twenty years, they'd kept it with them. Loosely translated, our name for ourselves— Chachapuris—meant walkers or those who walk the earth.

We watched the necklace swing like a pendulum, transfixed. The night it had been given to me, I'd been at the height of my abilities. I remembered how good that had felt, however briefly.

"Julia," John said softly.

"What?" I asked, still staring at the necklace, the last trace of my heritage.

The gold suddenly caught a beam of light, and showers of sparkles shot across the stark white walls. As the gold piece slowly twirled, the lights traveled. I held up one arm to catch the lights and watched them play over the back of my hand. My entire body felt illuminated, all my worries briefly banished.

"This is still who you are," John said. I turned to look at him, the lights playing over his cheekbone. "Trust it. You can control it."

I had the feeling of déjà vu, that I recognized this moment, that I had been here before.

I exhaled.

Gently, I took the necklace from him. The room went plain white again.

"That's who I was." I dangled the necklace over the drawer of my bedside table, lowering it gently, then closing it back in the dark. "I have to stop. It's too dangerous to be different."

"It's still a part of you. It's okay to miss them. They're your family."

"I don't."

His phone vibrated on the bed somewhere near my hip. We'd been ignoring his phone that had been blowing up with texts and he'd just missed a call. This time, I picked it up and saw a text from Allie: Where are you?

John glanced at the text before putting his phone face-down on the bed, knowing I'd seen it.

"You need to get back to the party," I said, before he could.

John stayed silent. He had gone completely still and was studying the room intently, like he was searching for something he'd forgotten. The look on his face unnerved me. I couldn't help it. I tried to read his mind. Then, as if he felt me doing it, he came to attention, made his mind go blank, and swung his legs over the side of the bed so quickly it surprised me.

He stood and walked across the room. "You still do *that*."

"How do you . . . I'm sorry. That's the hardest thing to control. It feels as natural as breathing." I saw him look around the room again, unsettled. "What's wrong?"

"I'm good," he said, shaking it off with a joke. "Why don't you read someone else's mind? Like my brother's."

"That would be 'tennis, August, tennis, where's John?, tennis.'" I smiled. "No, it's always been just you," I said softly and then wished I hadn't said anything.

"But why me?" he asked, suddenly serious.

"I don't know. Because you're special," I teased. Hopefully not as special as my father believed.

"Are you sure other people from your group can't read minds?"

"Not that I know of." If that had been the case, Angus, my oldest friend who had also been a Lost Kid, would have somehow found out and told me.

I got off the bed, picked up the packet from Stanford, and walked over to John, noticing for the first time that his eye color had changed, the tiny green flecks had become more prominent.

John opened the bedroom door. As if he knew exactly who I had just been thinking about, he said over his shoulder, "I keep thinking Angus is going to show up any minute."

I followed him from the room, surprised he was worried. "Why would you even think that? He can't come back here. Everyone has seen the video. He launched himself from a three-story balcony causing an earthquake and a human stampede. He and his parents were lucky to get away from the police."

"Everyone *everywhere* has seen the video. You're here, and that's why he'd come back." In the usual John fashion, he'd told me his feelings and then had started to walk away.

As soon as we entered the living room, we caught the Fords' new dog red-handed, lounging on my low-slung couch, one front paw dangling on top of the other. The rescue dog was Taro and Kathleen's answer to an almost-empty nest. He quickly barreled off the sofa and hurtled around obstacles to reach John before running into his legs.

"Spirit!" John bent at the waist and lightly wrestled the dog back and forth between his hands, a tactic to avoid talking about Angus more. Spirit's tail wagged crazily, making a hollow thump as it banged against the glass coffee table.

"Want to leave Spirit here?" I offered.

John hesitated. "That's okay. He's my cover story. I said I would take him out with me to get ice since he wouldn't stop barking after the neighbor's dog went crazy."

Spirit was getting hyper, beginning to jump. John scooped up the long, sleek dog and put him over his shoulder like a giant baby. Spirit gave me a doleful look.

I walked John to the kitchen and set the packet on the counter as I studied my phone, which Stuart had linked to my security system so that I could view the surveillance in and immediately around my apartment. I watched the outside hall, ready to tell John when it looked empty and he could exit unseen.

"Wait, what else was in there?" John asked, pointing to the envelope.

I spilled the contents onto the white marble counter. "It's information on some program I can apply to called the 'Institute for Progressive Learning.'"

John set Spirit on the ground. "'A learning environment committed to fostering innovation, deeply rooted in Stanford's pioneering spirit of the West,'" John quoted from over my shoulder. "They want you," he said, suddenly happier. He pulled his phone from his pocket and scrolled. Next thing I knew the apartment was shaking with the sounds of "California Love" blaring from the speakers.

"Hey!" I said, laughing as he sang every single lyric. "Turn it down! Yes, I know you know this song." I finally had to jump up and grab the phone he held high over his head. I hit pause.

"Look," I said, before he got too excited. "I don't know if they can get over the fact that I'm the daughter of the Oracle of Austin, the billionaire who disappeared off the face of the earth with sixty people and is now wanted by the FBI. That's not the kind of attention Stanford wants."

"All that shit is dying down. I walked in here easily," John said, putting his phone back in his pocket.

"Are you sure?" I asked for probably the fifth time, changing the subject. "No one recognized you?"

"Seriously, it was fine. It's UT graduation. Downtown's packed. Let's go out tomorrow night. I am so sick of pretending that we're not together." He reached out and stroked my hair. "I want to make it up to you about the party."

"We can't."

John shoved his hands in his pockets. "Yes, we can. So what if someone takes our picture and finds out we're a couple? Is it me you're ashamed of?"

He'd said it flippantly, almost like he was joking, but there it was. It was John's only vulnerability as far as I could tell—his fear that I would lose interest, that he wasn't good enough compared to the Puris. Angus, specifically. He couldn't forget how I'd unceremoniously dumped him last year while Angus looked on. At the time, I'd wanted my family to take me back more than anything. But in the end, I'd wanted John to take me back more.

"It's not you. It's me." I hoped he knew I meant it. "You and your family's privacy is way too important." It wasn't just that, though I wouldn't tell him. I didn't care if pictures were taken. It was that I was worried my father would see them.

"We'll be careful."

I didn't want to say no to him this time. *Fuck the paparazzi.*

I didn't want Novak to know I had a boyfriend, to even put John on his radar, but maybe I was wrong to think Novak was watching me. He had much bigger things to worry about than to closely keep track of the daughter who'd always been a thorn in his side.

"If I pick the place?" I finally said.

"Okay, but you're not paying."

John made a move to go, but I reached for him again, bringing my lips to his. The kiss deepened, and I wound my arms around his neck as his hands wandered my back, down to my lower hips. He set me onto the barstool and stood between my legs, leaning into me. Spirit started barking.

Breathless, I pulled away. I put my hand under his shirt. I never wanted to stop touching him. It was addictive, his broad shoulders, the definition of his chest from all that tennis. John captured my hand to stop it.

"Don't," he said. "Not if I need to go."

"Stay," I said, accidentally, wanting to take it back immediately.

"Come with me," John said, matter-of-factly, like it was so easy. He kissed the side of my neck.

"I can't," I whispered, reluctantly. John let go of me. "We're going to California soon. And before that, I'm going on tour with you. No matter what, that's not going to change."

A minute later, I was alone again, and the apartment was too quiet. Seeing the papers splayed on the counter, I gathered them all and dropped them into the tall, silver trash.

Back in my bedroom, I leaned against the doorjamb, arms crossed, trying to look at it from John's perspective. What in this room had been bothering him? Maybe he was just restless in my luxurious and empty apartment since it was the only place we spent time together.

I turned and walked back to the kitchen. Every day I told myself I wouldn't do it, but then I did. Like cheating on a diet. Without touching the trash can, I focused and raised the metal lid. *Ahhhh*. Before the guilt set in, the rush felt fantastic. Then I began to sift through the papers at the top of the trash, retrieving every page from Stanford.

JOHN

Three broken hairbrushes. A shattered terra-cotta rabbit's head. Really, Julia? Broken shit everywhere. When you asked me to open that drawer to read the Stanford packet, I thought you wanted me to see that you were using your abilities. Did you really think I wouldn't notice?

I love you. I notice everything . . .

Chapter Three

Southwest Regions Private Wealth Management wasn't located in a downtown high rise in a high-end office suite. It was
in the suburbs, tucked into a nondescript limestone building
behind a store that made knockoff mid-century furniture.

"Donna?" I called as I stood in the entryway. No one was
in the office because it was Sunday, but the front door had
been left unlocked for me.

"Hi, honey!" The singsong voice came from her office.
I followed it, walking on the industrial carpet through the
abandoned cubicle center to meet Donna at her door.

"Hey! How's it going?" Donna gave me her big wave,
holding her hand high in the air.

If she wasn't six feet tall, she was close, even when wearing
flat, clean, white sneakers as she was today, paired with pristine white jeans instead of her usual workweek business suit.
When I'd first met her in the chaotic weeks after my family's
departure, when she'd come to the hotel room where I'd shut

myself in, she'd been wearing black pumps that made her thrillingly tall like my stepmother and sister.

She had appeared immediately when I'd finally called the number on the business card paper-clipped to the stack of legal documents I found in my bedroom the night my family left. The card had read, DONNA WILLIAMS, VICE PRESIDENT, SOUTHWEST REGIONS PRIVATE WEALTH MANAGEMENT. I had been scared to call the number at first. I felt besieged by the press and had been relentlessly questioned by the FBI about my father's possible whereabouts and finances. The estate was being held in contention and likely would be for years. For a while I'd lived off the cash that had been left with the documents, but I soon needed more money from the large trust fund my father and stepmother, Victoria, had set up for me to access at age eighteen. Because it had been set up a decade ago, the FBI couldn't touch it. Donna had mentioned that there wasn't any evidence of a similar trust for Liv, only me. Apparently my separation from the family had always been a consideration.

That night we'd met, Donna had arrived at my hotel room and spoke in financial lingo with such a knowing and confident tone that I'd signed with her immediately. She'd talked about how she would sort out my complicated finances, but that, first things first, she'd make sure I had an income going into a checking account. She went above and beyond and arranged for my apartment at the W, the right credit card, and most importantly, a lawyer to push back against the FBI. John excluded, Donna was the first outsider to gain a large amount of my trust. A cynical part of me knew she was gifted at making her clients feel like they were friends, but I also wanted to believe that maybe we were.

"Look at you!" Donna said. "You are a beautiful sight, but you need some sun. How was it out there? Anyone harass you?"

I followed Donna into her corner office that, in contrast to the firm bland exterior, was impressively upscale with a Damien Hirst piece hanging on the wall. Her desk was also a work of art—a large piece of glass on two steel sawhorses. From what Donna had told me, the contrast was intentional. She had a lot of clients who preferred a discreet, low-profile firm. She said my father must have heard of her through word of mouth and that was why she received an email invitation to a Dropbox account that dated back to the day my family left.

I cleared my throat. "No. I didn't run into anyone. The parking lot was empty. Thanks for meeting me so early."

Donna began sifting through a file. "Okay, I have some papers for you to sign—shifting money from savings to the distillery investment we talked about."

I got busy on the paper-signing train. When I was done, I leaned back, flexing my right hand, feeling comfortable in this office and with Donna. She didn't know much about me personally, but she made my life run smoothly, which was by nature pretty personal. I liked letting her boss me around and, once in a while, pretending I was being mothered.

"Let's talk logistics for California."

"Yes, ma'am," I said, smiling.

"All your bills and credit card statements will still be sent here. You have your car. You're going to need somewhere to live. I'm thinking you're not going to live in a dorm if they accept you."

"Correct."

"Ready to get out of here, huh?" she smiled. "Okay, so would you like an apartment or a house?"

"I don't know." I hadn't thought too much about what California would be like. I'd been waiting on Stanford for some reason.

"Anything in Silicon Valley is going to be an investment. Just think on it." Donna gently removed her Gucci reading glasses.

It seemed like we'd completed business for the day, but I wasn't ready to leave yet just to go back to the hotel. I got up and wandered around the room, looking at the many tchotchkes around her office, all interesting and perfectly displayed.

Donna stood up and joined me. "You like these?" She picked up one of the small ceramic windmills from a collection. "They were my dad's."

"I love them," I said, thinking again of my necklace, my only sentimental item.

There was a pregnant pause. The meeting was obviously over. Maybe because I just didn't want it to be or maybe because I knew it was time to understand my own finances, I said, "Donna, can I have hard copies of my account statements?"

There was a momentary surprise in her eyes. "Of course. You've got your laptop. I'll send you a Dropbox invite."

"Do you mind if I look at the hard copies? I'm still paranoid about the FBI breaking into my stuff."

"Sure. I'll have them messengered to the hotel. But remember what your lawyer told us? It's extremely hard for them to put a US citizen under that kind of surveillance. That said, they're smart. They're probably still watching you to see if your friend contacts you. The good news is that means Agent Kelly is still around!" She laughed.

"I can't believe you like him. Aren't you dating a player from the Spurs?"

"Nah. That ended. I told you what I found out about Agent Kelly? All that Iron Man stuff?"

"You should ask him out."

"To him, I'm the enemy. Your lawyer and me. All we do is try to block him."

"You can tell he's annoyed he was ever assigned to my case," I laughed, feeling good, joking around with Donna.

"Oh yeah, he's annoyed. He was an accountant. He's just interested in the money. He doesn't strike me as someone who believes in all the voodoo shit they were saying about your dad. Or the rumors about your friend and what he did to that bar." Donna paused for a moment, and then said, "Well, if you have any questions, just shoot me an email. Better yet, call me. I'll miss seeing you so often once you move. You'll be all caught up in that Silicon Valley lifestyle. Those California boys! Or girls. Sorry, I don't mean to presume. When do you take off?"

"I'll probably be there by late July."

"I can line up places for you to look at then if you'd like?"

"Sounds good. Thank you so much, Donna."

"A little free advice: you're on your way now. If your friend tries to contact you, ignore him and forget that he ever tried. Do not get pulled back in."

"He won't contact me. But yes, I hear what you're saying."

I then realized Donna was looking at me strangely and I was standing in front of the suddenly open office door. It dawned on me that I may have screwed up and opened the door without touching it.

Like a true professional, she calmed her expression in a split second. Amazingly, she only said, "Be safe, Julia. I'll be in touch."

JOHN

I was really looking forward to our date even if we were in a private room. It had been so long. I was also planning on surprising you and taking you to a show at Stubbs later in the night if I could convince you. I didn't know if I should get you flowers. I actually asked my brother if I looked okay. Of course in his opinion, I didn't. He and August started making fun of me because of how nervous I was, which made me even more nervous . . .

JUNE

Chapter Four

I stood at the glass dining room table in my apartment in front of the files Donna had provided, a beam of sunlight from the setting sun bisecting the papers. As soon as I opened the folder, I was drawn in, feeling a connection to my family so acutely it was as if they were in the room. Finances were my last tie to them. I enjoyed seeing Donna, but the price I paid was maintaining a link to my family that still felt too close for comfort. I missed my sister so much, I felt like I couldn't acknowledge it or I wouldn't be able to keep moving forward. It happened far less frequently, but there were still some mornings when I woke up and thought I was in the house on Scenic Drive. With Liv. With all of them.

A text lit up my phone, bringing me back to the present.
At the restaurant.

Finally, it was dusk. Quarter to eight on an early summer night. I closed the file I'd been reading. I switched off the light over the dining table and looked out the living room windows from behind the gossamer drapes. I could still see the outline of Lady Bird Lake.

From the brevity of John's text, I could tell he was semi-annoyed by the complicated instructions I'd given him. Go to Lamberts. Take the underground tunnel across the street to the restaurant where we're really going. Stay in the basement. They'll show you to the private dining room in the wine cellar.

I was annoyed myself. It was a beautiful night. I was tired of being cautious. I looked down at the strapless dress I wore. It was pretty. I actually felt pretty. All I wanted was to see my boyfriend and be outside without worrying.

I decided to walk. *What the hell?* It was only a couple of blocks.

The lobby was packed, the evening's activities getting underway. I walked through the hotel like I had important business and then out onto the street. There had been no paparazzi. Outside, it felt earlier in the evening than it had indoors. The shine of the streetlights and the humidity made me feel part of the world again. I cut around a large group walking en masse to the Congress Bridge to see the bats take flight at dusk.

There was a strange familiarity in the air. Flooded with an unexpected lightness and warmth, I slowed my pace and walked like someone enjoying the evening instead of some-one on a mission. Just as I rounded a corner, I drew up short, almost running into a small group of three teenage boys at a standstill on the sidewalk.

I stepped to the side and briefly looked over to see who the group was gathered around. The man's face was blocked, but I glimpsed grimy clothing and rapid hands demonstrating a card trick.

Oddly the street was very quiet, devoid of many pedestrians. Shaking off the feeling of discomfort, I crossed the street and entered into the stately, red-brick Victorian building, once a general store and now a historic landmark that still bore the name J. P. Schneider and Bros on the facade.

"Hello," I said politely to the hostess. When I began to explain that I had reservations in the "vault" across the street, I watched her burgeoning realization that I was a VIP.

She led me downstairs, through the underground tunnel beneath the street that connected the main restaurant to the basement of the building that had once been the owner's second store across the road. Of course, it was Donna who was in the know about the vault.

"Thank you," I said a second too late as she handed me off to the proper restaurant staff. I was too busy staring at John who was seated at one end of a long table with a distant, preoccupied look on his face.

"Hey," I said, curious what he was thinking about. John instantly hid his expression and gave me a smile.

He stood to greet me. "You look pretty."

I was about to ask what was wrong when something prickled at the back of my neck. I whipped around and saw, behind the server, a bald man with a beard, in a black T-shirt and black trousers positioned with his iPhone held high. The scene seemed to freeze as if already caught in a picture. There was no sound or motion as the flash illuminated John and me in a surreal circle of light.

"Hey!" I exclaimed.

The man ran up the staircase located to the left of the cellar. To my surprise, the server got in my way, blocking the exit, pretending it wasn't intentional.

"Move," I said, putting my hands on the server's shoulders to push him to the side. "Goddammit." I bolted up the staircase to catch the man, needing to grab his phone and that photo at all costs. I hurled off my shoes so I could run faster, sending them clattering down the stairs behind me.

"Julia, what are you *doing*?" John yelled from behind me.

All was serene when I arrived on the ground level of the restaurant above. Diners looked up as I stood, wild-eyed, scanning every inch of the space. Moving to the entrance, I whipped open the heavy door onto the sights and sounds of downtown.

Across the street, in front of Lamberts, two men writhed on the pavement, the slighter figure pinning down a larger one while clenching a fistful of hair.

Barefoot, I darted across the street, dodging the oncoming cars. Drawing closer, I recognized the dirty clothes of the person from the street. When I neared, he didn't look at me. He simply extended one hand with the phone, like he knew I would eventually come and take it. I saw ghost images of tattoos on his arms that looked almost erased. Automatically, I reached for the phone, the object I'd been hunting, confused by how he knew what I'd wanted. As soon as my fingers touched it, I felt the electricity—that expansive, encapsulating energy. I knew before I knew.

The photographer squirmed away from the loosened hold and took off, running full speed. The boy with the warm, gold-toned skin and the flawless face that looked familiar yet different set against dark hair, stood more slowly, almost reluctantly, refusing to meet my eyes. He began to lope down the street, away.

I felt the swarm gathering.

Standing by myself, I squinted into the sudden onslaught of what felt like a hundred flashes though there were only three photographers. It was nonstop, white lights blazing. Instinctively, I put up an arm to shade my eyes and tried to go deaf to the cruel things they began shouting.

Where's your father?

How do you feel about living off stolen money?

I glanced across the street. John was watching the melee and me, frozen in the headlights. Our eyes caught. I saw both how helpless and pissed off he felt before I snapped my gaze away. He was supposed to casually walk away if this happened. That was the prearranged plan.

He would think I was crazy for chasing that man after I'd said the key was to ignore them—the gawkers, the paparazzi. But from the direction that man had aimed his phone and where he had been looking, I knew he had been more intent on capturing John's image than mine.

I turned my head to the right, narrowing my eyes to search for the boy now blended in to a group of pedestrians traveling away into the fold of the city. Like he could feel my longing and decided to throw me a crumb, he looked over his shoulder at me once, his blue eyes dancing.

Angus.

I headed straight for my hotel's parking garage. Listening

to the sound of my own shallow breathing, I waited in my current car—an old white Prius, the one car that had been left behind in my family's underground garage on Scenic Drive, the garage that had once housed ten vehicles. John was sure to be expecting me at his house, but, when I had seen the mystery blanket in my backseat, I had waited to take off.

My back door opened and shut.

"Drive."

Hearing his voice for the first time in six months, my heart raced with joy and fear. Glancing in the mirror, I saw him flatten himself across the compact backseat, pulling the rough grey blanket over his filthy clothing.

"Have you been sleeping in here?" I asked, incredulous. Since my part-time bodyguard, Stuart, mostly drove me, I hadn't touched the car in months.

"Go," he said, his voice muffled.

I heard my own shaky inhale, a hyperventilating sound.

"It's okay. It's just me," he said.

"I know."

At the first light, I fidgeted. It was dark, but I was terrified that once we were at a stop, paparazzi would see us and hold a camera to our window.

I headed for the freeway. Once we were traveling at seventy miles per hour, I saw the grey mass rise up in back.

"Jesus, Julia. You don't have any gas," Angus said in his familiar joking, cutting tone. I wanted to face him to make sure he was real. "Pull off after the airport. It's quiet by McKinney Falls."

South of the airport, I picked an exit at random, finding my way onto a more rural road. I pulled over and stopped the car partway into a ditch of long, brown grass. I quickly turned the car off. Everything went dark and quiet. Angus got out, stretching his long legs.

"Let's walk."

"Are you crazy?"

He started sauntering along the road, the night sky lightened by a bright moon. We traveled alongside the shrub-like trees that wouldn't do much to shield us should any car approach.

"Stop," I finally said. Angus halted, twisting to face me.

I launched myself at him, and we hugged.

"I know," he said, holding me tight across the shoulders, rocking me slightly back and forth.

"Oh my God." I breathed into his collar. After six months of separation, of not seeing my own kind, I allowed myself to sag into him for just a second, letting him support me.

"You're good. I've been watching you." Never, ever in the past would we have been this demonstrative. But my guess was he'd been through as much as I had since the last time we'd seen each other.

"Tell me what happened when you left the ER that night," he said, referring to the last time I'd seen him, trapped and broken in a hospital bed.

When I'd said good-bye to Angus that night, I'd believed I would never see him again. Novak had banned Angus and his parents from joining the rest of the Puris for Relocation because of Angus's stunt, even though Lati, Angus's dad, had been my father's best friend. Safety in numbers and the preservation of the group were the main tenets of the Puris so the ultimate punishment was to be cut away. Angus's family were left to evade the police on their own and to find a way to hide from the world.

Angus should have never made a public scene, but he'd done it for me as much as for himself. He'd distracted my Puri friends from discovering my relationship with John.

I stepped back, putting some distance between us. "I stayed behind. I snuck out the day they left Austin, and no one tried to stop me. After that, it was interviews with the police, the FBI, moving to the W. That's it."

"And being in the news," he commented wryly.

"Yes. Lots of that." My eyes raked over every inch of him.

"I know. I look like shit," he said. Angus was dirty and worn out, wearing stained jeans that were ripped with gaping holes at both knees, his grey T-shirt dotted with dark stains. His hair was dyed a flat, chocolate brown, his only other attempt to disguise himself besides the laser tattoo removal that was incomplete.

"What were you doing out on the street with those stupid cards? You're insane."

"It wasn't working just waiting in your hotel garage," Angus shrugged, one corner of his mouth tilting up in a half smile.

"Tell me what happened to you. That night in the hospital."

Angus started walking again, crunching gravel beneath his feet, his gait loose. I had no choice but to impatiently follow. Tough roadside grasses switched at my bare legs.

Angus's voice became flat as if reporting events that had happened to someone else. "My dad paid a nurse to wheel me out the back door. A chauffeured car was waiting with my mom. We drove for almost twenty-four hours to Los Angeles. They've been guests on the estate of a wealthy inventor in Bel Air ever since—turns out that was my dad's plan B. He knew there were these connoisseurs of the unusual out there. In exchange, my parents are asked to occasionally perform for guests, like exotic birds taken out of their cage." His omission of detail made it clear everything was far worse than he let on and he didn't want to talk about it.

"That's revolting. It's also unsafe."

"My dad had to make a deal quickly."

"But you left LA," I said.

"I told them I had to find a better place for us. I wasn't handing control of my life over to someone much dumber than Novak. Why'd you stay behind? For him?" Angus stopped. He lifted a hand and grazed my cheek with his fingertips as if I were precious and he wanted to make sure I was actually there.

"Yes. And no, especially after I found out that Novak was lying to us. You were right—he wanted us to lose our abilities."

"He was your father. You couldn't see it." Angus shrugged generously.

"Was he really that threatened by us?"

"Definitely by you and me. His illegitimate half-Puri daughter shouldn't have been more powerful than his full-blooded one."

"He was always priming Liz to be the next leader."

"And he just hated me." Angus laughed at that memory.

"I was so jealous of the other group. They were finally learning all the Puri secrets. But I actually believed in him. I really thought our time would come. Just later." I was disgusted by Novak, disgusted by myself for having always chased his approval.

"And here I thought you stayed for me," Angus said lightly.

I touched his arm apologetically. "At first I thought I would look for you right away. It's been so much more of a circus than I imagined. I keep trying to quit my abilities, but I can't seem to stop and there are so many eyes on me." I shook my head. "I knew we would find each other, but I thought maybe it would be twenty years from now."

"What are we going to be doing twenty years from now, Julia? Hiding?"

I understood. I knew he'd made a public spectacle because he'd been scared to go on Relocation—of the restrictions, of losing his ability to move freely—but now I heard disillusionment in his voice.

"Not me," I said adamantly. "I keep jumping through the FBI's hoops, trying to earn citizenship in the regular world. I want to just live an ordinary life. I'll stop using my abilities. I'll figure it out."

Angus snorted. "That sounds miserable. And impossible. We're different. At some point, you're going to get caught." Angus put his hands low on his hips, elbows jutting out at his sides. "That's why I've come to get you out."

I almost smiled. Angus thought he was the hero who had arrived to save me.

Angus continued, "This whole time, how have you not seen that Austin is the absolute worst place to be?" With a swift scorn that took me by surprise, he said, "You know you're endangering all of us."

"What do you mean 'us'?" I squinted at him.

"Me, you, my family. Puris disappear. That's what we do. Remember what Novak said to my dad at the hospital? He will be watching us, making sure we give nothing away about the Puris and where they're hiding. Like you said, you can't quit using your abilities. Here you are, in the spotlight, keeping the attention on him. How long until Novak intervenes?"

I didn't like this shaming, and I wanted it off of me. It was like I could physically feel it as it began to seep into my conscience. "I haven't done anything. The FBI knows nothing."

"Novak doesn't know that." Then Angus paused dramatically, cocking his head. "You want him to find out what you've really been hiding?"

"What are you talking about?" I demanded, reassuring myself that I had examined all of my choices from every angle. That was all I did, every day.

"You're not as safe as you think you are. You know, your boy is radioactive." He started walking to the car.

"Excuse me?" I asked, annoyed.

"My dad told me about Novak's mind-reading vision." Angus was walking fast now to irritate me.

"What about it?" I asked carefully, trailing just behind him.

"Novak's vision—that he'd be able to hear someone's thoughts—someone not from the group but similar enough to us. That person was destined to come with us for Relocation, whether they wanted to or not. It's a numbers game for us Puris. They were the new blood we needed since we've inbred to the point of extinction. Just another resource to bring below . . ."

"Stop walking." I yanked on Angus's sleeve. We stopped

right under a telephone wire that crossed the road, eerily thick with hundreds of still black birds that watched us.

"I don't like it out here," Angus said, his ears pinning back.

"Let's go."

Back at the car Angus swiftly slid into the backseat again, slouching low. I stared straight ahead. My hand shook when I started the engine. Last winter, I'd confessed to Angus that I'd read John's mind.

"Don't you think it's a little coincidental that you read someone's mind when Novak was on the lookout for that to happen?"

"No," I said, barely seeing the road in front of me as I pulled out of the grassy trough, streams of insects swarming in the beams of light.

He waited for me to say something, but I stayed quiet.

"So Liv was right about everything she said to us that night—about your boyfriend not flinching when I pushed him and how she rose from the dead when he touched her."

Denial seemed the safest thing. But Angus would see right through me.

"He's not like us." I omitted the last thing that had happened six months ago—John's maybe–vision of the group's hiding place.

"You stay, Novak's going to find him."

My impulse was to scream at Angus to shut his mouth. Instead, I flippantly said, "There's nothing for Novak to find."

"He's having you watched. You have to know that."

"Even if he is, I have been so careful. We never go out in public together. Until tonight."

"Oh, come on. I've seen you trying to be careful, but Novak has got to know by now that you have a boyfriend. God, he probably has someone at the W, reporting to someone else who reports to him. If you're near *John*"—Angus spat out the name—"and he does the slightest thing in public that makes him seem like us, Novak will find a way to get to him. You've led your father right to him."

"John isn't—"

"You're prodding the beast, Julia. You have to leave for the summer. Just until it's safe."

I had no choice but to get gas. I pulled off at an exit and drove into an eerily deserted industrial area. "Why the summer?" I could feel my brain scrambling to make sense of the information.

"My dad told me where the group is hiding."

"Stop! Don't tell me, Angus. I don't want to know."

"They're underground in—"

"Stop talking! I mean it!" I uselessly covered my ears with my hands, letting the car drift smoothly into the next lane. I let it go. Down to the millisecond, I intuitively knew how much time I had until we smashed into the median. Angus knew it too, but it never made it any easier for the passenger.

"Fine!" he said, impatient. I placed my hands back on the steering wheel. "But you need to know one thing."

Angus paused, giving me a last opportunity to shield myself. I remained silent. Finally Angus spoke, "They have a hard deadline. I know because my dad is counting the days until he knows he'll never see Novak again. It's September first."

"Why September first?" I searched my mind for the relevance of that date.

"That's when a mining company begins work close to where they're hiding. At that point, they need to seal themselves in if they don't want anyone to come across their spot."

Angus rose and rested his chin on the back of my leather seat, speaking softly, close to my ear. "That means Novak only has until September to keep tabs on you and to search for people like us."

"What did Lati say? Did Novak plan to search for one person specifically or many?" I refused to name John in this scenario.

"Both." Angus's voice became mocking. "No one believes him by the way—that there are others. But the bad thing is, you and I know he's right. And deep down Liv knows the truth about your boyfriend. Even if you talked her out of it."

We were silent. "You're going to need to leave soon," I finally said.

"Yeah, for sure. And you need to come with me."

"This is because you're lonely. Obviously. You were even doing cheap magic on the street. Trust me, I know—"

"No, I'm trying to keep Novak far from the Puris who are still left above ground," Angus said with a sudden force, uncaring that he'd just served up more information than I ever wanted. "Don't you understand? The closer you are to John, the better the chances that Novak will find him and abduct him and punish you. You need to separate from him if you want to protect all of us. It's only for the summer, until they're gone."

"We're fine! I'm about to leave Austin. I'm going to be on the road."

"What do you mean 'the road'?" Angus made quotation marks with his fingers.

"It'll be good—nine tournaments in nine different cities across the US for the next eight weeks. I'm going to be using cash only. I can stay under the radar with John."

"Wait, so following him around the country to watch him play tennis is safe? People aren't going to start clueing in to your presence?" Angus laughed in my face.

I obstinately shook my head, but my tone was gentle. "I'm not going to leave him. There's no reason, Angus. He's not one of us."

"You have blinders on. What about that guy taking pictures? Something has you scared."

"I'll just be more careful." I didn't know for sure he'd been after John's picture.

"Why would you risk his life and ours? After this summer, you're free and you can decide what—or who—you really want. Lie to him if you need to but leave with me." He lowered his voice to almost a whisper. "Come on, Julia. Come now. You know it's the right thing to do."

The quiet weighed between us. I slowed and edged the car over to an old gas station. The fluorescent lighting was startling. Angus abruptly flung open the car door, and the smell of gasoline permeated the car's interior.

"Make up your mind soon. I don't think you have as much time as you think."

The car door slammed. When I whipped my head around, he'd already vanished somewhere in the dark.

JOHN

I keep thinking about the night you were missing for three hours, after our failed date—was that when Angus came back?

It had to be. That's when everything changed. When you finally showed up at my parents' house, I was so incredibly mad at you. We'd done that camera drill before, but I was just over it. When you wouldn't even look at me in the street—what if I denied your existence in public that way? And then I had to roll in early on what was supposed to be a big night, and my whole family felt sorry for me. It really made me second-guess who I'd become.

I was especially pissed because I was going to tell you at dinner all about what was going on with me. Everything I couldn't explain, everything I was hiding from you. For months I thought I was losing my mind—I looked up schizophrenia—but I kept it to myself because I knew once I told you or my family, I would have to deal with it. But of course deep down I knew there's you and your family and everything you all can do, and it seemed like you were rubbing off on me. I was going to tell you that night. I was ready . . .

JUNE

Chapter Five

~⚮~

"Eight to six." John snatched the putter from Alex's hand and lofted it into the rusty disc golf basket. The dangling, waving chains gave a piercing clang a moment after John released the disc. "Nine–six. Go."

The irritating jangle echoed my mood.

Alex retrieved the putter and missed. "Whoever gets to fifteen first."

"No. To ten," John said flatly. "Didn't you used to be good at this?"

Alex laughed. "Shut up." He picked up the disc and was handing it to John when I walked out of the shadows and into his line of vision.

"What the . . . !" Alex exclaimed. He put a hand over his heart. "You came out of nowhere."

I was about to touch Alex's shoulder in apology but pulled back, unsure if that was too friendly. "Sorry. I heard the chains so I came straight to the backyard. It's late. I didn't want to bother your parents."

I looked to John. In the dark of their backyard, a cock-eyed outdoor fixture the only source of light, he leaned forward and lightly tossed the disc right into the basket.

"Hi," I said when he straightened.

"Hey," he said normally as if he'd known all along I would appear out of the dark in his backyard at ten-thirty at night after being MIA for three hours and not answering his call or text. But he didn't make eye contact when he walked past me to the basket. In a moment, I'd worry that he was mad. Later, I'd worry about Angus being in town. At this second, I was so happy to be reminded that this was my real life now.

The back door opened, and from the house, a smoky voice I didn't recognize called out, "Boys! It's too loud. You'll wake the neighbors."

They knew better than to attempt even one last throw. John and Alex stopped the game and walked over to the woman who held the door to the kitchen partway open. John looked back to me, as if he was daring me to follow.

"Grandma, this is Julia," John said, outing my presence.

With no other choice, I walked into the brighter light of the patio. I'd been counting on John thinking it was too late to invite me in.

I joined them in the cramped kitchen, brushing past John's grandmother, who held the door open with one hand while dangling a dark brown cigarette in the other.

I reached out my hand. "It's nice to meet you."

She certainly didn't match the stereotype of the tiny, silver-haired Asian grandmother I had pictured in my head. Her age was impossible to guess, her skin was barely lined, and her jet-black hair was gathered in a low twist. Flicking her cigarette outside, she blew clove-smelling smoke out the back door before turning to face me. Her nails were perfectly manicured and painted a chic black.

She didn't answer for a moment, sizing me up. I had on the strapless dress that was sexier than what I would have preferred to be wearing in front of John's parents and grandmother. When I glanced down, I saw bits of dirt stuck to my bare legs and fresh scratches from the highway grasses. I surreptitiously rubbed one leg against the other.

"I'm Jade," John's grandmother finally spoke. I looked away first. I now understood where Taro and John got their poker faces from.

"Mom, can you close the door when you're done? Spirit's going to make a run for it again," Taro said from where he and Kathleen were standing at the counter cleaning up after a late dinner. "Hi, Julia," he said.

"Hi, honey," Kathleen said to me. I could feel her trying not to look at Taro.

Unblinkingly, Jade peered at her son. "Why can't you leave him in the backyard? He's a dog."

"He climbs over the fence. We still need to figure that out."

"Your house is too small to have a big dog in it."

John had said his grandmother liked to dig at his father for choosing to be a math teacher instead of an investment banker like his uncle.

"You live in Chicago?" I asked Jade in a cringe-worthy voice that sounded like I was at an audition for the role of "polite girl at dinner party." I was always afraid I'd slip into what sounded almost like a different language—speaking too fast, in shorthand, the way the Puris often communicated with each other.

"I do," Jade said, bending to put out her cigarette in a potted plant on the doorstep. She closed the door and reached just behind me to the dining room table to retrieve her red wine glass, lipstick marking the rim. "When my husband passed away, I thought about moving to Austin to be near my grandsons and my son but it's too hot here and I can't leave my friends."

"You've always lived in Chicago?" I could hear the shade of an accent, and I was trying to find out if she'd emigrated from Japan.

Jade said, "no" without expounding.

"She moved from Peru when she was a child," Taro said, filling in for her brusqueness.

"What?" I asked, too rudely.

"She came from Peru?" Taro repeated, unsure if that was what I was asking.

I took a deep breath, trying to put the brakes on my racing thoughts. "I didn't know that." I glanced at John. He knew that was where my people came from.

John shrugged. "I forgot."

"There's a small Japanese population there that came looking for work," Taro said. "They mostly farmed and mined for gold. That side of the family lived there for a few generations."

"I hear you're going to Stanford," Jade interrupted, deflecting attention from herself.

"No," I said quickly, though my head was still on Peru. "My application was late, so now I need to go for an interview in person this summer." This was a strange coincidence. Not just Peru but also the connection to gold mining.

"You'll get in," Jade said.

An understanding seemed to pass between us.

"Thank you," I said. "We'll see, I guess . . . "

Jade still watched me. She had the same high cheekbones as Taro and John.

"Come on," John said to me, pointing in the direction of the living room. I noticed he wasn't touching me.

John led me to the hunter green sectional, out in the middle of everyone and everything. I perched on one end, and John planted himself on the other, leaving more than ample space between us.

"Are you mad at me?" I asked, very softly, though that much was obvious. My paranoia worried that he'd somehow sensed I'd been with Angus.

John's silence made me take the only action I could. I searched his thoughts.

I can handle someone taking my picture. What, you'd rather be arrested than be in a picture with me?

I jerked back. John had never done that before, and it was disconcerting—communicating this way with him. I had silently communicated with the Lost Kids, but it had never been the other way around with anyone. John watched me. He knew I was listening. He also knew I couldn't reply.

I mouthed, *What are you doing?*

"I know you didn't want my help, but I wanted to do something," he said aloud, thankfully. Even if what he had just done was an easily explainable guess on John's part, after Angus's warning, I didn't like it.

"I know. But it wasn't bad. The last photographer lingered for a while. But then more people showed up. I guess there must be a bunch of preteens who have some use for my photo. I called Stuart and waited for him inside."

"That's where you were?" he asked. As in, *that's where you were for three hours?* And it didn't answer why I hadn't texted him back. Knowing John, he would never ask.

I hated Angus for forcing a secret on me. "Yes," I said, stepping over a line.

John watched me for a second like he knew I was hiding something and then stared down at the low, square coffee table. He was stressed, and I realized he was not only mad, but he'd also been worrying. When he focused on me again, I saw that he'd decided to trust me. In that moment, I knew I wasn't good enough for him.

John moved closer to me on the sofa. "I don't care if we're on every magazine cover together." He sounded like he was challenging me, but it was also a pretty romantic thing to say.

John's parents and Jade were still in the open kitchen, not even pretending they weren't listening to our conversation.

"I do care," I finally said, knowing he would be annoyed. But I wouldn't tell John what had really scared me—that the man who had taken his photo hadn't felt like paparazzi. At that thought, I felt the truth of Angus's warning before I shoved it down.

I expected John to grow suddenly distant the way only he could when we disagreed about being a couple in public. He surprised me by silently saying, *What is going on with you? There's something you're not telling me.*

"Okay, lovebirds," Alex said, entering the room, "you

know Mom and Dad are standing right there." His expression was strange, as if he didn't like something he was seeing.

I drove two hands through the sides of my hair and stood up. "It's almost eleven. I should go. You've got to leave early for Dallas tomorrow." To Kathleen and Taro, I said, "Sorry for the late visit."

Taro set down the sponge he was using on the dining room table. In profile, he looked exactly like John, except for the grey running through his black hair. "You know you're welcome anytime, Julia."

I cleared my throat. "Thank you for having me," I said.

You don't need to be so nervous around them.

I turned and stared at John. Now he was making me nervous. He stood up and draped his arm around my shoulder, as if he was trying to tell me that I belonged.

Kathleen stood farther back at the sink and remained quiet. What were they supposed to say to me? I'd disappeared halfway through the graduation party for their son, and then tonight I'd ended John's date with me before it started.

I was sure I came off as a freak. I didn't know what to say that would make me seem like a normal, likeable person. Everything I said to them came out sounding odd.

Then Kathleen surprised me by crossing over to us, wiping her wet hands on the back of her jeans. She wore an orange T-shirt with a lion mascot on it from the school where she worked. When I'd first met Kathleen, she'd been easy for me to sum up as a strict mother and a competent school administrator. Now I had a fuller view of her, how self-possessed she was, how her presence made every room she walked in to better. I thought of my severely elegant stepmother and how

Kathleen had become so much more beautiful to me. John made jokes about keeping his parents happy as long as he won matches, but as an outsider watching Kathleen and Taro with their kids, I knew they cared beyond just supporting Alex and John's ambitions. They were just in a tough position because sports scholarships and being debt-free could make a huge difference in the boys' lives.

John moved partially in front of me, like he wanted to shield me, which proved to me he was worried his mother didn't like me.

"That must have been frightening tonight," Kathleen said in a sincere tone, the one I was sure she used in her vice principal job.

"It was fine. I'm used to it. I just don't like dragging John into it." Lately, the few times I'd seen her, I'd wanted to receive some of the caring she showed her kids and even August. But I knew I was different. I didn't invite that in people.

Kathleen nodded, agreeing with me completely. I should have been happy she backed me up in front of John, but illogically I was a little offended.

"Julia, if you need it—John's probably told you—my sister lives on a farm in Ohio. She'd be happy to have you if you wanted to go somewhere private this summer."

I was taken aback at both the kindness and the suggestion of a change in plans. After a second, I said, "Thanks for the offer, but I think I'll weather the storm. Things will get better when I leave Austin, I'm sure." I watched John for his reaction to his mother's words.

Don't be offended. Of course they think you'll be a distraction on tour. In their minds I've worked so hard to get to the top of the food chain in juniors tennis and I could do some real damage this summer.

I not only understood exactly what he was silently saying, but it was also more textured than hearing him speak aloud. I felt closer to him. I could better feel him and his emotion and intent in the words he was saying. It scared me how quickly I preferred it.

"You deserve a fresh start, Julia. I hope this doesn't follow you to California," Kathleen said.

There it was. The worry that I would hold John back if I went to California too.

I didn't breathe for a moment, and John grabbed my hand.

It's not you. They just don't like your situation. Or me going to college with a girlfriend. They want me to make the team when I try out at Stanford. If I somehow get cut, I lose my scholarship next year. They're not stupid, they know where I really go at night. They probably even know about the practices I've skipped.

What I wished I could say to Kathleen was that I knew my situation was not normal. I wasn't normal. But I was trying to be. I was doing everything I could to be.

"It won't always be like this," I said, knowing I couldn't guarantee it.

It was bold, but I looked Kathleen in the eye and made a firm resolution I meant to keep whether or not she believed there was anything to an eighteen-year-old's word. "I won't interfere with John's plans."

"I'll walk you to the car," John said, likely uncomfortable at the shift to talking about him in front of him.

"No, stay inside," I said. "We're going to have to be more careful again."

"I don't want to go backward," John said.

"Me neither. But it's out of our control. For now. I just want things to be normal. If we lay low, we'll get there faster. Now, I really better go. You all need your sleep."

John put a hand on my shoulder.

How to kiss someone good-bye in front of their parents and brother and still make it count?

I leaned in and made sure to take in every sensation when his lips touched mine, my hand squeezing his bicep to steady myself. To everyone else, it would have appeared as a quick peck on the lips.

John pulled back. *We're together. You're going on tour with me. That's not going to change.*

"It was nice to meet you," his grandmother said, interrupting our silent exchange.

She then dropped her gold-plated cigarette case, but before John could reach down and grab it for her, she beat him to it and it was back in her hand.

My pulse quickened, and I worked to hide the shock that I knew had passed over my face.

It was so subtle that no one else but me or a Puri would have caught it. The gold case had lifted up a quarter of an inch to meet her hand.

Jade didn't even seem aware of what she had just done. She touched my back in a good-bye gesture and exited the room.

John asked me, "What?"

I automatically shook my head that nothing was wrong.

"I'll see you in Dallas?" he said. "If I get to the finals."

"You'll get to the finals," his mom called out. "Your grandmother wants to see it."

I gave John an automatic smile and evaded his question. "Sleep well."

He repeated, "You're coming to Dallas."

I looked at him, at his family, framed for one last second the way I'd always pictured them before it all splintered apart in my mind.

"Of course. Good night."

When I arrived at my apartment, I bolted to the kitchen, the den, the living room. Every single room where I'd hid something that I'd bent, broken, or pierced.

I snatched up pieces, running back and forth to the trash. There was so much more than I remembered, I finally yanked the white trash bag out of the can and carried it with me all around the apartment, searching wildly in the backs of drawers, behind the few books I had, in the dirt of the potted banana tree.

The evidence was appalling. What had been a way to soothe myself, what I'd considered just a light application now and then, was a complete lie. This had been a daily habit.

A white china plate that I'd neatly serrated in three places balanced in my hand. I tipped the jagged pieces into the trash and one shard sliced my palm. I hauled the trash bag behind me like a demented Santa Claus and something sharp poked through the bag and grazed my bare leg.

I'd told myself I would slowly fill the trash with them over time in case anyone was going through my garbage, spying on me. But if I was honest, these remnants were my trophies. I double-bagged the trash and left it in the kitchen.

I went to the bathroom and started the shower, then looked back to my bedroom. Something about the way the room looked made me pause. I stared at the bed and the lamplight glowing against the white walls. John had been standing in this same spot the other day when he'd studied the room as if something was bothering him.

I've seen this room before.

Last year, while we'd sat in English class, way before I'd moved in, before we'd ever gotten together, John would think about us lying on a white bed, taking my clothes off piece by piece.

It was this exact bed without a headboard, in this exact room.

In his thoughts, light poured through the windows just like it had the other day. I'd thought it was John's private fantasy. Now I knew he'd been seeing the future.

Now that Angus had introduced the idea, I saw the signs everywhere. *And what about that stuff that Jade could do or seemed to know?*

I sank onto the cold hardwood floor, the sound of the shower water running in the background. I wiped at the trickle of blood coming from my calf, then squeezed my eyes closed.

I'd done this to John. I knew it. Maybe there'd been something there all along, because of his background. But I'd pushed him over the edge.

Ever since my family had left, Novak's was the one voice I'd tried most to repress. But now his voice echoed in my ears, *One of us would hear this person's thoughts and know he had the potential to become one of us completely. He was key to my direct line. He was meant for Liv.*

I'd never believed that, not in all these months. But recent events had me reconsidering. Like a layer existed just beneath the one where I was living, I could run my fingers over the floor and feel the textures of the carpet in Novak's office, hear his words, and vividly experience the chill of fear. My mind was back in my family home, reliving my final conversation with my father. I had been petrified, harboring the knowledge that I knew the person who Novak wanted.

I opened my eyes to break the reverie. For the first time since entering the apartment, I noticed the red message light on the house phone provided by the hotel. Only one party ever used this number.

I couldn't shake the feeling of something pulling me down from this sunny world into a dark place waiting just beneath.

JOHN

I don't know when I first felt you reading my mind. Or when I was first able to stop you. I guess I took pride in shutting you out. But that night at my house when you met my grandmother, I didn't plan it out ahead of time. I just knew I could communicate with you in a new way and when I did it, my head was so clear.

It was obvious you wanted me to stop speaking to you silently. So right then, I decided to let you ignore my unexpected actions if you wanted. I wasn't going to bring it up again.

It was strange to suddenly feel like I couldn't be myself with you . . .

JUNE

Chapter Six

❧

I sat through the usual onslaught of questions that I'd answered a thousand times at the FBI's nondescript beige building in a North Austin office park.

Have you heard from your father?

When did you find out your father was stealing money?

Where is the water they've stolen?

My head heard the words, but my mind was somewhere
else. With John. Terror hit me right in the heart whenever I
thought about him and what I was going to do. Which I'd
been doing nonstop, even while listening to that unexpected
message from Agent Kelly.

Though the FBI was a minor threat, it was still one that
needed to be managed. The timing of Agent Kelly's call was
the only thing that worried me, but I reminded myself that
the FBI would have surrounded us had they seen Angus and
that this interrogation I was now enduring was most likely a
routine annoyance.

Agent Kelly was clean-cut with black hair and amber eyes—Boy Scout-attractive, clearly in great shape beneath his conservative work attire. He was so serious I couldn't imagine he had a personality when he wasn't at work. I'd done my research like Donna: Agent Kelly was thirty-seven and from Salt Lake City. He'd started his career with the FBI in Denver.

I'd thought I would make it out of Austin without needing to give another interview. I'd already knocked down so many sessions with the police and the FBI, one by one. Last winter, I'd been amazed each time that I made it through without giving something important up.

Now the FBI dropped its bomb.

After all of these months, Kendra Wilson's body had been found. I should have been worried about lying again to Agent Kelly, but I was relieved the meeting had nothing to do with Angus.

"We have an approximate timeline of when she went missing and when she passed away. Did you see Miss Wilson any time in November or December of last year?"

I began to speak, and my lawyer put a hand on my upper arm. Her name was Kathryn Caspar and she'd been right at my side, answering my questions, guiding me through the countless interviews, and countering the FBI at every turn since last December. She never wavered in her assertion: I was a young girl from what they could only approximate to a cult, and I had no knowledge of the inner workings of the operation or where my family members were hiding. I'd escaped and deserved a chance to proceed with my new life.

She and Donna had worked hard to prove the veracity of

my story so my assets weren't seized. Donna sat on my other side, present so she could answer any financial inquiries.

Kathryn scrawled on a piece of white paper. *September?*

I nodded, lying, protecting my family. My father hadn't wanted Kendra to die. That had been an accident. His crime was concealing her death and disposing of Kendra's body after an accident on our property.

The real crime had been when Novak had hired her as his assistant. I'd heard his regret—not that she'd died but that he'd been wrong. He'd thought he'd finally proved that there were people like us out in the world who could withstand close, prolonged contact with us. Kendra had lasted longer than the other assistants he'd auditioned to take into hiding. But ultimately her mental health deteriorated, just like theirs.

"As she's informed you over and over again, the last time my client saw Kendra Wilson was in September when Miss Jaynes went to visit her father at his downtown office."

Though it had been a police investigation, Agent Kelly still suspected it was me who gave Kendra's parents the anonymous tip in March, informing them that their daughter had passed away. The search had been renewed because of that tip. Then as months went by, the investigation lagged with only her poor parents trying to keep Kendra's name in the news.

Agent Kelly tried one more time to speak to me directly. "Before I ask the next question, I want to remind you that lying puts you in violation of Title 18, United States Code, Section 1001, which makes it a crime to knowingly and willfully make any false statement in any matter within the jurisdiction of the judicial branch of the United States."

I nodded.

"So, Miss Jaynes, the body was discovered in this area, right near the Pennybacker Bridge. Have you been here before?" He held out a stack of photos, and Kathryn took them. We quickly looked together.

I shook my head, concealing my surprise that Kendra had been buried in the Lost Kids' old stomping ground.

"So that's a no? You've never been here before?"

"Correct," I said. I didn't feel bad about lying. They had found her. That was the important thing.

"There was an unidentifiable marking on the body, so now the FBI has a hate crime investigation as well as the financial crimes investigation." Agent Kelly seemed angry, as if he were about to start shaking his head at the depths of my family's depravity.

Now the presence of Linda Martinez, the young woman next to Agent Kelly who had been introduced as being from FBI headquarters in DC, specializing in hate crimes, made sense.

Agent Martinez pushed a picture in front of me. It was a close-up, so I couldn't tell which part of Kendra's body the marking was on. It was an intricate fractal pattern that looked like some kind of symbol or family crest. I'd never seen it before, but I had no doubt someone from my family had etched it. Perhaps it was a Puri marking I wasn't aware of. There was so much I didn't know about our history, all of which I'd been told I'd learn one day, but that would never happen now.

I shook my head. "I've never seen this before."

"She was badly interred. And we had those rains this

winter." Agent Kelly threw that out and watched me. I kept my face blank even though inside I was appalled that whoever it was from my group who'd covered this up hadn't shown the courtesy of burying her correctly. Agent Kelly looked at me with slight disgust, like he knew I was lying and he wanted to prove it. I couldn't mess up in front of him the way I had with Donna the other day when I'd thoughtlessly opened the door with my mind. Now that Agent Kelly had surprised me, I was on edge knowing Angus was in the vicinity.

"We're done here, right?" Kathryn said.

"One last thing." Agent Kelly unfurled the map of the world in front of me once again. I'd seen it what felt like a hundred times at this point. Kathryn sighed along with me.

"Really, guys?" Kathryn said, leaning back and crossing her arms over her blue silk blouse.

"Just see if you can remember anything new. Anywhere else you went on vacation or on a trip with your family," Agent Kelly said.

I looked up at him. *Rafa*, as I'd heard his fellow agents call him. Rafael Kelly. There was something different about him today. Because of the recent discovery, he was reenergized about my case after months of coming up short.

I focused on the map in front of me, seeing all the work I'd done on it. Every place I'd ever been to all over the world, always at an exclusive resort or a private island, was marked by a red dot. I hadn't held back when they'd asked. My family would never settle somewhere we'd been before. And I knew they would never let themselves get caught.

Agent Kelly spoke. "They have to be in the United States if they're tapping into the aquifer."

My family's water assets could have rivaled Nestle's with how much fresh water they had ended up controlling.

"The aquifer spans all this," he pointed to a gigantic area including parts of Colorado and Texas. "We're also tracking suspect building supplies being shipped piecemeal to the Yukon."

I almost said, "What about New Zealand?" Donna had told me it was an open secret that some American billionaires were making doomsday preparations in case they needed to flee a natural disaster, nuclear threat, or French Revolution–style class war. New Zealand was the choice destination for real estate purchase because it was a First World country, self-sustaining, and far, far away from the rest of the world.

Instead I said, "I think I've remembered everything," though I continued to look at the map. *Where were they?* Where was my sister right now, right this second? I had a sudden longing for her. It was hard to believe they were actually somewhere you could see on this map. In my mind, they lived in a whole other dimension now.

"What about your biological mother?" Agent Kelly asked. "Have you been in contact?"

You could have heard a pin drop. All eyes trained on me. "No."

"Can you please speak up?"

"No," I enunciated and shook my head for emphasis.

"Do you think your father will contact her?"

"No." I gave Kathryn a look, prompting her.

"I think we're finished here," she said, flattening her hands on the conference table. In silent agreement, Agent Kelly reached across the table and gathered the photos, taking his time. Kathryn stood, and Donna and I rose as well. Agent Kelly and his partner escorted us out of the conference room. As we walked the long hall to the exit, I actually heard Kathryn attempt some chitchat with Agent Kelly. Donna, not to be outdone, chimed in as well. I'd observed that Rafael Kelly was extremely shy when not in his official role.

After, at the exit, Kathryn gave a cursory wave. "I'm off. Julia, I'll call you if anything more comes up, but I think we're good."

"Thank you," I said and expectantly turned to Donna. I waited for the very temporary but welcome escape of her usual sunny chatter, but today I sensed some impatience in how she was standing—one heel lifting up and down, her body tensed.

I didn't linger, reminded that I was a paying client and not her friend.

JOHN

When I arrived in Dallas and we got together again, I could tell something was different. You were different. You seemed sad, and I wondered if it was because of me. You're hard to understand.

In the past, you've made self-deprecating comments about how you're so different from your perfect family, less than them somehow. I don't think you see yourself. You are every bit as striking and self-contained and intimidating in your own way.

Sometimes, after we've been apart for a few days, I see your tattoos and your glowing blue eyes and dark hair and I'm almost scared to touch you, you're almost too beautiful. Now you're of two worlds and I can feel the tug of each on you. I hope you know that I don't expect you to change just to be with me.

I can't imagine what it would have been like to be the black sheep in a family as insulated as yours. I love how my parents actually make you nervous because you like them so much. You're never nervous that I can tell otherwise. Annoyed, sad sometimes, but not nervous . . .

JUNE

Chapter Seven

I quit cold turkey. Like I should have done the second my family left.

My first resolution was to stop being lazy and cut out all the bad habits. I got up to switch on lights. I pulled open my drawers. Manually doing all the little things took twice as much time. But I still felt okay. My old rash hadn't even flared.

"Julia?" Paula called through the door. I'd forgotten today was her twice-weekly day to clean the apartment.

"Hi, Paula." I backed away instead of welcoming her, no longer sure if I should be in such close quarters with outsiders, having no idea if I was doing anything to them the way I had with John. I had assumed that since I was only half Puri, and John seemed to be fine all throughout our senior year, I just didn't have the same effect on outsiders. Now it seemed I might have been wrong.

After John, Paula was the person I was physically closest to on a regular basis. I'd enjoyed getting to know her, and even found excuses to talk to her when she was busy. I knew all about her five-year-old twin daughters and their family life; I'd let myself become too interested. I suddenly worried that reading someone else's energy—which was impossible for me not to do if I was in a conversation—was cheating as well.

"You okay?" She looked around. The trash bags from my last cleaning frenzy were stuffed and sitting out in the living room, and there were bits of debris and glass on the floor.

"Oh, yes." I waved a dismissive hand. "Just packing. Don't worry about those. I'll remove them." I walked away from Paula, isolating myself to a whole new degree, trying to get as far from her as possible.

How long would it take to kill off my abilities for good? Maybe if I stopped them in myself, they would stop developing in John. I didn't know if it would work, but that was all I could think of to do. That and stay away from John in the meantime.

Novak had claimed we could influence certain, predisposed outsiders to become more like us. In traits and appearance, Novak's handpicked assistants had gradually come to vaguely resemble us—Kendra most definitely—until they abruptly broke down psychologically. Now I couldn't stop thinking about that happening to John.

But what about Jade? If she had similar abilities, she seemed fine using them, and no one in her family seemed worse for wear. But I couldn't take the chance that John was exactly like his grandmother.

Paula began sweeping glass from the living room floor into a pile, and I gently closed the door to my bedroom, taking a seat on my bed, tucking my legs under me.

"John," I said softly when he picked up my call.

"Hey, baby." His voice was tired and husky.

"Did you make it through semis?" I asked.

"Yes. That was a rough one."

"Why?" He never complained about his tournaments being hard. He rarely complained about tennis, period, even though I knew he hated it. I shifted and stretched my legs out in front of me, brushing a streak of dust off my shorts.

"Only because I was tired and it was hot. I somehow volunteered to take my grandmother to the airport at 4:30 in the morning."

"What? She left? I thought she was supposed to stay if you made the finals."

"She said it was too hot. So Alex and I played cards and just never went to bed."

I smiled, picturing the whole thing. I loved that the brothers were so close in age, like Liv and me, but they never competed over important things. Games—cards, pool, darts, horseshoes, anything they could get their hands on—were a different story.

John cleared his throat. "By the way, my grandmother liked you, and she hates everyone."

"Really? That's nice. You're her favorite, right?" It had been obvious to me just from the way Jade looked at him—proud.

"Oh, yeah."

I laughed that he had no qualms admitting it. Now would be the time to ask more about Jade but I found myself not filling the silence. Why scare John when I had a plan to stop it all?

"Julia," he said.

"John," I said, a smile in my voice.

"When are you coming to Dallas?"

I was quiet.

"Look, I know you're mad because otherwise you would already be here. And we would have talked before now."

"You could have called me too." He'd texted me to see if I got home okay and to tell me when he'd arrived in Dallas, but it was rare for us not to talk for one day, let alone three.

"I'm sorry. I shouldn't have been so blunt about my parents. I hope I didn't hurt your feelings. I was just pissed that our night got ruined. I'll tell them today that you're for sure coming on tour this summer."

Oh. I realized it was the perfect thing to hide behind now. Maybe even for the whole summer.

"I don't want to put you in a bad position . . ." I said.

"You're the love of my life. Who cares what they think? I can do it all."

"Maybe they're right, maybe this summer you need to just finish what you started how many years ago? Ten? More?"

"What are you *talking* about? We aren't changing plans," he said, getting more upset than I'd heard in a long time.

"It's only two months." I hated hearing myself play it off like it wasn't a big deal.

There was silence for a moment.

"Are you serious?"

For a second, I entertained the fantasy that maybe I was crazy. It had been late that night. Maybe I hadn't seen any of what I thought I'd seen at his house. Maybe he hadn't had a vision of this bedroom a year ago. Things were the same as they'd always been.

"I love you," I said, wanting to smooth over what I'd just said.

I could sense more than hear his sigh of relief.

Then it was like every color in the room flipped to neon, the air shifted so drastically.

I whipped around and watched the entry, waiting. Angus came to stand in the doorway of my bedroom.

His hood was down and his translucent eyes glowed as he put a finger to his lips.

"I love you too," John said on the other end of the line. "So get in the car and come to Dallas."

I watched Angus give me a slow smile when he saw I wasn't startled. At any other time, I would have replayed John's 'I love you,' over and over in my head, enjoying the thrill because he rarely said it.

"Are you there?" John asked, annoyed.

"Paula just walked in."

"Got it," John said, his voice carefully neutral. "Call me back."

"Bye," I whispered and ended the call, my eyes never leaving Angus's.

I began shaking my head, speechless. He made a gesture like he was driving a car and slipped out of the room.

I waited ten minutes before I gathered my bag and keys and walked to the entryway.

"Bye, Paula," I called, waiting to hear in her tone that everything was normal, that she hadn't seen Angus.

"Bye, Julia," Paula's voice rang out from the second bedroom.

Angus had snuck by her. As I made my way down the

hotel hallway and then into the elevator, I glanced out of the corner of my eye at the security cameras, knowing they were hidden in the lights, in the corners of the walls.

How had he done it? How had he gotten around the codes?

I realized, scarily, he'd done it simply by walking into the apartment. In plain sight. Most likely right behind Paula. Which meant others could do it.

"So?" he asked from the backseat the second I ducked in and closed the car door, the sound thundering through the empty garage.

It was so confusing to see Angus. John knew me, but he didn't understand how I'd been raised or what it felt like to rein yourself in every time you left home. Living in this state made me feel like I was trying to survive on an island. Now suddenly, out of nowhere, I wasn't alone.

"So what?" I asked.

"What's your answer?"

I didn't respond.

"Julia, I can sense that dude from a mile away. I know when he's been in your apartment or even near the W. A month ago, when I first got to Austin, it wasn't like that."

"I don't feel it." Maybe I was too close to him all the time.

"You need to get far away from him."

"I made a decision. I'm stopping everything. It worked with Roger and Ellis." At that moment, I decided to go all in with Angus, just the way I used to.

"Yeah, Novak neutered them. But that took months of them not using. Your best bet—his best bet—is you staying away."

"I know," I said, admitting finally that I had to leave.

"So what are you waiting for? If you're with him and he has abilities, Novak will find him through his spies, through his visions, who knows how else."

I listened, aware Angus was trying to hijack my life. "So now you have respect for Novak's power?"

"I don't understand why you haven't already left."

"Because I'm trying to figure out the best way to tell him!"

Angus leaned back against the seat. Then, as if he had a new idea, he said, "I can do it."

"No. You won't," I said, deliberately using an unworried tone to treat Angus's words as an empty threat.

"I'm serious. Every passing day hurts us. If you don't tell him, I will."

"You know I would never, ever let you talk to him," I cut Angus off.

"Then stop putting it off," Angus said in a sudden biting voice, letting me know that he was deadly serious.

AUGUST, two months later

JOHN

I couldn't wait to see you in Dallas. Getting you out of Austin felt so right, like it was the beginning of our real life together. It felt like everything was headed in a good direction.

I remember being nervous about you being with my parents so much on tour, but I told myself it was going to be fine. We were only months away from going to California and having true independence. I know high school couples who go to college together mostly don't work out, but we're not most couples . . .

JUNE

Chapter Eight

◦◦◦

I'd left while it was still dark to arrive in time to watch John play in the finals of the Texas State Open. It was only the first few days of my own private rehab, resisting impulses that were second nature. The side effects were terrible—the headaches, the rash that had appeared this morning, the depression. It was worse than almost two years ago when I'd first been told by Novak to stop using my abilities. Of course any restraint then hadn't lasted very long. I'd pretty much always cheated.

I arrived at the tennis center, a sprawling complex in the suburbs of Dallas, a checkerboard of courts with a grey-shingled pro shop in the middle. It was the start of the out-of-town summer tour we'd once planned on. I was an hour early. No one was there except staff who scurried around, setting up the entrance table, adjusting the board, and putting up nets.

I went into the women's locker room and waited, knowing this may be the last moment when things could possibly still be the same. We could still carry out our plans for this summer and then move to California. I could warn John about Angus, I could decide Angus had it all wrong and my father was long gone. If John had any abilities, they were so slight anyway, and I could tell him how to make them go away.

My eyes popped open when a small group of women and girls walked into the locker room.

It had to be time. I kept my eyes to the floor, wending my way past the group who began conferencing around a large, square bench in the center of the locker room. As I walked by, everyone looked up. Even if I wasn't recognized, people always paused and took note of my presence. It wasn't me specifically as much as their subconscious recognition that I was somehow different.

Opening the door, I almost slammed directly into John's chest.

John put up his hands to stop the collision. When he saw me, his dark brown eyes lit up and his hands automatically curved around my shoulders. I was leery of onlookers, realizing we were in the center of the action and now John was noticeable as a player who had advanced to the finals.

"Hi, Julia," John's mom said from just behind him. "We're checking in and then, if you'd like, come sit with us. Alex is coming up."

"Thanks." I was aware of John's hands on me in front of the crowd and his mom. "I'm going to hang back though," I said reluctantly. I'd told John I'd come but I'd have to stay in the background.

"Gotcha," Kathleen said as if she just remembered my

situation. I felt like I'd just lost the imaginary point I'd gained from showing up.

Kathleen turned to John. "Hurry, okay?"

I could tell she was nervous for him. She walked over to study the board, looking at her son's name in the finals box, giving us a moment to say hello after days apart.

"Hi." I smiled.

"I can't be separated from you like that," John said decidedly, as if it were something he simply refused to do again.

The black cloud swiftly rolled in.

"Did you used to say that to all the girls?" I joked. I wouldn't discuss anything serious until after his match.

"You know I didn't."

"I missed you so much." I inched back to look at him. I automatically reached up to touch his high cheekbone, my fingers nearly brushing his long lashes, unable to stop even though we were in public. His tan skin was so smooth, without a single pore. His eyes still had the green flecks toward the center, but otherwise, John looked the same as he always had. I relaxed a little.

He kissed my palm, his hands moving to my waist then sliding down until his fingertips grazed the top of my back pockets. I inhaled sharply, my head tilting to the side as I let myself feel his touch.

"Guess who I'm playing?"

"No," I said, starting to laugh.

"Yep. He's turning seventeen this year so he's in my bracket."

"Where is Alex?"

"Probably giving himself a pep talk in a corner somewhere."

"Be careful. Don't kill each other."

"He's the one who needs to be careful."

"Has Alex ever beaten you in a tournament?"

John looked over his shoulder, pretending to be distracted and avoiding my question. I had to stop myself from smiling.

"Can I drive home with you after this?" John asked, suddenly pensive, changing the subject. The Fords would be home for a few days before their next trip.

"Of course," I said, curious. Why did he want to talk to me? I needed to say something too. "Is something going on?"

"Nothing." John looked like he was about to say more but then he shook his head.

"It's so good to see you." It was. Even better than seeing Angus who I'd worried about for six months.

I stared at his full lips. Forgetting myself in public, I stood on tiptoe and touched my lips to his. I didn't deepen the kiss, but it was enough to make us both feel a little out of control. I could hear John's heartbeat begin to race.

"John! Let's go!" Alex called.

John made an annoyed sound, and we broke apart. He looked over his shoulder at his brother and then back to me.

He frowned. "You look like you haven't eaten in days."

"I'm fine. Good luck."

"I don't need any!" John joked as he walked off.

I found a good vantage point on a top bleacher of the center court, which must have sat about two hundred. The Ford parents were down below, courtside.

As the match began, I was so relieved to see that John was good, but he wasn't perfect. He wasn't exponentially better than Alex.

At first I thought the matchup of the brothers would be funny, but then I saw why Kathleen had her hands close to her face, as if she wanted to cover her eyes. The boys slammed the ball at each other as hard as they possibly could and threw their entire bodies into returning shots they otherwise would have let go.

John kept a consistent lead, but Alex kept coming back before John knocked him back down again.

John began to pull further ahead and placed a shot into the far corner of Alex's side, into the last inch where the ball would have been called in. There was no way Alex could get it, but he still lunged for it.

I heard a pop. Then Alex suddenly went down and grabbed his knee. John's parents stood.

The umpire ran over and John was second in line, coming to kneel at his brother's side. John reached for Alex's knee. I stood and then quickly sat back down, unable to see anything now that Alex was surrounded.

The crowd murmured.

From what I knew from playing soccer, it was most likely Alex's ACL. If that was the case, he was done. He'd need surgery and he'd be out for months, missing out on playing his senior year when he needed tennis to earn him a scholarship.

Of course it had to happen when John was playing him. Alex's fierce competitiveness was probably why it had happened.

While I waited for Alex to be carried off the court, I hugged my upper arms and wracked my brain, thinking down the line, wondering if there was anything I could do—somehow secretly pay for Alex's surgery, or college, how to convince John he wasn't responsible—when the entire stadium erupted in clapping and a few whistles.

I raised my head and was confused to see Alex limp lightly off the court, John just behind him.

Unable to move a single muscle, I let the crowd empty the stands and continued to sit where I was, up high in the sweltering heat, watching John.

❧◦❧

I stood off to one side, near the men's locker room, watching Alex pace gingerly as he waited for his brother. Alex and John had both changed and gathered their gear. Alex snagged John's sleeve as John tried to walk past.

"What the hell, man?" I heard Alex whisper to John.

"What?"

"What was that?"

John looked up and saw me nearby. "The match?" John asked his brother, sounding sincere. But then I saw in John's eyes that he was covering. He knew.

"I blew my knee out," Alex stated.

"You didn't blow your knee out."

"I did. I've never been in so much fucking pain." Alex leaned closer to John. "What did you do when you grabbed my knee?"

John retreated. "You're the one who suddenly stood up and started walking. It was nothing I did."

Alex stared at John. Then, again, "What did you do?"

John suddenly jumped all over his brother. "It was a shitty match. Let's just go." John blew off Alex and started walking away.

He half-turned to me as he passed by. "I'm going to go find my parents and tell them I'm driving home with you." He was upset.

"Of course." I could hear myself say the words, but I felt like I was floating somewhere above my body.

John strode off toward the clubhouse.

Alex came to stand next to me, snapping me back to the moment. "Did you see it?" Alex asked me directly, almost accusingly.

"Sort of," I lied. "I just saw you go down." I was a wreck. The trembling in my hands hadn't stopped.

"I don't know. He just pried my hands off my knee and put his hands on it like he knew what to do. And then it was like a fire was put out."

Over and over again, he kept stretching out his knee. He looked confused, and he walked over to a patch of shade. I followed.

"Have you noticed how he shifts sometimes?" Alex said.

"Shifts?"

"I don't know. He'll suddenly go into a mode where he can do everything. And he looks different or maybe he just seems different. It's like there are these moments where he becomes this tennis god or he can win easily at any other game he plays. Then this crazy thing just happened."

"When did you start noticing something unusual?" I shouldn't have asked because Alex looked at me, suspicious.

"Here and there last year. And then a lot lately."

"I don't know about your knee. Maybe it was phantom pain. Your brain thought you'd hurt yourself. And the other stuff—I think that's just John. He's really good at everything." I wanted to lead Alex away from where his train of thought was headed. But what did he mean, "here and there last year"? What had I missed?

"Is it you?" Alex's eyes glazed with tears of sudden mistrust and fear. "Is the stuff they say about you true?"

"I don't understand what you're asking." Really I didn't know how to respond.

Alex backed off, unsure of the position he was about to take. His instincts were ahead of his brain. "Nothing. I gotta go."

"Want me to drive?" John asked as he approached the car. I noted how he avoided looking me in the eye. The tennis center was far quieter than it had been even fifteen minutes ago, only some of the smaller courts still housing matches. John bent low and undid his shoelaces, making them even looser.

Across the parking lot, Kathleen and Taro waved good-bye, trying to catch our eye as they got into their Accord. As their car drove off, I saw Alex in the backseat, craning to catch a last glimpse of us. I turned my attention to John, who had risen and was staring at me since I hadn't responded to his question.

"Can we sit down for a second?" I asked, reluctantly. "I need to talk to you."

"What? I just want to get out of here. We can talk in the car." It struck me that he wasn't curious as to what I wanted to talk about.

"Let's talk now." I tilted my head back and looked in the sky, knowing I was on the brink of changing everything.

"Okay," John said in a cautious tone, steeling himself.

I'd had time to pick out the spot under the awning of the

main court. No one would be able to see us or hear us unless they began walking down the bleachers, and then we would spot them coming.

He waited on the bench. If I sat next to him, I wouldn't be able to see him, so I chose to stand in front, keeping us face-to-face. John's hair had already dried in the heat. He pulled up the bottom edge of his black T-shirt to wipe away a drop of sweat on his face. Then he fidgeted with his shoes again. He looked everywhere but at me.

"So what happened down there?" I started.

"I don't really want to replay the match."

"Your brother blew out his ACL."

"What are you talking about?"

"Did you intentionally fix it?"

"That's crazy," John said dismissively. But he didn't deny it.

"Remember Liv at Barton Springs?"

"Of course." His eyes snapped to mine at the rare mention of my sister's name.

"You touched her that day and she leapt up from being essentially dead."

"I thought that was you," he said.

I could see in his eyes he was slightly scared, wanting to hear me continue to connect the dots but not sure he was ready to make it real.

"It wasn't me," I finally said.

John scrubbed his face with his hand. Then he rested his forearms on his knees and looked at me, but still, he didn't say anything. I began to wonder how long he'd been alone with this.

"I'm pretty sure that was you," I began explaining.

"But it was because of you being there?"

"Maybe. I don't know. But it wasn't me."

"That's impossible."

"John," I said, gently, wanting him to admit it.

I reached out to touch him and he dodged my hand, the only sign that he was scared.

"You're different than when I first met you," I began. "For instance, how do you know when I try to read your mind now? How do you block me? I know you pictured my bedroom at the W months before I lived there. Admit it, you realized that on the day of your graduation party. And today you reminded me of what happened with Liv. . . . So you seem to have this healing ability and these visions of the future. What else is going on?"

John stood.

"Stop. Don't walk away. This is important. Look at me," I ordered.

John sat back down and stared into my eyes. I settled next to him and took his hand. I remembered when I told him who I really was, about what existed beyond the realm of his imagination. Now I had to tell him he was part of it.

"Just tell me what's been happening. I've seen it, but tell me what you've been feeling."

He looked at me for a moment longer. "Fine. Yes, I feel like I'm going through some shit right now."

"What do you mean?"

"I just thought everything was going my way. I've been super focused. I got into Stanford. The smartest, hottest girl on the planet is my girlfriend."

I squeezed his hand. "Did something happen?"

John looked off in the distance and then back to me. "I can see details that were invisible before."

"Like?"

"If I look down at the ground, I can see every individual speck of dirt or sand. I also hear sounds I shouldn't be able to hear—like Spirit's heartbeat. I've been feeling like I'm going crazy."

"Why didn't you tell me any of this?" I asked, amazed he had been holding it in. Then I saw that John was watching me warily, worried about my reaction.

"I almost did a few times. I thought about bringing it up that night we went to dinner. But if you didn't believe me, I would have felt like . . . I don't know."

"Of course I would have believed you!"

"I also thought maybe I was hallucinating and I was scared to know that for sure. But I feel amazing. I feel so calm. I did anyway."

"What do you mean you did?"

"Just now, after Alex stood up, it was such a high. It made me remember that I'd had that exact same sensation at Barton Springs. I'd written that off because it was a long time ago and everything happened so fast—I met you for the first time, then your sister almost died, and then all of a sudden we were at the police station."

I squeezed his hand hard. "Come on. Let's get out of here."

"Tell me, Julia. What the fuck is it?"

John got back into the car, holding two drinks in one hand

from the rest stop convenience store. We'd just passed Waco, about a hundred miles from Austin. I was relieved when he closed the door. I was in a hurry. I'd noticed the same black Chevy Tahoe driving behind us for miles and now it was parked at the rest stop as well.

"Did you know this could happen?" After having a few minutes to himself, John had had time to think of more questions.

I shakily started the car, taking the iced tea from him with my other hand. I watched him fidget with the lid of his orange Gatorade, the only sign of how nervous he was. While he'd been inside, I'd thought about how I was going to say what I had to next. It was the worst part.

"My father thought we had an effect on certain people, but I thought I was different. You didn't think to tell me your grandmother was from Peru, just like my family?"

"Lots of people are from other countries."

"But it's good—we're young enough. From what I've seen in myself and other Puri kids, when you're our age you can either develop it and make it stronger or leave it alone and it goes away. So I think there's still time to make it stop. I'm counting on it."

"What are you talking about? I have this feeling like everything is right in me. Like I'm complete. Does that make sense?"

It made perfect sense. I'd felt it for the first time when I'd read John's mind.

John spoke quickly, nervous about what he was asking. "I want you to help me figure this out."

"No." I shook my head vehemently, taking my eyes off

the road. "You do not want to be one of us. You will be hiding for the rest of your life. Even from your own family. Trust me. It's not worth it."

"But what would have happened to Alex if I hadn't done that?"

"It's not going to work. It will get you in trouble."

"How? I would be so careful."

I had expected John to be wary and out of his element, ready to drop it. I had not anticipated that he would push back.

"Don't go down this road. I've lived it: all fun and games until it's not, and then it's lonely. Do you know how scared I am? I never quite know what I can do and if I can control it. I live in fear of messing up in the exact wrong place. You know I've done that before. That's how we met."

"Healing people isn't fun and games." John reached out and ran his hand down the length of my ponytail. "You see your abilities as a bad thing, but they can obviously be used for something good."

"I want to stop somewhere to talk to you." I scanned for road signs that would tell me where I could pull over. I checked the rearview mirror—no Tahoe behind me.

"Why?"

"There's more."

John watched me for a moment and then looked around at the signs on the freeway. "Cameron Park. I've played disc golf there. Take that exit."

I followed his directions, driving a distance off the freeway. Checking in the rearview mirror, I didn't see any cars behind us. I wound my way into the park. We were just outside the Waco City limits, but suddenly, we were in a quiet oasis, thick with cedars and oaks that provided a cover of shade.

Together we silently agreed to walk down the dirt path through a thicket of shadowed woods ahead, the reverberating rattle of cicadas present in surround sound. We reached a lookout, a limestone pavilion shaded by the surrounding trees. Below, at the bottom of the steep cliff, lay the Brazos River bordered by cypress trees, their trunks rising from the water, casting shadows.

I turned to face him. "I didn't want to tell you any of this because I didn't think it mattered."

"What?" John asked warily, but still he rested his hands lightly on my waist.

"Like I said, my father thought there were people out in the world—a select few—who had the potential to become like us. Novak's been trying for years to change people and it never worked."

"What do you mean?" John dropped his hands to his sides.

On the river, kayakers drifted by in the blazing afternoon sun, their laughter echoing up the rock walls.

"He believed some people sought him out because they were drawn to his energy, that it tapped in to something that was already in them. Then he reasoned that, if they spent enough time in his presence, they would begin to evolve."

"Why would he want to change them? You hate outsiders."

I wanted to get this over with. "Novak didn't hate all of them. He'd watch for someone he thought showed promise and then hire them on as his assistant—Kendra was one of them. Novak hoped they'd make the jump and he could take them into hiding with the rest of the group." I knew he could hear my voice shake. This was the part I hadn't wanted him to ever know about.

"Why?" John asked.

"We're becoming extinct. We—they—need more people. An expanded gene pool."

John's eyes widened. "So they took people with them to repopulate?"

"I'm not sure. I know Novak was looking, but no one else in the group believes there is anyone like us and they were getting impatient with his search."

"What happened to the people you mentioned?"

"They would seem so similar to us—match us in intelligence, kind of begin to look similar to us—and then one day, they would have a psychotic break. Like changing was too much. I think my mother may have been one of the first people Novak experimented with. I don't know what happened to her though."

"So you think I'm one of these people? You're worried I'm going to have a psychotic break from being around you?"

"Yes, I think you are one of these people, and yes, I'm worried. I've never been this close to anyone but you, especially for an extended period of time. But I'm also worried about something Novak said to me the night I left."

John didn't say a word, his eyes flat, waiting.

"He told me he'd had a vision: he or Liv were going to read someone's mind and so they'd know without a doubt that they'd found one of us. Finally."

I watched John's eyes as he realized the eerie accuracy of the prediction.

"It sounds crazy," I said in a soft, placating tone.

"But I'm just me," he said. "I'm not—"

At that moment, for his sake, I wished I could go back in time. I was sorry for John that he'd ever crossed my path.

"I know," I said. "I felt the same way when I heard my father say it. But I can't deny that I've read your mind, and he predicted it—or, well, something close to it. And now I can't deny that you're doing these things. For the first time, I'm admitting my father is right. I think it's clear you're one of these people. And the fact that your grandmother's family lived in Peru for a few generations. It's too much of a coincidence. I don't know if you have a connection to the Puris or . . . I don't know."

"What about my brother or my dad?"

"They're pretty exceptional people. I don't know. Maybe it's lying dormant in them and the right person or circumstance would bring it out. Maybe it's in everyone and my people just figured out how to tap into it."

John shook his head uncertainly.

"You said it felt like fate the day we met, like we recognized each other. And you've had visions yourself. Since the day my family left, I've been scared Novak could be right. You thought it was paparazzi attention I was worried about? Really, it's any photos my father might see of you and me together. I've been trying to hide you. I scour the internet frequently, making sure we were never caught on camera together."

"But they're gone."

"Apparently, they aren't gone until the end of summer."

"Where did you hear that?" John asked sharply.

Dammit. I could never mention Angus's name. I'd already

said too much about Kendra. "It was something my father said the last night I saw him. Novak is still searching for you until then."

John shook his head, still acting like I was crazy. I remained quiet, watching him wade through my logic. "What do you think would happen if he found me?"

"He'd take you," I said bluntly. "Your family would never see you again, and I wouldn't be able to find you. My father used his money to build a place where he can contain the entire group. They won't be heard from ever again once summer is over."

"It's underground, isn't it?"

"You saw it that day. You had a vision. When we were in my old bedroom the day we went back to the house."

John must have seen the look on my face because he reached out as if I were the one who needed comforting.

I cleared my throat. "Everything has happened pretty much just like my father said. Oh, except in his version, you and my sister are supposed to be together." It wasn't funny. I crossed my arms on the ledge of the lookout and buried my face, not wanting John to see how helpless I suddenly felt.

After a long silence, John gently smoothed my hair back from my temple, tucking it behind my ear, trying to get me to look at him. "If you're sure he's right, why did *you* hear my thoughts, and why did I fall in love with you and not your sister? She was right there that day I met you."

I looked up at him, feeling slightly better.

"So I'm the future of your species, but I'm here. With you."

"Don't even joke about it. You are not the future of the species."

"I still can't see it—that they would want to pluck me out of obscurity. I'm no one." A group of four men appeared, hauling two Yeti coolers. I straightened. John said hello to the group and then pulled on my sleeve so I would follow him out of the now-crowded pavilion.

John started up a narrow wooded path that led away from the lookout, and I walked behind him, worried about everything. We found a small, sun-dappled clearing with a lone bench. I sat and John stopped to stand in front of me.

I started with the easier part to talk about. "I have a way I think we can keep you safe."

"How?"

"You have to immediately try to stop using your new abilities." When he looked like he was going to argue, I preempted him. "Even I don't have complete control over mine. God forbid you do any of this in public, which you already have. When you do these things, you build a different energy. If any Puri passed you on the street, they would know."

He began to walk around the small clearing. "It's not like I have control over this. I don't think I can stop."

"I think you can if we're apart."

He snapped his gaze back to me.

"People in our group are stronger together, almost like we feed off of one another. I believe I'm having an effect on you, that I bring this out in you."

"But this is all just pure speculation."

"It's somewhat informed. It has precedent. True, Novak may never come back. Your abilities might not be dependent on me at all. But I'm not going to risk it. We need to separate until September. Just for the summer, until Novak is gone."

"Why can't we stay and fight it? He's a wanted man."

"No, staying apart, hiding even, is the only way," I said, immoveable. Then, I added, "You need to trust me."

John knew me well enough to know he wouldn't convince me otherwise. "What would you do? Stay in Austin?"

I concentrated on the ground, crushing acorns beneath the tip of my shoe. Reluctantly, I said, "I don't know. Maybe I'll move early. Get out of Austin finally. I've got to get a grip on my own abilities. For me to go to college, I have to stop using them. I don't think I can have you and them."

"You will be in California at the end of summer, right?" For just a split second, I saw the mistrust he had when it came to me.

"Of course. Once the danger is gone, we'll be together. I promise." As soon as I said it, I thought of my sister and promises I'd made in the past and hadn't kept.

I waited for John to look at me. I stared into his beautiful eyes, knowing this was one of the last times we would be this close for a good, long while. I made another promise I knew I would give every ounce of myself to keep. "I'm not going to let him find you."

We both watched as a small red fox suddenly danced out into the clearing, crossing in front of us, before swiftly disappearing back into the woods.

I waited in my car across the street from John's house. He didn't look back when he closed the front door behind him.

I rested my head against the car window, alone for the first time since that morning.

We'd taken our sweet time getting back to Austin after the conversation in Waco. John had insisted on driving, as if he were trying to gain control over at least one small thing in his life. I'd been worried he might be in shock because he was so quiet on the drive and he drove the speed limit for once.

"I'm sorry," I'd said at one point.

"Why are you sorry? This isn't your fault."

The grey freeway blurred by and the air conditioner blasted.

"I could have stayed away from you," I said.

"Yeah, that didn't seem to work." He half-laughed. "By the way, you can't blame me for fantasizing about you in class. I guess those were just visions of the future. Not my fault."

"I don't know. I don't think I own that bra. Wasn't it really lacy?" I teased, wanting to make him blush. I was so happy he was talking to me and even kind of joking.

John smiled, just slightly. "Well, it doesn't sound like you stopped reading my mind at those moments. I thought you were supposed to be wary of outsiders?"

"I should have known right then that I would end up doing every single one of those things with you." I ran my fingers through his hair. He briefly leaned into my hand.

"Thank God you can't read my mind anymore."

"Don't be embarrassed. Ever. Okay?"

I'd wanted to keep looking at him the whole trip, seeing him in a bit of a brand-new light. When I thought about the things he might be capable of, I felt my attraction to him grow, if that was even possible. I told myself to stop it. John was John. We didn't need anything more in common than what we already had.

I watched the dark house for a few minutes before I opened my car door. As I exited to move to the driver's side, I saw a black Tahoe drive by. I had a glimpse of a bearded man at the wheel.

Maybe it wasn't the same Tahoe I'd seen earlier in the day. There were a million of them on the road. Maybe it wasn't the same bearded man who'd tried to take the picture of John in the restaurant cellar.

I was about to do something I shouldn't. Agent Kelly always gave me his card when I saw him. Sure enough, I found two at the bottom of my bag.

I dialed his number, my first contact with him without the aid of my lawyer.

"Agent Kelly," he answered on the fourth ring, out of breath as if he'd been working out.

I cleared my throat. "This is Julia Jaynes."

There was dead silence on the other end.

"Yes," he said.

I had the thought that I'd just experienced the most surprise Rafa would ever show.

The concierge gestured for Agent Kelly to proceed into the meeting room I'd arranged at the W. It was a Sunday night and Rafa looked like he'd dressed in a hurry.

"Hello," he said formally. He didn't try to shake my hand.

I didn't give Rafa the chance to sit down.

"Here's the phone," I said, handing him the cell phone Angus had given me that night in the parking garage. I'd wiped it down to get rid of Angus's fingerprints.

"It's probably just paparazzi," he said. Still, he'd come to meet me.

"I know. But there's something about it that feels more like surveillance. I'm sorry if I'm wasting your time and it's your people who are following me. If not though, I thought you'd want to know," I said, hinting that it could be Novak.

"You said this man dropped the phone?"

"Yes," I lied. "I took it because he was using it to take pictures of me. It doesn't seem like the kind of camera a professional would use."

Rafa took the phone from me and put it in a baggie, treating it like evidence.

I stood up to leave.

"Thank you for reaching out," Agent Kelly said. "I'm sorry you felt threatened by this person."

I wanted to roll my eyes. He had to know I'd felt threatened for months by everyone and everything. Him especially. I wasn't sure why my knee-jerk reaction had been to call him. He'd just suddenly seemed like a tool I could use to keep this photographer away from John. At the end of the day, I was most likely just paranoid about the Tahoe.

"Anything else?" he asked, pressing me.

"Nothing," I said, eager to get upstairs and finally crash.

"I may want to talk more about this if it leads to anything." He held up the baggie.

"Fine." I wasn't about to tell him I was leaving for California. The FBI had never told me I couldn't leave the state.

He would probably be alerted as soon as I boarded a plane anyway.

We stood across from each other, eyeing one another. I didn't feel like a young girl around Rafa and he had never treated me that way. I felt like his equal and his adversary. A small part of me appreciated it, as if it were the proper respect anyone under investigation was due versus being treated like either a criminal or a celebrity who was famous for nothing except being famous. But I knew it was also dangerous that he took me seriously.

"Okay, then," I said.

"Would you like me to walk you to your door?"

"No. No, thank you."

"Are you alright?" That wasn't a very Rafa-like question. His questions were usually black and white. I sensed it was a Sunday-night question, an away-from-official-business question.

"Yes," I nodded.

"I can tell that's not true."

I said nothing more and left the room.

JOHN

What you told me about myself didn't seem possible, but when I listened to you talk, you had this way of making complete sense. You had me convinced that our separation was the logical next move.

But I had this problem. Any time we were apart, things we'd discussed, experiences we'd had, it all felt like I'd made it up. Most of all, you didn't feel real.

When you showed up at the graduation party, it was almost shocking to see my two worlds collide. Shocking in a great way. There'd become such a clean divide between the land of Julia and the Fords.

So when we said good-bye for the summer, I already didn't trust that you'd come back. You'd disappeared before. I tried to play it cool like I trusted this separation was temporary but I was freaking out. I was ready to ask you to run away with me, marry me in Vegas . . .

Chapter Nine

Standing in the narrow driveway, John positioned a large bag full of extra rackets into the packed trunk and then closed the back door.

"I guess this is it," he said, walking around the car, talking to his dad outside his home. From the doorway inside the Ford house, I watched Spirit, who was off his leash, follow John everywhere he went. There were sounds of children playing on the playground across the street and the faraway heaving of garbage trucks.

"You going to be okay?" Taro asked.

"Yeah," John said. "I'm fine. This won't affect the way I play if that's what you're asking."

"I'm asking about you. Not your game."

"I'm fine. It's not like we're breaking up."

I backed away from the front door.

"Hey, I think we need to say good-bye," Kathleen said to me, entering the living room. "We've got to get out of here if we're going to get to the hotel in Lubbock at a decent hour."

"Okay." I lingered, not following Kathleen out the door to say good-bye in the driveway. It took her a second, and then, to her credit, she understood. "Want me to send him in?"

"Thanks, that would be great."

"Bye, Julia," Kathleen said. I smiled and she smiled back. And that was it. I didn't like that Kathleen might be thinking that she was saying good-bye to me for good. But there was nothing tying me to her son now. I was giving up my apartment in Austin today, and on the horizon there was only a Stanford interview with no promises attached.

I surveyed John's house. He was coming back for a few days here and there before heading off to his first semester at Stanford, but today was the beginning of Austin no longer being his home. It was where we'd met. I'd thought of this year as hard and our future on the West Coast as holding all the promise, but some of the sweetest times in my life had taken place in this house.

"You ready?"

I swung around to face John. His eyes were dead of emotion, which was why his parents were worried. Without my abilities, I couldn't stop feeling everything while John acted like he felt nothing at all.

"It's two months," I said. "That's it."

"This feels wrong." John looked at his feet before raising his eyes to meet mine. We had wasted the last five days arguing over the phone.

"I know," I conceded. John was pissed we hadn't seen each other since I dropped him off post-Dallas. I'd agreed to this brief good-bye, surrounded by his family.

The front door blew wide open, and immediately, heat

rolled into the air-conditioned room. We looked at each other, not touching.

"You're acting like you have to handle this alone."

"Can we not?" I could see John already wasn't feeling great physically. "Don't let this get in the way of playing, okay? You got where you are because of years of working hard, not because of how you briefly changed."

"Don't worry. I know how to focus even when I don't care."

"Start caring. You told me how important this summer is."

"Promise me you won't keep any more secrets," John said, as if this were a new requirement.

"The same goes for you."

We were quiet for a moment.

"I have something for you," John said, attempting to be nonchalant.

"Really?" I was excited. John never gave me anything. I knew it was because I already had everything and he was worried I wouldn't like something he bought. But I would absolutely love any present that came from John.

He reached into his pocket and pulled out a gold bangle.

I took it from him and slipped it right on my wrist. By its weight, I could tell it was solid gold. I glanced at John and realized he was uncomfortable. "I love it. I'm not taking it off."

"It's my grandmother's. She gave it to me to give to you," he said, brushing it off.

My heart was splitting in two.

"I love it," I said again. It was now my favorite possession. I smiled. I found John's nervous apathy adorable. To make him more nervous, I played with the bracelet and remained silent, looking up at him expectantly. He didn't disappoint.

"You know this kiss needs to last us for two months?" he said.

Each of us waited for the other to initiate our last kiss. I often waited for him to make the first move, like I always wanted confirmation that he was still sure about us. Today, I closed the distance. John touched his lips to mine and slid both his hands through my hair, holding me still. The kiss deepened. He was kissing me like he didn't think he'd ever see me again. I stepped back, breathless, startled that one kiss had somehow been more intimate than any act we'd shared.

"Have faith in us," I said.

"Have faith in yourself," he said right back, looking me straight in the eye. It seemed to come from a place of warning. Like he knew something I didn't.

At that moment, a cloud passed in front of the sun. Just for a second, the room was cast in shade.

"See you in California?"

"Yes," I said. "Definitely."

For the last time, I punched in the code and let myself into my apartment, ready to close the door and finally let loose after holding it together in front of John. Abruptly, I was blinded by intense light and felt a sudden surge throughout my whole body.

Angus stood in front of the large living room windows, shades fully up.

I put my hand over my heart, which felt like it was beating out of my chest.

"What's wrong with you? You didn't know I was here?"

"God." I took a deep breath. "No, I didn't." My senses were dulling. I didn't like not knowing what was coming next. It was hard to believe that was how most people lived. Like sitting ducks.

"Are you crying?" Angus asked in disbelief.

I didn't bother answering.

"We agreed to take a break." There was silence and I knew just from our proximity, Angus had no choice but to feel the pain I couldn't manage to bury.

"What do they say about the first cut being the deepest?" Angus began to sing.

"Shut up."

He stopped and laughed softly. "So, what does he know?"

"Everything. Except about you being back."

The apartment was in disarray. The pristine furniture provided by the hotel was surrounded by empty boxes, exposed cords and a dirty floor with some spare change and dust. The movers had packed everything of mine up and put it in storage.

Angus gripped a piece of paper in his hand. "Did you see this?"

I walked over to him and grabbed his hand, pulling him away from the windows and into my bedroom. "The FBI watches me. And paparazzi."

"I'm not worried."

"What do you mean *you're not worried*? You're crazy. And what about me? I'm harboring a fugitive."

"I can feel them coming. I've become good at hiding. What's your plan?"

"San Francisco. I fly out tomorrow morning."

"Cancel it. We're driving."

"No way."

"I have a fake ID. I rented a car. Come on, you need me, Julia."

"No."

"Yes. I know when the FBI is around. I'll know if Novak comes back. I can protect you. I'll even help you find your mother. Look. Did you see this?" Angus thrust the paper at me.

It was a copy of the documents I'd made Donna print for me. I hadn't looked too closely at everything yet.

"I was bored so I started looking through these file boxes. Not very safe there."

"Nice. So?"

"Your mother's name is listed here—Blackcomb. Novak sold her some property for cheap just before he left. Nice truckload of money you have, by the way."

I read the statement. Elizabeth Blackcomb had paid a small sum to a company called Edgewater. Donna had mentioned I was the owner of a small real estate firm by the name of Edgewater Holdings. From what I knew about real estate prices in California, the amount paid didn't seem like fair market value.

"That's gross," I said. "She and Novak have some sort of agreement."

"Looks like this is just south of San Francisco."

"Do you think he gave her this property as a gift?"

"I'm sure. Don't you think?"

I sat down on the edge of my bed.

"Maybe—"

"What?" I demanded, impatient.

"Maybe you should check out your mother."

"No."

Angus sat beside me. "Don't you want to know who she is? Remember how my dad said Novak thought your mother was one of us at first? So there's a precedent. I'm just saying. I'm curious."

"No."

"If you find out what happened between them, maybe that could help you. Outsider, Puri. Why didn't it work? What if finding her would help John?"

"It hasn't come to that. Yet."

"Oh, I like how now you'll consider it if it's for him. What do you know about her? You've done research since you found out who she was, right?"

"Let's stop, okay?"

"Why are you so resistant?"

"Why do you think?" I demanded loudly. Up until this past year I'd believed my mother had been one of the Puris, someone who had been left behind at the last Relocation, for reasons I'd never know. But then the FBI agents who had been investigating my father had cornered me at school and told me the truth. That my biological mother was just a regular human. And I'd finally had to come to terms with why I'd always felt so different, and so excluded, from the rest of my family.

Angus shrugged his shoulders. "You keep telling me that's all you want. To be like normal humans. Why wouldn't you look for your mother?"

My excuses sounded lame to my own ears.

"Come on, Julia. Let's go to California."

JOHN

We should have stuck together. But we didn't know any better. The tournaments were such a great excuse to be together.

The sudden prospect of a summer apart was crushing. It was a lose-lose scenario—we couldn't see each other and I was supposed to stop using any abilities. The very first day we were apart, I saw a kid at the motel get hurt when he did a backflip into the pool and hit his head on the side. I had the instinct to help before his parents came over but I stopped myself. That sucked . . .

Chapter Ten

I had one last thing to do before I left Texas.

Legally, the house was in limbo and not mine. But it was easy to let myself in. I entered the master code into the keypad on the front gates and walked downhill along the manicured driveway, noticing the groundskeeper had left the garden lights on during the day.

I hadn't been back since I'd visited with John less than forty-eight hours after my family had left, needing to see for myself that they were gone. I'd felt tense on the drive over, but now I didn't sense any trace of the people who used to live here. It was just a house now. A giant, empty showpiece of a house.

This was where I had lived my entire childhood—completely removed, as if on a different plane of existence from the rest of the population. I hadn't even felt like part of the same world. I couldn't remember what that was like anymore. It seemed like something out of a dark fairy tale or like it had happened to someone else.

This was the last place I'd seen my sister. It was like visiting a gravesite. I chose to stay in the driveway, shaded by the lush green trees, listening to the silence except for the rustling of leaves in the hot summer wind. I was scared how intensely I might remember Liv if I went any closer or, worse, that I wouldn't remember her at all.

Angus was down the street in the idling car, blocks away from this place that could still have eyes on it, counting down the five minutes I'd asked for. I took a few steps backward, then turned and walked out the gates, away from the glass house.

Bye, Liv.

I walked alongside the greenery at the edge of the winding road, head down until a car slowed and drove up next to me. Angus never fully stopped and I effortlessly got in, closing the door as he accelerated.

When we left the Austin city limits, I turned around one last time, watching my childhood become a blur in the distance.

"Yo! Are you up?" Without waiting for an answer, Angus began blaring music, ready for me to come out of my shell.

I was vaguely aware of the wide, grey highway lined with strip malls and office parks, a sea of color and cement flying past as we headed northwest. I rested my head against the window and kept my eyes closed.

"I'm up."

"If you're not going to talk this entire road trip . . ."

"Sorry. I'm not feeling well." That was an understatement. I felt like crap. Mentally and physically.

"What's wrong?"

"You know that feeling when you stop doing the extra-sensory stuff? At first you're miserable and then it's like your body gets mad?

"Yep."

"My body is mad."

"Then why the fuck don't you do something about it? You're away from him. You can do whatever you want now. You're free."

Angus seemed elated, happy to be hitting the road.

"Ha. No."

"Why would you torture yourself? It's not going to work," Angus said bluntly. "We physically couldn't stop using our abilities before. It nearly destroyed us when we'd try."

"Remember, I'm not exactly like you." Even I could hear the hint of shame in my voice. "It's too hard to live out here and have it."

"You are going to die of boredom."

"It's better than living a double life."

"I'd rather live a double life. No, I'd rather be where all of our people are."

I looked over at him, surprised. "Are you serious? After everything you stood up for, now you're saying you'd be okay with living in a vault under Novak's thumb?"

"Without Novak," Angus mumbled in a low voice.

"Well, that's not going to happen."

"You look like shit. Go back to sleep," Angus said, like he wanted to change the subject. Then, he switched off the music and said in a softer voice, "Rest. You're with me now."

It made me want to laugh. Angus said this as if he weren't a fugitive, putting me in danger. But I knew what he meant.

He was a Puri and I knew how he operated. He was the only person I could hand the reins to, and it felt so good to do it after so long. But I'd made him agree we would part ways when we arrived in California.

I studied his profile for a second longer.

"I'll wake you up in Brownwood."

The name meant nothing to me. I didn't know any of the towns we were zooming past. I'd flown privately everywhere and had no sense of how the state or the country felt when you traveled by car. It felt like we were dropping off the face of the earth, getting lost. The thought gave me some peace and I closed my eyes.

I drifted in and out of sleep. Brownwood, Abilene, Sweetwater. Angus kept driving, not disturbing me even when I was awake. It wasn't like him to not talk.

At one point, Angus stopped the car and mumbled about stretching his legs. I felt hot and cold at the same time, and I could barely raise my head. The headlights partially illuminated Angus in the distance, in a field of wind turbines, looking up at one. He suddenly leapt up, but, of course, it was too high off the ground. I wasn't used to seeing him look like a stick figure, so small next to the giant structure. But then, not to be defeated, he walked backward a few paces before taking a running leap at it. This time, he clung onto the bottom blade, swinging his legs to push him and the windmill into motion. He dropped to the ground, having used his outrageous strength so he could presumably see the windmill in action close up and feel the thrill of the motion so near his body. This was what I thought I saw. It may have been part of a dream.

⤜⚬⤛

It was dawn when I decided to stay awake for good.

Angus watched as I straightened my legs and lifted my arms to stretch.

"Hey. You feel better?"

Miraculously, I did. "Yeah, actually. Feel my forehead. Do I feel hot? I think I had a fever."

"See? If you let go of this shit, you're going to start getting sick like they do. And you can't even go to a doctor." He felt my forehead and then lay the back of his hand on my cheek. "You're fine."

The air smelled crisp and felt dry. "Are we in the mountains?"

"Yep. We're getting pretty high in altitude. Welcome to New Mexico."

We'd left our home state for good while I'd been sleeping. Maybe I shouldn't have been surprised that it felt like a giant weight had lifted.

"It's beautiful." Relief settled in as I surveyed the sudden natural beauty around me—the pine trees, the low green grass dotted with craggy boulders. I wanted to get out and explore. "You must be ready to stop."

"I could drive for days without stopping, you know that." We both could. I would have thought I'd need food. I worried that maybe Angus's presence was shifting my balance back to the Puri side.

"I should check my messages and call John."

"You can disappear for twenty-four hours before your boyfriend starts to worry."

"I don't like that he thinks I'm already in San Francisco."

"It's safer that way. Holman, New Mexico. We're making tracks," Angus pointed with his chin to a passing sign.

"Let's get out to San Francisco as fast as we can, okay?"

"What does it look like I'm doing?"

I shifted in the seat and dug my new burner phone out of my bag. It lit up with voice mails. I'd retired my usual smartphone for the trip and set up call forwarding through a service that claimed the utmost discretion. My cheap plastic phone showed me that Donna was a missed call, and Rafa Kelly had called me directly at my personal cell number. He wasn't supposed to do that. There were no calls from John.

"What are you going to do once we get to the Bay Area?" I asked Angus. After the tumult of the past few days, I was only now thinking about where we were headed and the plan in front of me.

"I'd like to stay close to you," Angus said.

"Angus."

"What? We're better off together."

"I'm trying to make a clean start. You're my best friend, but I can't do it with you around. You know that."

"I'm only thinking of your happiness."

"And your own."

"And mine. We are always going to have more in common than you and he will. He'll never know you like I do."

"No," I said with finality.

"What if you're in love with the part of him that's like us? When that's gone, is he going to be enough for you?"

"That's why I fell in love with him. He's not like us."

"You know you're tampering with him the way Novak did with us, right?"

"If you feel sorry for him, why are you helping me?" I snapped.

"Because I don't like John. I don't want him around. Mostly, I don't want Novak to win. I like that wherever he is, people finally doubt him and his stupid visions. I don't want them to find out Novak is actually right."

"But then what happens if enough people doubt him?"

"There's a power vacuum. Novak gets overthrown. The family can decide for themselves what they want to do next." Angus said it like he'd given this scenario serious thought.

"Where do you want to stop?" I asked, steering the subject away from a futile fantasy.

"Let's get close to Taos at least. I've always wanted to see it."

Chapter Eleven

⫷❦⫸

The shower spray felt like hot, stinging needles on my skin.

The bathroom tile was a dusky, old-fashioned pink, the sink a marbled pink-and-white seashell. We were in a retro hotel, but one we'd paid for dearly from my stash of bills. Against all my arguments to stay outside of the city, Angus had positioned us in a mission-style revival hotel in historic downtown Taos.

I'd left the shower gel I'd brought on a shelf above the sink—right next to the hotel soap. If I looked long enough and hard enough, I knew I could knock one over and roll the other toward me. It would be so easy.

It felt like play-acting when I made myself manually shut off the water and soak the bath mat and the bathroom floor in order to use my hand to retrieve the shower gel. But I made myself do it. It was this kind of thing I was painstakingly having to get used to.

The bathroom was small, hot, and steamy, and I would

have preferred to get dressed in the cooler bedroom. Angus was out there though. I dried off and put on the fresh clothes I'd brought into the bathroom and wrapped my hair turban-style with a thin white hotel towel.

"Your turn," I said to Angus when I opened the bathroom door. He was stretched out on top of one of the queen-sized beds, a Native American print on the bedspread.

Angus stared at me, looking at me from head to toe. I was wearing a pair of white shorts and a white tank top.

"What?"

"Nothing. You reminded me of Liv for a second, wearing all that white."

We hadn't spoken of her yet. By avoiding the subject, the specter of our friends and my sister had only gained strength and made it even harder to discuss now.

Angus went first. "What did she say to you when you left?" he asked intently.

I cleared my throat, hoping to keep any emotion from my voice. I told myself I was just reporting facts. I listened to myself say, "I waved through the window. I thought she was going to call for someone to tell them I was running, but then she just waved back."

"I'm sorry," he said.

"Yeah." My voice lowered involuntarily.

"She will always be fine. She's Novak's princess. I'm sure they have the one thing he promised—total safety. Now they never need to worry about anyone finding out who they are."

"Yep." I didn't know if I wanted to continue the conversation and stood there, silent. After a moment, Angus leapt to his feet and walked toward me. I was at the threshold to the bathroom, trying not to think about my sister, and Angus put both hands at my waist to move me aside. The touch startled me, and we looked at each other, face-to-face, his light-blue eyes reminiscent of the entire family whose absence loomed over me.

"Do you think about her?" I asked.

"Of course. I think about the boys. I hope they're happy. If not, I can't even help them. They looked up to me as their leader and then I fucked that up." Angus's eyes seemed to pale. I'd never seen him cry, but I knew the lightening of the iris was one step before. He stopped himself and his eyes returned to their usual color. "Move over. I've got to shower."

I wandered to the window, pulling the curtain back to peer out. I felt like an outlaw, holed up. I stared down onto a town plaza bordered by art galleries, boutiques of Native American jewelry and crafts, expensive restaurants housed in picturesque pueblos, and other buildings with Spanish colonial architecture.

Once I heard Angus start the water, I quickly picked up my cell phone and listened to my messages for the first time in twenty-four hours. Rafa wanted me to call him but didn't say why. Donna checked in with an update on some rentals. There were two more missed calls from Rafa. It was uncomfortable feeling insecure where John was concerned.

Finally, the very last message was John Ford's. "Hey. Call me." His voice didn't sound mad or affectionate. It was all-around neutral. I hated that.

I looked to the bathroom door while I tried calling John, wanting Angus to stay put. The shower water was on, but Angus could still hear everything I had to say to John.

John answered on the fourth ring with a business-like, "Hey."

"Hi!" I said, a tad over-brightly. At that moment, the sound of John's gravelly voice was my favorite thing in the world.

"Hold on." It sounded like he was walking away from a group. A door closed. "Okay, now I'm good."

"Are you at the clay thing yet?"

"Clay Court Championships? I am." He sounded like he was congested. "Actually, I have to go in a sec. We're headed out to the tournament."

"You okay? Do you have a cold?"

"I'm fine."

He had to be feeling out of sorts, and I wanted to press him about whether he'd kept his agreement to stop using any abilities, but I didn't want to seem like I didn't trust him.

"*I'm* not fine," I said. "I miss you."

"How's the Bay Area?"

"Everything sucks without you. I keep replaying in my mind that time we were lying on my floor, listening to Dire Straits on those new speakers." I was smiling at the phone.

"Please don't bring that up."

"Why?"

"I'm in the hotel bathroom. My mom's right outside." Then, "Is it true what they say about California? That they know how to party?"

"The West is pretty wild," I said right back, his reference making me laugh. I heard the shower water stop and I got up off the bed and uselessly turned my back for privacy. I wanted to end the conversation so I didn't have to outright lie.

Thankfully, right then, I heard Kathleen and Alex calling to John impatiently.

"I'll call you later," he said.

"Knock 'em dead."

"But not too dead. Okay, I gotta go."

I heard John answering someone's question as he hung up the phone, leaving me hanging.

There was Rafa to think about and how I was going to handle the three phone calls he'd made. I decided to put it off. I could also call Donna tomorrow.

Angus came out of the bathroom in a burst, the door hitting the wall, steam curling into the room. He'd had the decency to put on shorts, but his upper half was bare.

"Hey!" Angus walked right up to me like he had been thinking of something he wanted to tell me while he was in the shower.

"What?" I flopped down on the bed and crossed my ankles.

"When I was away—"

"Yes?" I prompted when he stopped mid-sentence.

"I just think you should know—I thought about you the most."

AUGUST, one month later

JOHN

Sharing hotel rooms with him? That's the toughest thing to get over . . .

Chapter Twelve

"We have to be very quiet," I had whispered, nervous.

"Very," John had said.

I squeezed my eyes shut tighter, willing the present to fade as the world sped past the car windows. The memory I had chosen to recall came back in photographic detail. Though I was still in the car with Angus, I could even see the city lights illuminating the quiet rooftop pool of the W.

"Someone's going to come up here," I had said, hesitating. "People always show up when you don't want them."

"I think at four a.m. we're still okay. Five a.m., things start waking up," John had said from where he stood in the water.

He moved his arms in unison, drawing them back behind him, trailing his fingers in the water, backlit by the pool lights. We'd spent the whole night together, but with a space between us for the first time in hours, I felt like I could finally look at him.

John had relinquished his clothes at the side of the pool before he got in, so confident that no one would stumble upon us. I had no such confidence and wore the black bikini I'd worn on the day we met at Barton Springs.

"What's up?" John asked when I remained standing by the side of the pool, the white towel firmly wrapped around me. He waded deeper and deeper into the water.

Now I had to make more of an entrance. I dropped the towel and actually heard him suck in his breath. More quickly than necessary, I took a few steps down into the pool, covering my body with water. I raised my arms and twisted my hair into a bun.

"Come here," he finally said.

"No, you come here," I said back.

John dunked his entire body underwater before wading over, coming to stand two stairs below me. We were the same height. I stood still, looking at the droplets of water clinging to his lashes.

"That's the bikini you wore that day," John said.

"You remember?"

"Oh yeah. It's burned into my brain. How you looked in it and you had those bedroom eyes . . ."

"Shut up." I laughed. Then, I said, "That's right, I caught you staring."

"You did. It's funny—knowing you now, you never wear anything that shows this much skin."

"Yeah, well . . ." I wasn't about to explain that it had been a last-ditch ploy to have Angus notice me, to notice me more than my statuesque, perfect-looking sister. I'd felt like a fool that day. I hadn't known someone else would be watching me.

"Can I stare now?"

I laughed. "No."

"Why?"

"Because it's way too small for me. It always has been. It's not even mine."

"Really?"

"Oh, yeah, no. It's my stepmother's. She was mad I was wearing it."

"Your stepmother's? Actually, I can completely see that."

"It was the only bathing suit I could find today. I need to throw it out."

"Why?"

"It's easier if I don't have anything that reminds me of them, that puts my mind back there."

"I'm not sure you can just wipe them from your memory like that."

I shrugged.

"But right now, you're with me and you should accept my compliment. And I love this bathing suit."

John ran his fingers down my side. It never failed to surprise me how many different ways he could touch me and how it made me feel. When I was with him, I felt like I could see myself in a prism; every time it moved, I saw myself in a slightly new way.

"Hey!" Angus shook me hard, and my dream-memory immediately receded.

I rolled onto my back and covered my eyes with my hand, not wanting to wake up yet. I yanked the sheets over my head, realizing that, for the first time in weeks, they weren't soaked with sweat.

"You sleep like a dog having a dream. Whimpering and kicking your legs."

"What do you know about pets?" I mumbled.

"The man in Bel Air has dogs." Angus seemed to drift away for a moment.

"Let me go back to sleep." I wanted to calm my racing heart in private. The dream had felt so real.

"No way. It took a full minute to wake you up. Let's get out of here, okay?"

"What time is it?"

"Seven."

I felt a stab of remorse. We'd missed our chance to leave while it was still dark out. So I said, "I'm going to sleep more."

"No, you're not. I actually got hungry and brought back some food. You haven't eaten or had anything to drink. It's just making you sicker."

"What did you get?" I asked, my voice muffled by the sheets.

"Donuts. Coffee. A bruised banana." Angus laughed. "You can have that. I was trying to be healthy."

I didn't make a move to get up. It seemed like so much effort, and I was still bone-tired. Waiting for further argument from Angus, I was surprised when he said nothing. Then, a breeze of refrigerated air chilled my body as he lifted my blankets and got in bed, flush up against me, spooning me.

"Angus!" I struggled to get away and got out on the other side of the bed, now the one standing over him.

"Well, let's go then. If we stay here, this is what we're

doing." He smiled and confidently crossed his arms behind his head, lounging in my bed.

"That's not happening."

"What?" he asked, innocently. "I just wanted to hold you. That's it."

I started laughing. "When have you ever wanted to hold anyone? You don't do that." The Puris have an amazing lack of affection.

"You'd be surprised."

"What does that mean?"

"Just because we were raised a certain way, doesn't mean we can't change. Look at you." he said as he reluctantly got up out of my bed and began gathering his clothes off the floor. I noticed he wouldn't look at me in my pajamas.

"I'm sorry," I said, feeling like I'd made fun of him.

"Don't apologize. Let's just leave." He was all business now as he zipped up one of his two small black bags, packed tight with bricks of cash.

"Lati gave that all to you?"

"No, I took it. He didn't want me to leave."

Of course he hadn't. It reminded me how dangerous it was out in the open for Angus.

"Stop going out to get food. I'll do it, okay?"

"Whatever. Just hurry up," he said, back to being an asshole.

"And green," Angus said as we approached the crosswalk. The light immediately flipped to walk and we kept going.

"Nice!" A man waiting at the light with two kids said.

"It's a talent," Angus replied.

We loaded up the nondescript Nissan in the small black-top parking lot across from the hotel. People were beginning to mill about, to-go cups in hand.

"I'll drive," I said, nervously adjusting my sunglasses.

"You still look like a wrath of God. I'll drive." Angus tossed the keys high in the air and caught them easily behind his back.

"I feel better." I did. I realized I had more energy today than I had yesterday.

"You know it's because of me, right?" Angus said, semi-annoyed. "You're better because you're in my company. That's the way it should be."

I hesitated at the side of the car. "Maybe this wasn't a good idea."

"What are you going to do? Take a bus?"

"I can fly out of here."

"Get in the car. You're just mad because I'm telling you the truth. We're better together. When you get those rashes all over your body, you could get rid of it in five seconds if you wanted. I don't know why you're being stubborn."

"You don't understand." I opened the passenger door and got in.

"What? You don't think I understand? I've been living out here for months. I know that it's dangerous. Look, all I'm saying is, if you let him go, you get it all. He's safe, you can be you."

"Just stop, okay? I can't have this conversation with you the entire trip."

Angus shut up and pouted. I decided not to speak until he did.

He drove north and I stared at the Sangre de Cristo mountain range, taking in the scenery from the safety of the car—the black and green ranges in the distance, all the sky surrounding us, the expanse of flat, rocky road.

"Wait, why are you getting off the highway?" I asked.

"Taos Pueblo."

"No. We aren't tourists."

"It's a UNESCO World Heritage site. Right here. We're seeing it."

Pissed, I shook my head.

"It opens in five minutes, we'll be the first ones, and we'll be in and out."

"Look at pictures online."

Out of nowhere, Angus rounded on me. "Do you realize we may never be back here? You think we have all the time in the world, but maybe we don't. Like you said, I may end up rotting in jail."

"I'm sorry," I said. "Jeez. I didn't know you wanted to look for America this trip."

"Aren't you curious? We grew up in a bubble. You realize that, don't you?"

"Fine. If you get arrested at a UNESCO World Heritage site, that's a good place to go down, I guess."

Angus ignored me and drove.

The road narrowed like a trail, leading us to the pueblo. In the tourism office, Angus spoke politely as he paid and accepted the two self-guided maps offered by the woman working behind the counter.

What he'd said about my lack of curiosity bugged me. I took my map from him and looked around at this living

Native American community. Signs stated no photographs of tribal members unless permission was granted, and *Restricted* signs were posted in some areas to protect the privacy of the residents.

I scanned my map and quickly read the history of the village, learning that it was currently occupied by 150 people.

"One thousand years old. At least," I said, observing the multistory adobe buildings under the blue sky with ladders at different points leading to upper floors. I was struck by the enormity of that number and all the history that had taken place in this spot. "It's hard to feel it."

"I can feel it," Angus bragged.

I continued to read aloud, "'Considered to be one of the oldest continuously inhabited communities in the United States. . . . Our people have a detailed oral history that is not divulged due to religious privacy.'" I paused. "Sounds familiar. So this is what it looks like when someone preserves their culture aboveboard. Do you think the people here like living in a fishbowl?"

"Hey, their culture is protected. And only members of the pueblo can use certain mountain land and their lake, so it says. Let's go in to the chapel."

Angus and I walked in to the chapel. Signs were posted everywhere asking visitors to show respect in this most sacred space. We stood together, not saying a word.

"Let's get on the road," Angus finally said. "This is too intense." He meant the energy he sensed inside. I wanted to feel what he was feeling, but I couldn't let myself.

On the way out, Angus stuffed a thick wad of cash into the wooden donation box.

"When did you become generous?" I asked, surprised.

At first I thought he didn't hear me, but then he said, "When I left Bel Air, I saw neighborhoods that were more like Third World countries, right there, in the same city. Just a few miles away from the estates."

Suddenly a soccer ball flew at my head. I deflected it with a glance, and the ball stopped in midair before bouncing down hard in the dirt. Jolted by what I'd done, I looked over to see a boy—maybe eight years old—staring at me, wide-eyed and stock-still. His bare feet meant he probably lived at the pueblo.

I stared at the little boy, not sure what to do. Angus grabbed my sleeve and pulled me to the exit.

"Dammit," I said, not bothering to complete my thought, beginning to beat myself up. "Why did I do that?"

"Because it's natural for you. Don't worry about it. Let's go."

As I saw the rash on my hands begin to recede, I chose to try and forget my brief lapse. It had been the first and only instance after being so good for so many days.

Tourbuses were arriving, releasing plumes of exhaust as they shuddered to a stop, a rude juxtaposition to the quiet pueblo. We drove away and didn't speak for miles.

An hour later, Angus pulled over. "I have to pee."

There were other cars on the road, but Angus didn't seem to care. He walked a distance. I looked away. There was not a tree or bush in sight. Just vast open space and mountains far, far away.

Out of the corner of my eye, I saw Angus begin to walk back to the car and I turned my head to watch him. Then he stopped. He stood, looking around, hands on his head, elbows wide. Without thinking, I opened my car door. I walked to Angus and stood next to him. I stretched my arms out, taking in the wide-open vistas and washes of pale pink and brown sandstone under the cloudless sky. Throwing my head back, I began to spin in circles.

JOHN

I'm still trapped, still thinking about you, and about how we got here. . . . I'll tell you about what happened while I was on the road.

Just before Clay Courts I began to feel like complete shit. Mentally and physically. I think, at that point, we'd been apart for only two or three days.

I put my head down, put my earphones on. I wore sunglasses and stayed in a fog: a kind of white noise daydream. I didn't talk much to Alex or my mom and they quit trying to talk to me. It looked like heartbreak, I'm sure. At that point, I was listening to your instructions. Because I've always been so good at following instructions.

I think I finally told you that I felt sick. It must be what kicking drugs is like. There was the pull of that thing that was calling me, that my body wanted to do, but I tried to shut off. I think you said it once: it was like this high that you were worried you'd never have again. No wonder you were breaking crap back in your apartment.

It was only about five days into the trip when I realized things weren't so bright or loud anymore. The car didn't have the smell of wet dog that no one else seemed to complain about. Almost all of my senses were dulled. I had returned to bland . . .

Chapter Thirteen

I floored it to one hundred, tearing past the mountain scenery, driving the way I used to in the old days. For a second, I pretended I was with Angus back when we were with the Lost Kids, driving recklessly in our lavish cars around Austin, trying to feel something, trying to get rid of our anger and helplessness as we watched my sister and the other chosen kids do the things Novak told us we couldn't. *Fuck him.*

Angus laughed, realizing he'd been enough of a bad influence and I was breaking my resolution. He never bothered with a seat belt. He rolled down his window and thrust his shoulders and head out the window, howling. His laughter was infectious, and inadvertently, I smiled.

"Keep a lookout for police!" I shouted to Angus.

He shook his head, conveying that he didn't sense a thing. No radar guns. No helicopters. No motorcycles.

Neither did I.

My body vaulted into high gear, adrenaline surging through my veins. I drove faster and faster, taking the curving mountain highway at deadly speed. It was like I'd pressed a button and every cell in my body was on track, my senses and reflexes working at full capacity.

The joyride didn't last long before two warning lights lit up the dashboard. One was the check engine light. The other was a foreboding exclamation point.

"Turn back to Durango," Angus said.

I slowed way down. "Why turn back?"

"This car is spent. It's perfect; we should ditch it anyway and change cars. We can buy a new one in Silverton."

"Why not in Durango?" I asked, rolling up my window.

"Because, baby, we're taking the train."

While we waited at the tourist trap otherwise known as the Durango and Silverton narrow-gauge railroad and museum, I felt confident there was no one watching Angus and me. Purchased tickets in hand, I walked by a couple dressed in gold rush–era costumes and shook my head. I looked at Angus as if to say, I can't believe you actually want to do this.

"Presidential class, just like you asked," I said, handing him his ticket. "Was this on your bucket list?"

"It sounds pretty cool," Angus said, completely unembarrassed. "I grabbed a brochure from the hotel in Taos. I've always had a thing for trains but I've never been on one."

With my hands on my hips, I surveyed the crowd and the vintage steam locomotive we were about to board. The clock on the wall of the station reminded me that John would be free by evening and he would know something was off if I didn't call. This whole trip was taking too long.

"We're going to get views you can't see from the highway," Angus said. "This will be worth it, I promise."

"We're wasting hours. This thing is going to go so slow I'm going to go out of my mind. The slowest fifty-two miles ever. Why do you always get your way?" I asked, half-annoyed that I'd let him talk me into it and partially resigned.

"Not in all things."

The train was already boarding. "Let's do it," I said.

We made our way to the presidential car. I'd given in to Angus on this too, even though two kids buying pricey accommodations was far more memorable. The dangers were so many and so pervasive—to John, to Angus—that they'd paralyze me if I continued to focus on them. All I could do was manage the here and now, just what was in front of me. On this trip, I wanted to fall off the map, just the way Novak could.

You can't find me. At least for today.

Angus and I entered the Old West. The presidential car was formal with wood paneling, patterned carpet, Victorian touches, and berth seating. Both of us went ramrod straight at the sound of the shrill whistle, and even I tried to stop myself from smiling as the train pulled out of the little station.

Everyone in our car looked to be retirement age, and both Angus and I kept our eyes glued on the window to avoid eye contact with the curious glances in our direction. Then they seemed to forget about us as we began the route.

"Come on," Angus pulled my arm once we were on our way. We exited onto the private, outdoor viewing platform— Angus's reason for wanting the more expensive car. We were at a high altitude in the rocky Colorado mining country, taking in vistas of the canyons and mountains dotted with pines that were inaccessible by car. The track was so narrow, the train felt so rickety, it was hard to believe anyone had ever dared to dream that this would work, that this was how they could connect the mines.

"Do people use this train to go fishing and hiking? Out here would be a great place to hide," Angus said wistfully.

"Who are you?" I asked but I was feeling awe-inspired as well. The route was going to cross southwest Colorado's Animas River—the River of Lost Souls—five times. "Look!" I cried out, involuntarily.

Even the people around us followed my finger, pointed at the river. "Bear," I said to the platform at large when people kept looking, unsure.

Angus started laughing, mocking me. I was an idiot. He and I could see the eyelashes on the bear while these people had to squint to see a huddled black figure.

When everyone lost interest, returning to their seats and their own window views, Angus nudged me. "Wasn't this worth it?"

"Maybe," I admitted. Was it possible not to feel guilty that I was taking in every sight and sound, using all the senses I was born with? When would I have this opportunity again? I decided to change course. Once I reached California, that's when I'd try again to quit. I'd have no choice.

As I watched the blades of grass rush in the wind and the dust swirl, I'd never felt so alive and a part of this world. And like myself.

Why would I ever want to change?

I shoved that thought right back down from where it came.

"Come on, J."

"I shouldn't." But it was a very weak argument at this point. It was hard to believe just three days ago I'd been so sick, detoxing from exactly what I was back to using.

"Whatever." Angus laughed at my faint protest.

"Okay, fine. Stand back." I focused hard on the sheer cliff high above us. It was a reach to use my telekinesis at that distance. I moved a small handful of dirt from above, and we watched it cascade down in a small brown trickle.

"I want to see a boulder."

"Nah, I'm not disturbing things here. That's a road up there."

Standing on the bank of a rushing, narrow stream, I surveyed the alpine valley, carpeted in wildflowers, situated below mountains that had once housed mines and were now abandoned ruins. We'd managed to secure a decrepit jeep in Silverton, and Angus had convinced me to go off-roading. We followed one of the old mining trails to explore the San Juan Mountains of southwest Colorado.

"Now's your chance to test yourself," Angus had said. "When have we been alone like this—with this amount of space?"

What ensued was a game. Angus would call out the name of an object that I had to move with my mind.

I had edged a decaying log into the middle of the narrow, winding stream, sending it down current. Like a sharpshooter, Angus watched for the individual pine needle that I moved apart from the rest. My all-time best was skipping a handful of rocks deep downstream.

Angus picked up felled trees like they weighed only as much as a heavy log. At first it was an effort for both of us, but in the fifteen minutes we dominated our surroundings, it got astonishingly easier and easier. We alternated, trying to outdo and show off to the other person, laughing like lunatics. Both of us were filthy from off-roading, with dirt in our hair and ears. But we stood there high on ourselves, thrilled by our own power.

"Imagine backpacking out here? We could do this shit all day," Angus said.

On the return ride to the San Juan highway, on our way to Ouray, another Victorian mining town nestled in the mountains, we had the attitudes of people satisfied after a great outlay of energy.

"You know what the best thing is?" Angus asked.

"What?" I said loudly. The open-air jeep made it hard to talk. My hair whipped around me as I took in the mountains, trying to make myself realize I was here and this was real.

"Novak couldn't take that away from us after all." He paused. "What do you think it's like?"

It took me a second to understand what he was asking. "Where they are now?"

Angus nodded.

"I don't know what Novak meant by paradise. Maybe it's like this? Playful? The freedom to use your powers all day long?"

The mood in the car changed at the mention of the group, a sadness bringing us down from our high.

Angus suddenly brightened. "What if you and I bought a cabin out here? I think we'd be safe." He said it like he'd just found the answer we'd been searching for.

"I can't, Angus," I said automatically. The light in Angus's eyes dimmed.

But then I imagined it. Falling off the face of the earth with Angus, in this most beautiful place, free from prying eyes.

The seed of this idea took root. It also meant John would be free to live a normal life.

JOHN

During the tour, my brother was as annoying as hell. Blaring his music, kicking up into handstands in our small motel rooms, asking me to check shit out on his phone. I'd lie down on my bed and put my forearm over my eyes and hope he'd get the hint. He reminded me of Spirit, how he followed me everywhere. He was with me All. Of. The. Time. But I also never wanted him to leave the room because it was something that felt normal. After all the subtle changes that had taken place over the past year, Alex and I were still the same together. Mostly. Now he was being careful with me, like he was worried about me.

When Alex finally blew up at me, I felt sorry for the guy. "You know this is our last summer together, right?"

After that, I made more of an effort.

Alex never talked about his injury. Which I should have known was a sign that he hadn't let it go.

JULY

Chapter Fourteen

We finished our journey in the dark, Angus driving full speed.

We pulled over at a roadside motel. Leaping from the open-air jeep in unison and walking side by side, I knew if anyone saw us, they would think we were trouble—dirty, deeply browned from the sun, acting like we owned the place. If only they knew one of us was an actual outlaw.

We walked the short distance to the motel office. "I'm getting my own room," Angus said evenly, as if he had a new resolution to distance himself from me. He had been acting cold toward me ever since he thought I'd rejected his proposal. I hadn't let on that I couldn't stop turning over the possibility in my head.

"Okay," I said slowly. "What about food?"

"I don't need it."

"Fine." I changed my tone to match his cold one.

Angus surprised me by reaching out and righting a strap of my tank top that had slid down my shoulder. I met his eyes.

"I'll still be on lookout," he reassured me, as if he were my protector.

"I got it," I said. It was true. When I used all my senses, I could take care of myself again.

We went into the dingy and slightly frightening motel office and came out with two rooms. Angus nodded to me, and disappointed, I watched him walk to his room at the other end of the row from mine.

Opening room number one with my jangling key, I let myself into the room. I tossed my duffel in the corner and then quickly picked it up off the floor. I found my phone and perched on the very edge of the thin, brown polyester bedspread wishing I didn't feel so nervous.

John answered on what felt like the last ring.

"Hey! It's me," I said, with butterflies in my stomach.

"Hey," he said, sounding groggy.

"Did I wake you up? I'm sorry!"

"Let me call you tomorrow. I don't want to wake Alex."

"Of course," I said softly.

"Bye," John whispered.

I put down the phone, disappointed but relieved I wouldn't have to lie to him. It was confusing; when I was with Angus, it was easy to be logical about the dangers confronting us, almost like I had a sharper sense of the importance of keeping John safe. But when I heard John's voice it made me remember how much I wanted him and how badly I wanted to keep the promise I'd made.

A string of disgusted profanity resounded just outside my

window. A child cried in response, then a slap and the crying abruptly stopped. I opened my motel room door.

Right outside was a woman standing next to a Mercedes SUV and a girl, maybe two years old, with wispy, tangled blond hair in a yellow sundress beside her. Before them on the ground was an iPad with a cracked screen.

The woman snapped her head in my direction and gave me a dirty look, not having the decency to look ashamed. The toddler swayed, trying to remain standing after the slap.

It was the little girl's helplessness that triggered it. Something in me couldn't take it.

"What are you *doing*?" I asked the woman.

I crossed to the little girl, bending so that we were eye to eye. By some instinct, I let down my guard. The worst was feeling her confused fear.

"Get away from her!" the woman shouted.

I whipped around. "No."

The woman glared.

"You're okay," I said and tentatively reached out to touch the top of the girl's head. If I were Novak, I would have been able to influence the tiny girl's feelings. Temporarily flood her with a different emotion besides fear. For once I didn't want to block out someone else's pain, I wanted to feel it. But staring into the eyes of the little girl, I hated that I didn't know what to do. And I understood what John had meant when he'd said that it was hard to walk away.

The woman reached down and snatched the child.

"Don't ever hit her again," I hissed the empty threat as the mother loaded her child into the car.

After they drove off, I decided to take a walk to cool

down. I traveled two blocks north to the small, shabby main street I'd seen when we'd driven into town. I could sense Angus inside a bar. He hadn't told me he was going out. He just couldn't seem to lay low.

Like something out of an old Western, two swinging doors led me into the town saloon. It was part tourist trap, part drinking hole, and one of the very few restaurants in the smaller, much less hospitable looking tourist town in which we'd found ourselves.

Scattered with peanut shells, the scratched floorboards were warped, and there was an etched glass mirror behind a long mahogany bar.

"Sit where you'd like," an older gentleman manning the bar called. "As long as you're not underage." This last bit was said without any real force behind the words. He had an extremely long beard, wore a yellowed white button-down shirt and suspenders in a seemingly reluctant effort to look like an old-time barkeep. The player piano in the corner had a piece of white paper taped to it that read, "Do not touch."

The entire bar was on edge—I could feel it. It was Angus. He had his back to me. He was sitting at a table in a corner, minding his own business like a good boy, or so it seemed. Then I saw the two young women sitting at the table next to his, leaning over and chatting with him. From the thick tension in the air, it was easy to tell that at least one young man sitting at the bar didn't like what was taking place.

"What's going on, *Tyler*," I said, sauntering up and using the name from Angus's fake ID.

"What's up," he said, dissing me publicly by keeping his eyes on the two women, who on closer inspection were either barely twenty-one or younger. One, with brown hair that hung stick straight past her shoulders, wore a red tank top and white shorts. The other had a short blond bob and wore a sundress and cowboy boots. From the pheromones dancing around them, it wasn't hard to see that they were very excited for a young stranger to drop into their bar on a Saturday night. I'd never seen Angus charm outsiders before. He'd watched them mostly, sometimes interfered with them from afar for entertainment, but I'd never seen him get this close.

I decided to mess with Angus. "Tyler, why did you leave me? I came back from my walk and there was no note!"

Angus looked both amused and annoyed. "Melody, you know me, I need to roam."

The name on my ID was Allison. He was going to get me kicked out if they checked. I tried to keep a straight face, rising to the challenge. "Seriously, Tyler, we can't go on like this." Now, the whole bar was watching. I belatedly realized Angus and I were both being ridiculous and cocky.

"She's so desperate," one of the girls murmured to Angus, shaking her head.

"Melody, go home."

Now I was getting pissed. "Tyler, let's go," I said in my normal voice, startling the girls out of their embarrassed laughter.

Angus had barely glanced at me since I walked in. Now he craned his neck to look at me. His glare said that he wanted me to leave him alone.

I heard a barstool scrape the floor and a heavy footfall behind us. I already knew which patron it would be. The young man with the longish, dishwater-blond hair who was attractive and knew it. His back had been bristling when I walked in, obviously possessive of one of these girls.

I faced him. "I've got this," I said gently to the stranger, trying to make him disappear. I could smell the alcohol on his breath.

I turned back to Angus. There wasn't any playfulness in his eyes when he looked at me. Intentionally trying to aggravate the young man further, Angus said, "I said, go home."

"You should both go." The young man grabbed Angus by the back of his T-shirt, holding it in one fistful, trying to yank him up. Angus didn't budge and rapidly chewed his gum.

"Let him go," I said sternly.

"Nick!" one of the girls said sharply.

With two hands, Nick moved me aside and grasped the back of Angus's chair, trying to dump him over.

Angus leapt to his feet and Nick was halfway across the bar before anyone could blink. Even I hadn't seen exactly what happened. The whole bar was silent, trying to figure it out. Nick was out cold.

One of the girls and a couple of guys from the bar ran over to Nick. Three others descended on Angus. I placed myself in front of him.

"Move," Angus said in a whisper-soft voice. I didn't know why but I listened. I moved to the side and watched while one man took hold of Angus's T-shirt by the collar and Angus let himself be hoisted to his tiptoes.

"Let him go," I said. "Now!"

No one paid attention to me. The man and Angus stared

at each other. I watched as Angus's eyes began to glow a light, light blue. I realized Angus was out of control, that he was going to use these people as punching bags to let out whatever pent-up emotion he'd hidden beneath the surface. The whole time we'd been together, since we'd reunited, he hadn't seemed like he was this angry.

In an attempt to save Angus, I did the lesser of two evils but still an evil. I sent the girls' wine glasses flying off their table. They landed on the floor in a spray of glass.

It would have better if I had actually touched the glasses before making them soar. The man holding Angus let go and backed up several feet. The girls slowly stood and scooted around their table, moving farther away from us.

Angus shook his head at the men, at the bar in general.

"Come on," I said.

Angus looked hard at the people watching us for a couple more seconds, then relented and began to walk slowly with me to the exit.

We'd almost made it out of the swinging doors when the bartender rushed toward us, then halted to keep a healthy distance between us.

"You!" His voice shook with so much emotion that I slowed to hear what he had to say.

"Don't come back." He pointed at us. "We've seen your kind before and you're not welcome here."

"What the fuck?" Angus muttered.

Once we were out of sight, we began running to the motel.

"Get your stuff," I said. "I'll meet you at the car in five minutes. Dammit. Now we need a new car."

"What do you think he meant?" Angus asked, fascinated.

"I have no idea. Go!"

"Sleeping Beauty!"

"What?" I snapped, shifting in the passenger seat. I must have spaced out. That's all I wanted to do now—retreat and pretend this road trip had never happened. It was too confusing. I had a plan and that should have been it. But thinking I could cut Angus out from the rest of my life was getting harder to imagine.

"Hey, no need to take it out on me. Let it go. I'm not worried. They can't prove anything."

I looked out the window. Every mile turned our mountainous scenery to desert as we descended into Utah. "We need to change cars in Salt Lake."

"Yes, we do." Angus seemed almost happy.

"Am I only contributing to your reckless thrill-seeking?"

"Yes, you are. Ha! I can't believe you were the one who made the mistake!"

"What if the FBI finds you? God, why did I do that?"

"Because Novak never taught us how to properly use our abilities. That's what he held over us—that he was going to teach us. Now, we have to figure it out on our own. And if you hadn't done what you did, we never would have heard what that guy had to say about 'our kind.'"

Angus had been fixated on that point, asking me over and over again what I thought he'd meant.

He slowed the car, taking in the barren, desert scenery. I noticed the wild rock formations in the distance. "Arches," he said, pleasure in his voice, pointing to the sign for Arches National Park.

"No, we're not going. I'm done with being tourists."

"What's waiting for you in California? No one. Nothing." Angus started putting his flip-flops on while driving, and the car jolted, slow and fast, in response.

"I have that interview at Stanford in a few weeks," I said, pulling on a loose khaki thread from my shorts.

"We need to look into that address."

"What address?"

"Your mother."

My stomach clenched. Lifting my elbow to the narrow window ledge, I rested my cheek in my hand.

Angus shifted, taking one hand off the wheel. "After what that bartender said, I really want to see your mother. What if there are more people like us?"

"John," I said.

"No. I mean that guy at the bar made it sound like *groups* of people. Like us. The way we were, I mean."

"Novak would have known."

"He's not perfect."

I prayed that was true.

"So, are you still in a rush to get out to Cali?" Angus raised an eyebrow at me.

"Fine," I said, pissed. Angus steered us toward Arches.

When I stepped out of the car, the panoramic view became real, finally capturing my full attention. There was nothing around us except space and sky and rock formations in the distance, standing like odd, giant ghosts. The world was so much bigger than me.

Angus put his arm around me, and I allowed myself to rest my head on his shoulder. We stood there, quiet, taking in the view, but it was also as if we were listening. If I wanted to forget my troubles, even temporarily, this was the place, under the enormous sheltering sky.

JULY

Chapter Fifteen

~⌒⌒~

"This way." I tilted my head to the entrance of the one story, nondescript branch of the Salt Lake City public library. Not one person looked up as we walked through the sensor even though it began beeping ferociously when Angus took his turn.

"Keep going," intoned an older man at the front desk, as if this were a normal occurrence. But my heart was still pounding.

I looked up for any cameras in the corners of the room. There was one old one. Angus wore a baseball hat, ignoring the sign that said please remove all hats. The screens of the two old Macs at the back of the small library faced the entire room. Angus whispered the address associated with Elizabeth Blackcomb, and I glared at him, annoyed he would think I wouldn't remember.

"What?" Angus shrugged. "I have no idea what parts of your brain you're acknowledging at this point."

I knew I needed to bury my abilities again—the scare at the bar had told me that—but I hadn't yet. I was putting it off, knowing how much it was going to hurt.

"Stop chewing your nail. It's slovenly. When did you pick that up?"

I hadn't realized it, but I probably had a whole host of new habits.

"I think we're a bit slovenly in general right now," I said, pointing to our wrinkled clothes thanks to driving through the night.

"Never," Angus said. For him, a pureblood, it was the truth. Me on the other hand . . . he'd reminded me I was all too ordinary in comparison to him.

I took a seat at one computer and Angus sat at the other.

"Let me do this," I said.

"Then do it. Just type it in and print out directions. See what a pain it is when you don't have a real phone?"

I quickly typed in the address and felt gross doing it, like I was going one step deeper, committing. Angus paced behind me, hands shoved in the pockets of his dirty designer jeans. Per usual, his actions spoke louder than his words and shitty tone and he came to stand behind me, putting his hands on my shoulders. It was becoming second nature to rely on him. I was growing used to being with him for almost every second of every day.

"Hit print."

"God, you are too much."

"What? I'll go get it. Where the hell is it?" Without waiting for my comment, Angus walked off in search of our printed directions. Good, he could hold on to them. I had another couple of days before I had to think about possibly finding her.

While Angus was across the room, I quickly did a search for John's tennis results. A photo of him at the Clay Court Championships popped up, taken just the other day.

I made it larger, waiting for the pixels to arrange themselves on the old computer. I scooted back in my chair to gaze at my boyfriend. It was a beautiful picture taken by a professional photographer.

John stood with one arm fully extended, racket held straight up to the sky. From the stance on his back foot, heel off the ground, it was clear he was serving.

The photo showed not only how attractive he was but that he was nearing peak physical performance. It hit me that John had the makings of the perfect tennis star: great looking, modest, and consistently getting results so far this summer. He should slow down. He was becoming too noticeable.

I scanned his results. Sure enough, he'd won the entire tournament. That was his first national tournament. And he'd said he wasn't comfortable playing on clay.

Angus walked up with pages in one hand. "Does it smell like peanut butter in here to you?"

I swiftly collapsed my search and cleared the history. "What, are you finally hungry?"

Angus lifted his shirt and rubbed his stomach, deliberately showing off his washboard abs.

"Maybe?" He looked genuinely perplexed, not used to the feeling.

"You at least need some nutrition. My dad—" I stopped.

I'd been about to bring up the chlorophyll drinks he seemed to endorse by always having one in hand.

"Yeah, yeah, I know what you were going to say." Angus glossed over my words for my sake. "Fine, I'll let you buy me something at a gas station." We were speaking in whispers; even more than whispers, I realized we were speaking the way our people used to—so fast and quiet it sounded like a code with our letters and sounds dropping and blurring

"I'm going to go use the bathroom," I said.

"Okay, hurry up. We need to figure out if we want to stay somewhere in the city tonight."

Walking partway through the dark, low-ceilinged library, I realized I needed my bag. I returned to the computer stations and found Angus typing furiously on one of them.

"What are you doing?" I asked.

He'd felt me coming and had already collapsed the window he was using. "Nothing. Weren't you going to the restroom or something?"

"Are you checking email?" I asked incredulously, brushing the hair out of my face.

"Get out of here, okay? It's how I stay in contact with my parents."

"Ah. Sorry." Of course. I hadn't even thought about that. I walked away, giving him some privacy.

When I returned, Angus was still at the computer. I stopped in my tracks and then spun around when I saw what was on the screen. I left the building for some air.

I was temporarily blinded by the bright daylight and sat on the edge of a brick planter in the shade to wait.

What was he doing? Why did he need to look at pictures

of her? I wanted to un-see all of them. His screen was filled with a row of images of Liv and search results that contained the words "seventeen, daughter, missing." I could look at the picture of John endlessly, but I couldn't, even for one second, look at one of Liv.

Eventually Angus appeared. "Why did you leave like that? I just wanted to see what was being said about the kids. Of course, she's the most famous one."

I didn't answer him.

"You can't even look at her?"

"That's not her," I finally said.

Angus stood tall in front of me, blocking the sun. "Oh, excuse me, you can't even look at *pictures* of her?"

I didn't know what to say. Angus watched me for a second and then took a seat next to me.

"What's wrong?" he finally asked.

I shook my head. He should understand how shocking that had been—it was one thing to talk about them, another thing to see a picture. I didn't know how to file them away, and every day I tried something new. Seeing Liv again toppled my house of cards.

"She's not dead," Angus said.

I shrugged.

"You feel like you didn't do right by her?"

"Are you saying I should feel guilty?" I asked, rearing back to look at him.

"Keep your voice down." Angus scanned the area around us. "No, I just wonder what it's like for them. If it feels right. I hope so. Who knows? Maybe we're the idiots and that was the place to be."

I stood. "Let's go."

Angus followed me to our newest car. I kept seeing Liv's face. One of the photos had been taken just before they left—a school photo. In her eyes, you could see the real Liv despite the fake persona all of us had inhabited at school. Her blue eyes had the spark that showed who she really was: joyful.

We drove aimlessly, searching for a place to stay. I knew we should check in to a hotel so I could call John and hear about his big tournament win.

"Let's just drive straight," I finally said.

"Really? What's the rush?"

"I want to get off the road. It's too hard to lie to him."

"Fine," Angus said. I was surprised he didn't argue.

"They're in paradise," I said it like I needed him to confirm it.

Angus didn't say a word.

Next stops: Reno and then San Francisco. Thirteen more hours total. It was easier to just get it done and finish this road trip.

It was hard to imagine not traveling all day, every day in a car, living with this strange kind of rhythm. We stopped briefly in Reno so I could stretch my legs and use the restroom. Angus got out to get gas, but other than that I was glad to see he stayed in the car. He still turned too many heads. Even in a hat, sunglasses, and dirty clothing, he looked like a movie star.

In a grimy rest stop bathroom, I used my elbow to run the faucet, washing my face and drying it with stiff paper towels. I looked at my flip-flops. I'd come a long way. Julia Jaynes from a year ago would not have been comfortable using a dark highway bathroom, with its leaking toilets and wet floors. Less than a week on the road was all it had taken.

Shaking my hair out of its ponytail, I tried to comb through the tangles with my fingers. There was no longer a trace of makeup on my face and I'd worn the same army green tank top for three days in a row. The designer clothes and diamond bracelet I had worn in high school were long gone. Maybe that should all be dropped permanently now. California was mere hours away. It was supposed to be a place for a new start.

When I exited the restroom, I had to navigate around two retractable dog leashes. Two older women with two poodles milled outside the bathrooms, talking while their little dogs sniffed the brown weeds.

"Sorry, Hon, can you get around?"

"Yes, no problem." I smiled slightly. One of the women suddenly elbowed the other.

"You know who you look like?" one of them said to me a second later.

I shook my head quickly, continuing to walk.

"That heiress. You know who I'm talking about, right?"

"From that weird cult they're trying to hunt down," the other woman said.

"Ha!" was my only acknowledgment. I walked to the car, got in, and locked the door. "Someone recognized me."

Without a word, Angus started the car and carefully drove out of the rest stop. Once we were back on the freeway, he sped up.

"What's wrong?" Angus asked, sensing my moodiness.

"I thought I was unrecognizable." I gestured to my dirty clothes. "I keep having fantasies that I'll go to college and blend in," I admitted, wishing I could take it back the second I said it.

"Yeah, that's never going to happen," Angus said bluntly. "You are who you are."

But I didn't want to be that person anymore. "I'm trapped. We're trapped."

"You look pretty free to me right now," Angus said, an edge in his voice.

I had to be careful because technically, I was a lot freer than he was. "Don't you ever get mad? That we can't just be like other people?"

"Am I mad I'm a Puri? No." There was a pause. "It's the honor of my life."

It was the most sincere thing I thought I'd ever heard him say.

It's a curse, I wanted to say. Angus didn't understand. He would have been happy if we roamed the world like Bonnie and Clyde for the rest of our lives. And even though I could see the appeal of that I knew that if I wanted to be with the love of my life, I had to make it work in John's world.

I was driving, three hours out from Palo Alto, when Angus said, "We'll drop you at your hotel and figure out a meeting place for tomorrow."

"What? Where are you going?"

"I said I'd see you tomorrow."

"So we have a little more time together?"

"Sure." Angus kept his voice perfectly unemotional.

I found myself getting worked up, already thinking about not having him nearby.

"You know you've been emotionally cheating on him, right?" Angus said, picking at me, the only indication that he didn't like the thought of us separating.

"*Emotionally cheating*?" I scoffed.

"Yep. What else do you call this? Sharing hotel rooms, being together twenty-four hours a day. I know you better than he ever will. Except in the biblical sense, but we can change that whenever you're ready. I'm a gentleman."

"You're not a gentleman." I tried to deflect by joking.

"Julia." His voice was serious, not letting me escape the conversation. "You're lying to him."

I was glad I could keep my eyes on the road. "*Angus*," I said, using his name in return. "You've given me no choice. When you showed up, you knew you put me in that position."

"Facts are facts. You're here with me, not him, and he has no idea."

"Way to push me away."

"I'm doing the opposite. I'm reminding you who you're naturally supposed to be with. You can't even be in the same room with him. Something's got to give. You change yourself or you change him. Or you do neither and stay with me."

That was so Angus. He had started out attacking me and ended with offering himself to me.

"You know—"

"I'm the one who can protect you. I'm the one who nursed you back to full health when you were making yourself sick. Just . . . how about you don't say anything? Not right now."

Right then and there I knew I should tell him we were done once we arrived in the Bay Area. If I wanted to start over for real that was the thing to do. But I didn't say another word.

JOHN

US National Clay Court Champion: John Ford. That was un-expected.

My spirits picked up a little bit, but I pretended things weren't looking sharper again.

Nightly, I was also playing and winning a lot of poker against Alex and some kids we'd known for years on the tennis circuit. Everyone's tell was broadcast loud and clear to me. I could see things other people couldn't. I was starting to have more fun, joking around with friends. Those are the fun parts of this thing—having people look up to you, winning every damn thing. No wonder you and your friends had an attitude.

Chapter Sixteen

I usually had to remember to blink for appearances' sake, but the clear California light gave me the urge. After being in the car for four days, the shopping center where we'd pulled over didn't quite feel like a real place. It was another new landscape, this time of palm trees and gentle mountains in the background, so different from where we'd started the trip.

"Park there," Angus directed. He'd helped me navigate off the 280 freeway at the Menlo Park exit, past my hotel on Sand Hill Road, and directly into the Stanford Shopping Center. The outdoor mall was enormous. I found a narrow space in a back row.

"Get out."

"What?" I asked, startled.

"Get out here. I need the car. You can get a rideshare back to your hotel." He wouldn't look at me.

"Already?" my voice sounded small. Our separation today had crept up too soon.

"Meet me here—I don't know—in two days at the—" Angus looked in the rearview mirror. "Outside the American Girl store. At noon."

"Two days? Why that long?"

"Get your shit in order, act like you've been living here, I don't know. I've got to go." Angus seemed agitated. He put his sunglasses on.

"Where are you going to go?"

"I'll figure it out," he said, exasperated.

I was about to say one more thing, to wrap up our trip, to say thank you. "I—"

"Go!"

Stung, I got out without a word and walked to the rear of the car. I unloaded my silver, hard-shelled suitcase and duffel and closed the trunk with a decisive slam. I didn't look back. I was just a girl in rumpled clothing, dragging a rolling suitcase with a duffel across my back.

I wended my way to the center of the labyrinth, taking note of the elaborate landscaping. It was the most manicured, upscale shopping mall I'd ever seen. I walked to the shaded middle with its view of Louis Vuitton, Ermenegildo Zegna, and a Tesla showroom.

I sat on a bench by an outdoor fire pit and beds of peonies, dahlias, and feathery green ferns, the sounds of shoppers echoing from the covered walkways. Not one person stopped to look at me. There was an international, cosmopolitan crowd here, and a girl burdened with an expensive suitcase didn't warrant attention.

Without removing my sunglasses, I wiped the stream of tears with the tail of my shirt. What was wrong with me? I would see him in two days. He wasn't abandoning me.

I reached for my phone. Surprisingly, there were no new voice mails. John hadn't called to tell me he'd won. He'd texted, and I should have called him hours and hours ago. I wasn't sure what excuse I would make. I looked around, feeling lost. I had nothing grounding me here. Not yet.

It was seventy-five degrees on a July afternoon. I could actually breathe. The temperate weather was a welcome shock after the triple-digit temperatures of Texas.

I took in the view of the rolling brown hills from the suite where I'd been hiding for the past twelve hours. Just over the Santa Cruz Mountains lay the ocean. I'd be following it when I drove north with Angus in a matter of hours.

When I'd checked in yesterday, I'd met my personal concierge and been escorted through the exclusive lobby for a quick tour. Donna had told me that the hotel was in the epicenter of the Silicon Valley tech world, on the famous road lined by venture capital firms, and she had arranged an extended stay. Thus, I found myself in a clubhouse of sorts primarily filled with men. If I was noticeable so far, it was because I was female. As I walked through the halls, I sensed an innovative and exciting energy—like a modern-day gold rush.

Novak would have fit right in as a youthful billionaire in a T-shirt, accurately predicting the next unicorn. For a second, I wondered if I could make it in this world, betting on where the technological revolution was headed next, using my instincts that were far sharper than the average person's. Maybe one option for me was to make a home right in this hotel if Stanford didn't work out. I pictured myself in the Rosewood dining room, multiplying my money.

It would be a way to pass the time until John was free, and waiting around for him in a hotel suite while he built his own life wasn't enough for me. I wanted to have a life of my own, and it somehow felt within reach, like I'd just had a taste of it on the road trip.

Around mid-morning, when I couldn't stand the room anymore, I ventured to the nearly empty gym. After an hour, I turned off the treadmill, grabbed a soft white hand towel and checked my phone, the usual one. It had been a relief to throw my cheap phone away. Of course, I had missed John trying to FaceTime with me.

I practically ran back to my suite, a bit put off to find that someone had been inside. The towels were replaced and my few things neatened. Quickly, I slipped the "do not disturb" sign on the outside of the door.

"Hey!" I hadn't even put my things down before I initiated the call. We hadn't really spoken since Taos. I held out the phone and John appeared on the screen, the first time I'd seen him in days. "What's going on? Where are you?"

"Still Florida. Where are you?" His voice sounded the same, maybe a little brusque.

"My hotel room." I wanted to tell him how I'd just arrived, how I couldn't believe what this place felt like—how the weather was cool, how the ocean and San Francisco were so close—but as far as he knew, I'd been here since the day

I left Austin. "I went to the gym," I said instead, explaining why I'd missed his call.

"Ah. This is the first time you've called me back in minutes instead of hours." Of course, John said it like it was an observation instead of an accusation. But I think he had picked up on my evasiveness. "That FBI agent called me. And my parents and my brother."

"What?" I nearly flipped over my chair when I stood up. I wanted to pace, but I had to keep holding the stupid phone. "Agent Kelly?"

"That guy."

"What did *he* want? Why is he bothering *you*?" I said, angry. Already my fresh start was going down the drain.

"He wanted to know where you were and when I saw you last. He said he'd been looking for you since last week."

"What did you tell him?" I tried to keep all emotion off my face.

"I told him what he wanted to know. What's going on?" John asked.

"I gave him the cell phone of the man who took your picture so he could look into it. I should have called him back right away. He obviously doesn't like to be ignored." I was kicking myself. I should have known he'd go to John and his family if he couldn't find me. And I really should have followed up.

"Let me know what Rafa says, okay?"

"I'm sure it was nothing. What's going on with you?" I asked lightly.

"Not a lot. Sleeping, playing tennis."

"Congratulations. I can't believe you won the tournament."

"Oh, yeah. That was pretty cool. I'm playing well."

"You're playing great. Maybe too great."

"I'm not throwing tennis matches. Tennis is the one thing I can do." There was frustration behind his words that reminded me of how Angus and I, and the rest of the boys, had felt a year ago—knowing there were natural instincts that we should be using, like animals caged in a zoo.

"You look much better," John said, interrupting my thoughts.

I surreptitiously glanced at the mirror above the desk for a better look. I'd forgotten that the last time he'd seen me, I'd looked like death warmed over. Now I had the glow. I didn't have the same hair color or skin color as the rest of the Puris, but if I had an identifiable physical marker that said I was a Puri, it was the glow. It had faded when they left and now it was back after being with Angus.

I turned away from the mirror and returned to my chair, trying to relax. "I am feeling better. I've gotten lots of rest." I felt like such a jerk, telling him to do one thing while I'd been doing the opposite.

John had purposely changed the subject because I knew he was uncomfortable with what he thought was complaining. He was too stoic in general. From reading his mind in the past, I knew he was a worrier but kept it well hidden. His parents had no idea of the pressure he felt. But, this time, I ignored the warning signs and let it slide because I didn't want him to argue with me. I just wanted him to keep doing what he was doing and get through it.

"Are you nervous about your interview?"

"Not yet. I'm trying not to think about it. I still have a

few weeks." I recognized how much the importance of the interview had faded in my mind.

But the mention of the interview made me realize we were beginning to make a dent in the timeline. I tried not to think that Angus was the one responsible for making time fly. I decided to go ahead and mention my first foray into searching for Elizabeth Blackcomb. I left the 'how' deliberately vague.

"Are you serious? What made you decide?"

More like *who* had made me decide. Guiltily, I tilted my head back and stared up at the crown molding while I gained control over my expression. Then, ready, I looked him in the eye once again. "I have the time, that's all. I'm sure it won't lead to anything."

He was perceptive enough to know that I wanted to move on. After a beat he said, "Call me if you find her, okay?"

"I promise I will."

For the first time since we'd begun the conversation, he smiled. Just a little bit. "Pretty soon we won't have my parents around. No curfew. We can finally take our time."

"I don't know," I joked, "you may be too busy for me with your tennis, your classes . . ."

"What about you? You'll probably be taking seven classes or something crazy like that."

As hard as I tried, I could no longer see it. There was an awkward pause I didn't manage to fill fast enough. John picked up on it.

"I gotta go," he said.

JOHN

The phone wasn't really doing it for either of us. So much of our communication was nonverbal. Like the way we naturally gravitated toward each other at Austin High—at the drinking fountain after tennis, walking to the parking lot together. I felt like when we spent time together, it was simply being next to each other.

It hurt when you didn't return my calls. Then Agent Kelly called me asking where you were, signaling that you weren't at the Rosewood.

I still don't know where you really were that first part of July . . .

Chapter Seventeen

At ten the next morning, after walking around aimlessly for an hour as planned, I saw Angus near the entrance of the American Girl store. When he saw me, he quickly walked a ways ahead, leading me through the parking lot until he got into a new car. One door of the maroon Hyundai was grey and mismatched.

"Where did you end up staying?" I asked when I slipped in beside him.

"San Jose," Angus said, sunglasses and hat in place. "How are you?" He looked me over.

"Fine." I shrugged. I didn't let on how relieved I was to see him.

"Miss me?"

I just shook my head and gave him a half smile. "Thanks for coming with me."

It was Angus's turn to shake his head in an "it's nothing" gesture.

"Hey!" I leaned forward.

"What?"

I watched a fit man in his thirties or forties with dark hair and sunglasses covering his eyes climb into a white Ford sedan five rows away. For a second I thought he looked familiar. Before I could get a better visual, he ducked down into the car.

I squinted and saw California plates. "Nothing." I settled back into the seat.

Angus seemed to know where he was going. He stayed on back roads to SR 92, then the car wound up the long switchback highway beneath thick redwoods and through a small town called La Honda. The change in temperature and scenery surprised me. Sunny and dry changed to shaded forest until we climbed a peak and came out into fog. Driving down Skyline Boulevard, we followed a ridge that ran parallel to the ocean far below the rocky cliffs. When I first saw the ocean I thought, *I'm here*, like I'd finally made it to a place I'd been trying to get to. The temperature on the dashboard dropped to the low sixties.

"You're not going to say anything?" Angus asked. We'd been driving for only twenty-five minutes since we'd left the shopping mall, but it felt like we'd traveled far away.

"I don't want to do this," I said after a long pause. "You're only pushing me because you're hoping you find another group of us."

"Yes." When he felt my anger building he added, "Look, I do think you need to know if she's like your boy and what happened to her after she spent time with Novak." Because he wanted whatever I found out to force me away from John.

"What if she's insane?"

"Then you probably need to know that too."

"We only have this address," I said skeptically.

I imagined Angus meeting this person and then forever looking at me differently—with just a bit of that Puri distance and disregard. The snobbery and mistrust were still inside me too, as much as John's family and Donna had made an impression on me. Other than the night of my last conversation with Novak, I'd never been so scared and nervous. If it weren't for John, there would be no call for this visit. I kept telling myself chances were slim that we would find her today.

Angus wasn't deterred. "What do you think she's like?"

My only impressions were from the pictures I'd seen online. The similarities I'd seen between us.

"I don't know. Maybe like one of the assistants? A girl he met and thought was special?" I thought of Kendra again. The guilt of not being forthcoming about how she'd died was still right there, riding alongside me. I hadn't left it behind in Texas.

"Remember my father said that Novak loved her? Wanted to marry her?" When I didn't respond, he said, "You are about to face her. You should prepare yourself."

I began to feel like I was going to throw up. Every part of me wanted out.

We reached our destination, a coastal town just south of San Francisco, and I paled as Angus began navigating the streets of a neighborhood. But we drove the same few streets for the next thirty minutes, unable to find the exact address we were looking for.

"It doesn't exist," Angus finally said.

"Let's stop." I was more than happy to have a way out.

"One more time, okay? We were right there. We must have missed it somehow."

"What if we find her?" I asked abruptly.

Angus paused, like he wasn't sure how to handle my fears. But then, so kindly, he said, "It's just information. We gather it and leave. You were raised by Puris. This isn't going to change you."

The tension in the car was white-hot as we drifted alongside the edge of a steep, rocky cliff enshrouded in fog. A bright orange traffic cone folded onto itself, disappearing under our tire as Angus slowed to a complete stop. The posh homes that lined the block across the street looked like oversized dollhouses, narrow and tall with decorative trim and large bay windows. They had a waterfront view but were far from the beach below. More traffic cones dotted the street in front of the slim pathway running along the cliff, succulents propagating in the sand and dirt every few inches.

"2330 Ocean," Angus said.

"That has to be close." I indicated the house number 2319 on the residence in front of us. The new pseudo-Victorian house was painted in yellows and browns. A telescope sat on a third-floor roof-deck enclosed by a white railing.

I led the way through the small picket fence and postage stamp–size lawn to the front door flanked by mullioned side windows.

Angus rang the doorbell. We waited. I chewed a nail, no longer breathing, letting myself go blank.

The door flung open and a woman wearing marbled purple

and white spandex and a midriff-baring American flag T-shirt stood in front of us.

She looked at us cautiously. A small boy in Ralph Lauren rode a cherry-red tricycle in the background.

"Hi," Angus said "I'm looking for an address for Elizabeth Blackcomb," he said, speaking for me.

Barefoot, the brunette stepped onto the patio. Almost eagerly, she softly closed the front door behind her. It was easy to tell she had fillers in her cheekbones. I noticed a dolphin tattoo on her ankle.

"She lives down there."

"Where?" Angus asked.

"The beach. There are stairs right by those cones. Is that your car?" We both nodded in response. "You're going to need to move it. Otherwise my husband will go ballistic. Are you guests?" The woman scrutinized us skeptically.

Neither Angus nor I knew how to answer. "We were just looking for her," I said.

"Good luck. You can't just go down there. Unless you pay thirty thousand dollars and wait six months."

"What's down there?" I asked.

"They call it 'The Cove.'" She held up her hands to make mocking quotation signs. "It's a commune. Elizabeth Blackcomb owns the beach from some grandfathered deal. That should be protected land. They shouldn't even be allowed to have it. And then they go and operate an illegal business."

Suddenly the door behind her opened. A much older man with silver hair wearing a polo shirt and holding the Sunday paper by his side said with no greeting, "You need to move your car. Didn't you see those cones?"

"That's street parking," Angus said calmly.

The man started to sputter. "You leave your car, it won't be there when you get back."

Angus's eyes turned a crystal blue. "You don't want to touch that car."

"Come on," I said, grabbing Angus's sleeve.

"Tell those covies to pick up their trash," the man belted, sounding unhinged.

We crossed the street to the car, and I now saw the battered steel lockbox with the faded number 2330 next to the top of a staircase. We'd walked right past when we got out of the car. Angus grabbed one of the orange cones and drop-kicked it across the street into the man's front yard. The man still watched us menacingly, cell phone now held to his ear.

"Let's go," Angus said as he stepped down onto the first stair.

"I don't know."

"Oh, yeah. Come on. This gets better all the time." Angus smiled and held out his hand.

"Of course this wouldn't be normal."

"What's normal?"

We descended into the mist, and the stairs continued on a relentless downward course. It was cold and damp for summer. We were stuck in the infamous Bay Area fog. It had been clear and warm just ten miles south. We walked down many stories of treacherous stairs. I was surprised when we were met at the base by a very elderly woman.

Small, tan, and weathered, she stood on the beach with a pair of binoculars. I wondered if she was bird-watching. She looked like she could have been one hundred years old, but she was obviously still spry with her salt-and-pepper hair in youthful long braids.

When she saw us, she picked up a chalkboard that hung around her neck.

She scratched: "*Private property. Public beaches nearby.*"

I squinted into the distance, and the beach came alive, images growing sharp against the ocean. A few people in wetsuits played in the surf as a light mist rose from the water. Farther down the beach were weathered bungalows on stilts, all a matching silvered wood.

"We came here to see Elizabeth Blackcomb," Angus said.

The woman paused and seemed to take another look at me. She picked up her chalkboard and took longer to write this time, at one point licking a finger to erase and start over.

"*There's a wait-list to see her.*"

"We'll wait then," Angus said, my spokesperson since I no longer seemed to have any words.

The woman tried again. "*She's in silence till Tuesday.*"

"We'll come back," I said, tugging on Angus's sleeve, heading to the stairs. I looked back over my shoulder when I'd retreated two stairs up. The old woman studied me hard. Angus was still waiting at the foot of the stairs, looking down the beach, trying to figure out what this place was.

"Angus," I said. He turned and joined me.

After we'd scaled the first major portion of the stairs, he said. "Stop."

"What is this place?" I asked immediately.

"It's got to be more than some kind of yoga retreat. Do you feel the energy down here?" Angus asked, some excitement in his voice.

"I do. It's different though," I said, referring to the aura surrounding our family.

"It's not as strong." In the distance we saw the little woman walking bandy-legged down the beach to a small group of shirtless men. One carried a small kayak over his head. "She's going to tell them about us." Angus looked at me. "You shouldn't have to wait until Tuesday. We came from fucking Texas to see her."

"No, I came to see Menlo Park."

"We came to see your mother. You should not have to wait. Come on, we can leave as soon as you meet her. And now I've got to meet this woman who has a wait-list."

I let Angus lead me back the way we came. We walked down the stretch of beach, staying close to the houses on stilts, using them as cover. I counted sixteen of them. We drew closer and closer to the large group sitting in a circle on blankets on the beach.

We stopped at the largest house and stood beneath it. From our vantage point, we could watch the group meditating below, closer to the water. Every one was dressed in white. I focused on the slender form of a woman whose dark hair hung loose to her waist, whose face was turned away from us. I couldn't take my eyes off her perfectly still back.

"They have to stand sometime. Do you think that's her?" Angus asked, spotting the same person. I wasn't sure if he saw my nod.

We waited. The sun was higher in the sky now, beginning to burn off some of the fog. I leaned against one stilt. It was easy to get lulled by the rhythmic, deafening crash of the waves. At one point we saw a couple struggling with chic luggage walk past, guided by the old woman. Meditation tourists, I guessed. The group would stir any second and then I'd have to do this. It wasn't too late to walk away. I still didn't know a thing.

"Angus." I was about to tell him I wanted to leave when all at once, like a herd, the group of thirty people rose. I watched in wonder as the woman I'd been studying turned in our direction and began to walk away from the ocean and toward the bungalows. The group fanned out, but a few people followed the woman with the streaming black hair, speaking to her and slowing her progress.

A well-heeled couple walked ahead of the group, reaching the house where we were waiting, unaware of our presence in the shadows. "We chose this over fourteen days in Mozambique? I can't feel my left leg," the man said.

The woman violently shushed him, and they walked up the outdoor stairs to the bungalow above us.

The woman I assumed to be Elizabeth and her entourage drew closer to us. I took a few steps deeper into the shadows.

"Let's go. Let's leave." I pulled back on Angus's arm.

"We're here now. Just do it. You have every right." He gave me a not-so-soft push out into the sunlight.

The procession was just going up the stairs. My movement caught the eye of one person.

She turned her head, never slowing her progress up the stairs. It felt like slow motion when our eyes met and an electricity passed between us. I saw in her eyes that she recognized herself staring back at her. Except for the color of my eyes. The same color as Novak's.

She shifted her gaze forward and continued walking.

"I'll go through the front and you go through the back, okay?" Angus said. "One of us will find someone to speak to before they kick us out."

Then Angus was gone. Up top I heard a sliding door close.

I walked farther out into the sunlight, stunned, picking up on the remnants of energy she'd left behind. She'd known I was her daughter. I could tell. Yet she'd hidden it as expertly as a Puri.

Right above me was my mother who'd just seen me for the first time since I'd been a baby. I'd just seen the person who had carried me inside her.

I was all adrenaline as I ran up the steps. No one was on the deck. I opened the rickety sliding glass door and entered the living room where a small group of people were assembled on mildewed wall-to-wall carpeting at the feet of Elizabeth Blackcomb. Elizabeth sat on a wicker chair with her legs tucked under her. She was dressed in white, and her hair, parted down the middle, draped over one shoulder. Elizabeth was skinny, making her beautiful face hard. She was scary in her remoteness. Her eyes were almost exactly like mine, narrow and heavy-lidded, except the color was so dark.

Two young men who looked like models, hair bleached from the sun, sat on the floor on either side of her chair. People dressed in yoga pants and loose blouses served plates of fruit and those who'd been served were eating silently. It was a light-filled room that didn't feel austere. It felt content. One of the beautiful young men in flowing pants and beads around his wrist handed Elizabeth a cup. She continued to stare at her lap as she took it.

Just then Angus appeared in the doorway opposite me.

At once a man stood and walked over to him. Angus looked like he was prepared to push him away and make a scene. Elizabeth still wouldn't come out of her shell even though she could presumably sense intruders in the room.

Angus saw Elizabeth, seated like a queen, willfully existing in another dimension, and then he looked back at me. He understood she knew I was there but wouldn't look at me. He dropped his hands to his sides.

Two large men, including the one who'd served Elizabeth, came to my side. They each lightly grasped an elbow to escort me out. Just before I made their job easy, I took one last look at my birth mother who was refusing to acknowledge me.

Fuck you.

And then I looked at her steaming hot tea cup, and from across the room, I jostled it. Tea splashed onto the saucer and into her lap. The movement startled her.

Instinctively, Elizabeth looked at me. She knew exactly where that kind of power came from. She'd seen it before. Maybe it was the reminder of Novak that made her unable to look away again.

Elizabeth watched them begin to remove me from the room, but I craned my neck, my eyes fastened on hers. She kept her gaze fixed on mine, pretending not to care. Then there was just a flicker of doubt. I saw the fight within, then the exact second she broke, letting the memory of me come flying back to her, her eyes becoming pools of vulnerability.

"Give them number thirteen." Her voice rang out like a shot, shattering the silence.

JOHN

And then there was the night at the La Quinta in Florida.

I'd made Alex go off to Chili's without me so, for once, I was by myself.

I'd been sort of absentmindedly running my thumb over a long scrape on my leg from the match. I looked down and the scrape caught my eye. I wasn't sure, but it seemed just a tiny bit shorter than it had been a few minutes before.

I wanted to tell you, but you didn't pick up. Then I decided it was probably counter to our agreement. But it felt so good. How would I attract unwanted attention by healing just myself?

Chapter Eighteen

―※―

"She can't talk with you until Tuesday. You wait here until then."

That was only two days from now. Even Angus didn't argue with the tall, blond man who led us inside number thirteen, a bungalow at the far end of the crescent-shaped stretch of beach.

"We don't have any of our stuff," I said, dazed, as I looked around the large studio.

"I'm not going to tell them that," Angus said to me as soon as the man left. "I have the feeling once we leave, we may never be let back in."

"I don't have any bars on my cell phone."

"You just met your mother. What do you care about bars on your cell phone?" Angus looked at me incredulously. Then he got it. "He'll understand when you tell him what happened. That you met her."

We both looked around the open room. It had a 1970s

vibe but had been painted recently and was much nicer than the bungalow where we'd seen Elizabeth. Obviously this was where they put their paying guests. A queen-size bed with a wicker headboard was off to one side of the room, two rolled yoga mats were in a basket by the front door, and ferns hung in macramé holders in the small kitchenette. A gigantic basket of fresh fruit sat on the small table pushed up against a window with an ocean view. The sun had officially broken through, warming everything, and the water sparkled.

Angus kicked off his shoes. "I don't think I want to leave."

"You feel safe here?" I asked.

"I don't see why not. It's a private, secluded beach where they're operating an illegal business. We'll move the car later—they must have a place for visitors to park. No one is going to call the cops."

He looked like a weight had lifted from his shoulders, almost like he'd just been let out of prison. He seemed more like a kid again.

"She's making me wait for two days to speak to her. This isn't a vacation," I said, trying to get his attention.

"Relax. She wants you here. We didn't know that your mother would be some goddess running a—what do they call this place?" Angus moved to the bedside table and picked up a thick, paper packet. "'Intentional community.' Julia, we have landed at an intentional community."

"Is that what this is?"

"Are you laughing or about to cry? I can't tell. Man, she knew exactly who you were."

"I look like her," I said, warming up my arms with my hands

as if that would help. I was still in shock, jittery, and hanging on every word of Angus's interpretation of the meeting.

"Yeah, but when you did that to her cup, she really knew—like that guy back in Colorado." Angus surveyed the room and was drawn to the window and the ocean beyond. "So this is what life after Novak looks like. I'll bet she wanted to forget all about him."

"Knowing what she paid, Novak practically gave this place to her."

"I'm disappointed though."

"Why are *you* the one disappointed?"

"Part of me was expecting to maybe find a group like us down here. I thought maybe your mother was one of us. But I don't feel it."

"She's just—"

"An outsider," Angus supplied.

I stared at some sand someone forgot to sweep.

"Something is up with her though," Angus continued, as if trying to make me feel better. "She's special somehow. Clearly. She has an energy all her own. Maybe it's all the meditation they do in this place and that's why it feels good here. Can you relax?" Angus walked to me and grabbed my hand, trying to loosen me up.

"No." I gripped his hand hard.

"Come on. This is at least part of the reason you wanted to come to California—to meet her. You can lie to yourself and say it's only for him, and I've been playing along with that. But this is your chance to open the vault—at one point, you never thought you'd be allowed to find out about your past."

"It was easier not knowing. I should have left it. I don't want to want anything from her."

"So don't want anything," Angus said.

I wanted to kill him. "You may not have any emotions, but I do."

Angus looked at me like I was crazy. "I have them. I just know how to control them. You do too. That's how we survive. If you need her to mean nothing to you, you know how to make that happen. This side of yourself you've been trying on? It's only opened you up to weaknesses that have made you unhappy. That's how I see it. And I'm sorry, but I'm happy. This place buys me more time to spend with you. I don't have to leave for a few more days."

I was flooded with relief.

Without touching it, Angus opened the thin bungalow door and walked onto the deck. "Get out here!"

I followed. I stood next to him, placing my hands on the peeling white-painted railing, feeling the gritty sand beneath my fingertips. The ocean lay at our feet. We watched as a couple walked into the water and then ran, laughing, then screaming, as the tide came in and chased them back up the beach. I looked up at the cliffs, trying to see any signs of life up top. But those mansions were too far up and out of sight. We were secluded in this cove and could be anywhere in the world. This was a place where it was easy to pretend anything you wanted.

"I'm going in!" Angus ripped off his T-shirt and ran down the stairs in a flash. He sprinted straight into the ocean and dove into a wave. Moments later, he burst out, white water shooting off of him. He let the momentum of smaller waves buoy him gently up and down. A man in a wet suit paddled in a sea kayak near Angus, holding up the haul of fish he was bringing back to shore, no doubt mystified by Angus's tolerance for the cold water.

I carefully kept my eyes on Angus, not wanting to watch Elizabeth, her back rigid, as she led a pack of strangers down the beach.

When Angus emerged from the water, I joined him on the beach. The sun was high in the sky.

"Dive in, Julia. Those waves are rough."

"I'll pass. I don't have anything to wear."

"I'm sure you can go naked and no one here would care."

I declined humorlessly, and we walked together back up the stairs to the deck. Angus turned on the rickety outdoor shower. It groaned and then made a loud sound as water spurted unevenly from the showerhead onto the deck. Angus turned his body around and around underneath, wiping the salt away with his hands. Obviously, the perceived charm of a reclusive beach community made customers willing to overlook certain signs of disrepair.

I cautiously watched as a bald black man walked up the stairs of our bungalow. He wore flowing drawstring pants, carried folded towels under one arm, and held a basket with the other hand.

"Maya wanted you to have supplies," he said by way of greeting. In the basket were toothbrushes and yoga clothes.

"Who?" I asked.

"Maya," he repeated.

"You mean Elizabeth?" Angus shut off the shower and shook his hair, spraying water like a dog before walking over to drip next to me.

"Yes," the man said. "What are your names?"

Angus and I hadn't even discussed whether I should use my real name to anyone other than my mother. "I'm Julia Jaynes," I said, waiting for the recognition in his eyes at my name, which had been splashed across the news and jumped from there into the zeitgeist. But there was nothing. No recognition whatsoever.

"And you are?" the man asked Angus.

"Tyler," Angus said, using the name on his fake ID.

"You're a couple?"

"Yes," Angus said at the same time I said, "No."

The man smiled slightly. "What brings you here?"

"Have you been sent to find out?" I asked.

"No. I'm curious." He nodded to me. "You're obviously a relation of Maya's. But you're the first she's let in. Are her parents well?"

I paused at the mention of grandparents and then jumped on the suggestion. "That's something I'd like to talk to her about," I said, not wanting to let her get away with an interaction by proxy.

"I see. Well, I'm Emmanuel, here to deliver supplies, but I also need you to sign these release forms."

"So if we drown in the ocean, you're not responsible?" Angus eyed him.

"Exactly," the man said pleasantly. So far he was the first friendly person we'd encountered.

"How long have you been at this—intentional community?" I asked.

"Years and years, my friend. You're the first young people I've seen in a long while."

"What about up there?" Angus asked, pointing to the bluff. "You see people up there."

"We don't leave. The world comes to us. At least the guests who apply to come visit. And the people who deliver our food and supplies."

"When was the last time you left?" No wonder he seemed to have no concept of the news.

"Oh, man, that had to be fifteen years ago. That's when I stumbled on Maya living down here. She was first. This community was all her doing. Slowly she filled some of the bungalows with her friends when the previous tenants left. And then some of us quit leaving the beach altogether."

Angus looked at me sidelong. Did her friends know she owned it? Remembering that the land came to her through Novak made me feel like this beautiful place was dirty once again.

Angus and I signed the waivers. The man still lingered.

"Yes?" Angus asked.

The bald man looked at us more intently, sizing us up. "This bungalow is reserved for registered guests. I'm not sure how long you can stay here. Until then, please, you're our guests like anyone else. Join us. Everyone would like to see you at the meditations. Young people are a breath of fresh air."

After the man left, we drifted inside. Angus plunked himself down into the giant papasan chair without a care, saturating the bright orange cushion with his sopping wet shorts. He seemed to sag with disappointment. "We don't know how long we have here?"

"It's not very welcoming," I said.

"Whatever," Angus said, as if he suddenly shook off disappointment and became practical again. "We're on a fact-finding mission. We already know the most important thing. Your father didn't ruin her."

"Or did he? We don't know what she's like or what this is."

"If anything, it seems like he created her."

"Do you think this is a cult?" With my birth mother as leader. The same had been said about my father.

"I don't know yet," Angus said. "That guy who's friends with Elizabeth and lives here full time just seems like a hippie. The 'guests' don't seem like cult types. More like rich people who wear shirts that say 'spiritual gangster.'"

That night, we went to the room where we'd first seen Elizabeth and ate plates of beans, rice, and mango while sitting in a circle on the floor. Small cushions were provided to the visitors who shifted uncomfortably throughout the meal as they tried to sit with their legs crisscrossed. Elizabeth was conspicuously absent. The room was quiet except for the crash of the waves that carried through the open windows. The curious stares aimed in my direction had a light, non-threatening quality. I either kept my eyes on my food or on Angus, who nibbled on mango and pushed the rest of the food around the plate.

As we departed dinner to walk down the beach to our bungalow, one older couple hurried to catch up to us. Angus and I stiffened.

"Hello!"

"Hi," Angus and I said in unison.

"Are you Maya's daughter? My wife wants to know," the man asked.

"Roy!"

I didn't know how to answer that.

"She is," Angus said, claiming her for me.

It was a fact after all. And those seemed to be getting harder to keep track of in this confusing place.

"Wow. I had no idea she had children," the woman said. They quickly fell behind when we kept up our pace, making it clear we didn't welcome conversation.

Later, when we switched off the lamps, I leaned against the wicker headboard of the queen-size bed under a white cotton coverlet. Angus began the night on the floor on a yoga mat, but eventually the hard floor sent him into bed next to me. It was more of a comfort than an annoyance since I was wide awake, knowing just down the beach there was someone who could finally tell me about my past. I was in a strange space—not wanting to wait but almost too scared to find out more.

JOHN

Whenever I had a second alone, I focused on that scrape. Each time I could erase a little bit more of it.

The next night, I could heal more at one time.

I used the same skills I used to block you from reading my mind. Quieting my mind to keep you from eavesdropping was the gateway.

Somewhere along the way, I became okay with not telling you about the healing. I started to throw myself all over the tennis court. I dove unnecessarily, looking to get some minor injuries. I'm sure my family wanted to ask, "What the hell are you doing?"

I imagined I could see beneath the skin. Going deep, seeing the cells repair. I started Googling anything having to do with people who called themselves healers. I wanted to email a few of them. I didn't though because I wasn't sure who was a quack and who might be for real.

You'd told me that being near you brought this out in me,

and that these extras would fade when you were gone. My whole life I'd been careful to do what people asked me to do. This was the thread I picked up to see how it might unravel—what if I could get better at this thing without you?

Chapter Nineteen

I refused to think of her as Maya. That was the name she'd used to remake herself after Novak left. I wanted who she was before that.

I was conscious of time slipping away as Tuesday approached, the day Elizabeth's "silence" would supposedly end. I didn't see her on the beach or at the meals, yoga classes, and meditations that consumed Angus and me. Though we kept a certain distance we'd begun to follow the schedule as an investigation of sorts. The community always welcomed us.

We knew how to be quiet. But this was a different kind of quiet. A quiet that wasn't eerie and cunning. It was just, for lack of a better word, open. Time took on a new quality after the third time I meditated on the beach. I had gone to the first meditation uneasily, only looking for Elizabeth, but something had happened. Everything had felt vast. All the worry, all the obsessive planning, it had fallen away.

I didn't bother asking if Angus felt it too. He'd become

more quiet. When he did talk, he mentioned the beach and how he could stay forever, listening to the waves.

That melded feeling, like we were part of a larger whole, and the rate at which we'd become comfortable were what caused Angus to mess up.

We were finishing our third and last meditation of the day. It felt like one second had passed, not one hour. For the entire session, I'd kept my eyes closed and felt as though I'd become part of the ocean, drifting in the waves. At the end of the session, my reality slowly came back to me— John, Novak, my currently empty hotel room—but it was hazier than it had been before. I didn't feel the same sense of urgency.

First, I heard a gasp to my right. I didn't immediately open my eyes, not wanting to make the abrupt transition to reality before I was ready. I wanted to savor the moment, the cool ocean air against my skin, the ebbing light further darkening the world beyond my closed eyelids.

Angus moved next to me, and my eyes snapped open. Everyone was looking at Angus. At first I couldn't comprehend what I was seeing.

Angus sat, angelic, his legs in crossed position, two inches off the ground. He floated.

"Angus." I smacked his knee with the back of my hand. Startled, he came down hard on the sand. The assembled group was watching us. Eyes were large, but no one said a word. Thankfully, none of the meditation tourists had come to this last event of the day. Only the residents were present.

"What?" Angus whispered to me.

"Well done," said Emmanuel who'd led the meditation.

He got up and stretched, acting blasé. The group took his lead and stood, glancing sidelong at Angus, shaking off the miracle.

Emmanuel shielded his eyes from the sun. "Maya said she'd seen that in India, at a temple once. You are an advanced creature already, my friend. Use it wisely." He clapped Angus on the back so hard that Angus's slight chest thrust forward.

"Can you tell me what happened?" Angus asked me when everyone else had left.

"You levitated," I said.

"No." He eyed me skeptically.

Worry about what people had seen took a surprising backseat. "What did it feel like?"

No one was grabbing pitchforks. Yet.

"That was . . ." I paused. "I don't even know what. Pure, I guess."

"Are you serious? Damn. Do we need to leave?"

"I'm not sure. They don't seem very excited." Which felt like a miracle in and of itself. I wasn't sure I could trust it was safe, but I wasn't ready to leave yet.

"I felt . . . I don't know . . . I wasn't even here. I was somewhere else." Angus was glowing.

"You are an advanced creature, my friend," I agreed. "I don't quite know what we should do next though."

"Look." Angus lightly touched my shoulder and pointed to Elizabeth slowly walking down the beach.

Novak would have approached us with an entourage, but Elizabeth came by herself.

"You ready?" Angus asked me.

The beach darkened as the sun set and Elizabeth closed the distance between us.

"Stay with me, okay?" I said.

"I'm not going anywhere."

"She won't call the police about us. I don't think she wants any trouble . . ." I said the words though I didn't know a thing about what she would and wouldn't do. She may be unstable for all I knew. Judging by the alert but calm energy of the people who'd surrounded us since we'd arrived, I would guess Elizabeth knew what she was doing. The question was, could she be special? Both Angus and I wanted to see something in her that could give us a clue as to why Novak had thought she was different.

Elizabeth was nearing. She was dressed in white linen pants and a white yoga top with an oversize cardigan falling off one shoulder. I resisted the urge to grab Angus's hand. Angus and I had never met an outsider who knew history we didn't.

"I saw you've been doing some tricks down here," Elizabeth called to Angus over the waves. Her voice was pretty, more pleasant than I remembered from the other day.

"It wasn't a trick," Angus replied.

"No, it wasn't. I'm sorry, that was the wrong thing to call it." Elizabeth tilted her head to indicate we should move away from the crash of the waves to better talk.

We followed her thin figure to our bungalow. Her hair hung loose and stick straight almost to her waist, tucked behind one ear. She looked like an apparition. I wanted her to speak to us again so I had an excuse to look at her.

Angus and I trailed Elizabeth up the stairs, watching her lead the way into the space Angus and I had shared for the past two days. Angus gently closed the door behind us.

Elizabeth faced us, placing her elbows on the counter of the kitchenette behind her. "I'm Maya," she said, looking at us both but definitely more at Angus.

"I'm Julia." I held out a hand to her.

I wasn't wrong—her reluctance was clear, when, after a beat too long, she came forward to take my hand. When we shook hands, I barely registered what it felt like; I was too consumed with the fact that it was happening.

Angus quickly shook her hand as well.

The three of us stood looking at each other. Was she going to speak? Confront us? No, instead she rested against the counter, keeping her gaze leveled on us.

I felt Angus look from me to Elizabeth and knew he was about to take over. I knew the right thing to do was to step out from behind him. I was grateful he had taken me this far, but it wasn't right for him to handle this moment for me.

"I think I'm your daughter," I said awkwardly, breaking the silence.

"Is he coming?" Elizabeth asked right back, not acknowledging what I'd just said. For the second time in her dark eyes, I saw a brief view behind the curtain, before the calm shield went right back up. It reminded me of John.

"Novak?" Angus asked.

When Elizabeth looked blank, I said, "My father?"

"He goes by Novak now?" Then she nodded as if, of course, it all made sense that he would change his name.

"No. He's not coming," I said. Something went out of

her eyes. Was it disappointment? Anticipation? Maybe it was only the fear. Her muscles seemed to relax, as if she had dispensed with the most pressing business.

"But you're here," Elizabeth said, sizing me up.

"Yes."

"How?" she asked. "Why have you broken off from the group? That's how you get your power."

What else did she know about us?

"I left," I said.

"And you?" she asked Angus.

"I was kicked out."

She looked me directly in the eye. "What makes you think they aren't coming to find you?"

"We're on our own now," I said.

"I'm very good at reading people, and I'm getting the sense that you aren't done with them."

"Why do you say that?"

"I also have good foresight, so maybe it's that they aren't done with you."

"Then you must have known I was coming." A sarcastic edge slipped into my voice. The stress of the encounter was getting to me. And the fact that she was scaring me all over again about things I'd been trying to forget.

"No, actually, I didn't see you coming." She straightened and crossed her arms protectively across her slight frame. Elizabeth looked wraith-like from far away, but where her sweater had slipped was a ropy, toned arm.

"Do you want me to leave?" Angus asked me.

"Yes, give us a few minutes," I said.

After Angus left, I looked at Elizabeth and she held my

gaze. I realized I could stare and stare at her all day. Over the years, I'd tried to imagine her, but that could not compare to standing right in front of her.

"Is he your brother?" she asked.

"No. He's my best friend. My only family left." I realized, to her, Angus looked so much more like Novak than I did. I wondered if she wanted to know whether Novak had more children.

Elizabeth sat on one of the stools pulled up to the counter, leaning her body to one side. She was so graceful, like she'd once been a dancer.

"It took me a while to get to the point where I didn't think about this," she finally said. She lifted her bare feet to rest on the bottom rung of the stool and flattened her hands on the tops of her thighs, pressing down. "Look, I'm not prepared for you. You were someone I'd play with in my dreams and that's where you stayed. And then finally I had to stop. I've spent the last eighteen years trying to rid myself of any expectation—that Chris would come back, that you would find me. I reminded myself over and over again that you people never come back. Even though he told me he'd find a way."

"*I* found a way."

"It's funny. You're exactly how I pictured you." Elizabeth studied me, but it was with remove.

I wanted to drink her in as fast as I could, used to how fragile life was, that people disappeared.

"I know you wanted to see who I am, and you managed to find me." Elizabeth gestured to the room at large, to the ocean. "But I'm not sure I can have this noise here. I built a new life. Your father and those people were a recurring night-mare for me, the thing that kept me from progressing for so long. When you and he disappeared, that was the end of a life for Elizabeth Blackcomb. All of that is to say, I don't know if you and your friend can stay here."

"I don't mean to ruin your life. I'm just trying to make sense of mine."

Elizabeth nodded in response. "That's fair. I'm just not sure I can open that door. Stay here tonight as planned, but as Emmanuel explained, I don't know how long I can host you."

She was unflappable. Somehow I couldn't hate her after her honesty. I almost wanted to be polite and let her go on her way. When she turned to leave, I saw a small tattoo on her exposed shoulder blade. It said "12-5."

"What did you name me?" I asked, right before she crossed the threshold.

"Excuse me?" She looked back at me.

"What did you name me when I was born?"

"Julia," she said. The screen door shut behind her, clap-ping open and closing once more.

Late AUGUST

JOHN

So Alex knew. About you, I mean.

I'm guessing that my parents saw you mostly as . . . actually, I have no idea. When I think about it, it had to be strange that their son was suddenly dating someone from a world of private jets whose father was a criminal. They had to be pretty worried that I'd disappear into a life so different from theirs, like I was a commoner marrying into a royal family, although, pretty much all we did was order takeout at your place.

I don't know if they ever thought too much about the other speculation that was in the news.

On the other hand, Alex and I had heard plenty of stories about your family. I think we even met one of you. On this last trip, Alex reminded me about this kid who played tennis with us and our coach when we were maybe twelve. He was very quiet and polite and an eerily good tennis player for his age. I remember my parents discussed him a lot and speculated about where he came from. He was only there for a month and then he disappeared. Alex said, looking back, he thought that kid was probably a member of your family. I bet you anything he was one of your friends.

This is all to say that Alex was prepped. And he'd spent some time around you. Maybe he'd seen you do something accidentally. So I think he was already living in this grey area of knowing and not knowing for sure about you.

I made the mistake of asking my dad about my grandmother in front of Alex. Then Alex wouldn't let it go. He reminded me about things we'd grown up hearing about my grandmother— that she was never wrong at guessing a baby's sex in utero and she'd correctly predicted the outcome of every presidential election since Kennedy. There were legendary family stories about my grandmother knowing exactly where my dad and his friends were hanging out and what they were up to.

Then this thing happened with Spirit when we went home for a few days. I took him for a hike on the Greenbelt with Alex, and Spirit came back sad and limping. When we got home, I sat with him on the couch and took a closer look. I rubbed one finger over a nail that had split down the middle and coaxed it to repair itself. I didn't realize Alex was standing behind me until I turned and saw him leaving the room.

He's so weird. He's always been an open book except when it came to outright discussing this stuff. And then he decided to talk to you instead of me . . .

Chapter Twenty

～∽✦∽～

We were closing in on three weeks at the beach. We felt lucky we hadn't been asked to leave. I hadn't lost touch with the outside world entirely but I was only checking messages to see that all was status quo with John. He and I were in a waiting place. It was like we'd both tacitly agreed that speaking on the phone only made the separation harder.

"I've never seen you smile this much," Angus said. His longish hair that framed his patrician profile was becoming even more sun-streaked by the California sun.

"Same with you." I sat across from him on a straw mat on the floor of the dining area.

Angus toyed with his papaya, which was shipped in cases every week from Hawaii.

"Who were you talking to earlier? When you went out in the kayak?" I asked idly.

"That guy in the boat? He was just fishing."

Nothing much happened at the cove and that was fine by me. "If you're not going to eat that, I will," I said, leaning forward.

Angus picked it up with his hands and held it out of my reach. I leaned forward to easily grab it just as Elizabeth made a surprise appearance.

"I'm starving," I said to her in explanation, suddenly excited.

She stood in a pool of light shining through the open window. She nodded to us and gave a half smile before moving on to the next "guest." As soon as she left, it was like the most exciting celebrity in the world had left.

I wondered if it was intentional, if she withheld her presence to make everyone eager for it. I didn't think so. Emmanuel had told me she preferred the quiet of her bungalow and spent hours of her day in meditation. This operation funded that lifestyle.

Angus let his powers flow, not entirely in private. I found I could use the rigor of the hours of quiet sitting and the subsequent bliss as a substitute for using my abilities. It wasn't lost on me that maybe I'd found an answer to the cravings, that this lifestyle was like methadone.

Very quickly, I realized I wouldn't be having any more private conversations with my mother. Elizabeth/Maya didn't treat me any differently than any of the others. The fact that she was letting me stay said something. Other than that, I believed her that she stayed firmly in the present and didn't feel emotional attachment. I kept telling myself that I had seen her look terrified when she first saw me. But now that seemed almost impossible to remember or believe.

"It's better closer to our house," the trophy wife said, standing at the very edge of her picket fence.

"Excuse me?" I thought I'd heard what she said but wanted to make sure she was indeed being friendly. All this time she'd watched me try, and sometimes succeed in, making calls.

"Stand on my porch, you'll get reception right here." When I hesitated, she added, "When Bruce isn't home, I sometimes let the meditation tourists come up to our porch and use their phones."

"Oh," I said, walking out of the sand and succulent overgrowth, across the narrow street. "I thought they weren't supposed to."

"They aren't. But they do." She held out her hand. "Carrie."

"Julia," I said, offering my hand. She pressed her palm to mine for just a bare moment. Her handshake was surprisingly limp for someone whose badge of honor had to be how in shape she was. Today she was dressed in spandex again and a tight waffle-knit long-sleeve that showed off her curves.

I followed her down the flagstone path to her front door. Immediately, my phone pulsed to life, and messages started rolling in. One from Donna. Two from Rafa, which made me mad since I'd asked Kathryn Caspar to handle Agent Kelly. I understood it was his job to stay in constant contact but every time I did speak with him, he didn't have any new information and neither did I. Since I'd checked two days ago, there weren't any texts from John. Curiously, there was a message from Alex.

"Do you mind if I make a phone call from up here?"
I asked Carrie.

"Go right ahead. I'll be inside." Carrie opened the front
door and I saw an older woman in a uniform tending to the
little boy.

"Alex!" I said when he picked up, sounding more enthusi-
astic to speak to him than I ever had in my life.

"Hey," he said in a voice that took effort to be hostile.

"What's going on? Where are you guys?"

"Los Angeles. What about you?"

I was in the same state as John. "Well, it's funny, I—"

Someone interrupted him, and Alex said, "In a minute."
Then, to me, he said, "Something's wrong with my brother."

"What? What's going on? Is he okay?"

"I'm just going to come out and say it, okay? All last year,
I was worried when he met you, but he was happy. Then I
liked you. So I think I pretended not to see some stuff."

"What stuff?" I asked, suddenly cautious.

"It's like he's changed from being around you. I don't
know. It's hard to put into words."

I settled gently onto the porch swing and began to rock.
I shouldn't have been surprised. They'd been roommates for
weeks now.

"He seems unstoppable when playing. He reminds me of
you somehow."

"What are you talking about?" I said dismissively.

"He was sort of—like I said, it's hard to put into words.
He just becomes kind of perfect."

That had my attention.

"Since you left, he's been moody, kind of lethargic.

Basically a total asshole. Which pisses us all off. Then he plays incredible tennis that's far better than I've ever seen him play. He'll suddenly seem temporarily better—happier, less tired. And then, not to offend you, but girls, actually all kinds of people, start coming up to him, like they want a piece of him. Then he withdraws and doesn't talk to anyone."

"I don't know, Alex, you know him, he becomes a head case about tennis. If he wins, he worries about how he's going to keep winning."

Alex ignored me. "I don't know what your deal is. I never thought the rumors were true—that you were unusual. A different kind of person. Now I'm guessing that maybe that is true. John must know, but he won't tell me anything. And now it's like he's different too. What is it?"

"Alex—" I started.

"Just tell me. Because he won't."

"I think what you're seeing is that I didn't grow up like you guys. I wasn't allowed to socialize outside my family. So that's why I'm different. It's not him. He's probably just spent a lot of time with me and become more secretive."

"That's not it."

"All I can say is, he's fine. I promise."

"What happened with my knee?"

"I don't—"

"It happened again. A few days ago, we went back home. Just John and I were at the house and Spirit got hurt. He was limping and John just held his paw in this really focused way. He didn't know I was watching. All of a sudden Spirit gets up, wags his tail, and trots away."

"What are you saying?" I indented one fingernail hard

into my leg. I looked out at the horizon, at the guardrails across the street protecting cars from the steep drop.

"I think John healed Spirit. And I know he healed me. You can call me crazy, but like I said, I know him. Even better than you do."

"Hey!" I heard John's voice in the background.

"Your girlfriend's looking for you," Alex said.

I was already clamoring for John, and said, "Hand him the phone."

Then he was on the line. "Julia?"

"Hi!" The last several times we'd spoken, the cell reception had cut in and out. On Carrie's porch, it was perfect. I looked behind me at the house, but Carrie was nowhere to be seen.

"Why are you calling my brother?" He was annoyed.

"He wanted to talk. Alex said you're on a winning streak."

"It's fine," John said brusquely. From John's voice, I could tell Alex was still hovering, wanting his phone back.

"Is it?"

"Yes. It's all good."

"John—"

"Trust me." Then, he changed the subject. "How's your mother?"

"Elizabeth," I automatically corrected. "I barely see her."

"How many weeks has it been?" he said, implying that he thought it was strange I still hadn't confronted her.

"I think it's enough to see she had a life after Novak."

"But why didn't they stay together?"

"She's not going to give me answers." For the first time, I thought about John needing answers from Elizabeth too.

She was his only example of someone like him who had presumably been living her life and then a Puri came in and swept through, like a tornado.

I walked away from the house a bit, worried about privacy. As I stared at some ferns newly planted in dark soil at the border of the picket fence, the line began to cut out.

"John?" I walked toward the house again.

"I'm here."

"Alex knows something is different. He called me."

He let out a frustrated noise. "Alex is all over me. In fact, he's standing right here."

"This will pass. I promise you. And then you'll be at Stanford. You can't let your guard down."

"Your interview is coming up," he said, blowing me off. From the clapping in the background, it sounded like he was at another set of tennis courts.

"What if I stayed here while you went to Stanford?" I tried to sound casual. The beginnings of a new plan had been in my mind, and I couldn't help but float the idea. I didn't know if Elizabeth would let me stay, but a little bit of hope had started to form. It would certainly be less drastic than dropping off the grid, trying to make it somewhere out in the wilderness.

"What are you *talking* about?" he asked, incredulous. Then I heard him whisper to Alex. I could tell they had to go.

"You should see this place, John. It's close to where you'll be. I'd feel safe here. It's hard to explain, but it suits me much better than a place like Stanford. The consequences if things go wrong . . . it would be safer for you."

"So you're proposing that we live two separate lives. Like we've always done."

"Julia! Come on. Now," Angus called to me from the top of the stairs, making a "cut it off" motion. I waved him away, and he put his hands on his hips for a moment before going back down the stairs.

"Who is that?" John asked.

"Someone from the community. I'm breaking the rules. I told you we're not supposed to use phones." There was silence. "John?" I said, unsure if he was still there.

"Yes?" His voice had hardened.

"I'm just trying to figure things out. We only have a matter of weeks now and then you should be safe. But I don't know about me—"

"I gotta go."

The line went dead.

"Ugh!" I said out loud, wanting to throw the phone.

As if on cue, the front door of the house opened. "Hey! Want a drink?" Carrie carefully juggled two highball glasses as she shut the front door behind her.

The fact that she had made me a cocktail showed how lonely she was. I took the drink from her, and she very carefully sat on the porch swing next to me, balancing her drink in front of her.

"Boy problems?"

"Yep."

"I remember those," she said.

We didn't swing as much as sway, sitting in a surprisingly companionable silence. The cocktail was sweet and strong.

"What's it like down there?" Carrie asked.

I thought for a moment, not sure if I was allowed to talk about it. "Perfect," I said.

"Why do you think people pay so much to go down there?"

"Well, they're looking for something, right?" I said.

"What is it? What is that thing?" she asked like she knew but couldn't put a name to it.

I looked out at the ocean. "Peace."

Late AUGUST

JOHN

No. What you said about staying with Elizabeth instead of going to school? That wasn't okay.

Right after I hung up the phone, as I was walking onto a tennis court, I had my third vision. They've all been fast but immersive, like I'm temporarily missing from my real life and in a new place altogether.

When I closed my eyes, I was floating over the ocean and came to the cove, rising up over the structures and the cliffs to the hillside and town above. I saw in such detail that, later, I easily found the location on the map . . .

Chapter Twenty-One

Angus was singing some song under his breath. It was after midnight. We'd just come in from a late-night walk on the beach and were winding down, getting ready to turn off the two small lamps that cast a yellow light over the center of the room, not quite reaching the edges. It was time for Angus to put his blanket and pillow on the floor since I'd kicked him out of the bed after the first night. I was gearing up to hear his usual complaints and make the offer I always made to switch places.

Suddenly Angus flew across the room and back out the bungalow. By the time I reached the door, he was gone. But in the darkness I could just make out two figures coming down the beach. The V-shaped light of a flashlight beamed before them.

"This is where she's staying," I heard Emmanuel say when they crossed in front of our bungalow. The other person was male and a few inches taller than Emmanuel. As they started up the stairs, I felt what Angus had.

I waited, heat radiating off my back, knowing exactly who it was and feeling all control completely leave my hands.

Walking farther out onto the deck, I stood near the top of the stairs to greet them. Emmanuel appeared first.

"I'll leave you two," Emmanuel said as John and I silently exchanged looks.

"I . . ."

I couldn't see his face clearly. He was still cast in shadows.

"I have to be back in LA by dawn," he said.

"You just drove here from LA?" I asked, sounding like I couldn't catch my breath.

"I did."

"Do your parents know?"

"No. Just Alex. I'll be back before they know I ever left."

"But we agreed . . ." Never mind my fear about him finding out about Angus, John was not supposed to be here. He was not supposed to be anywhere near me.

"One hour isn't going to hurt me." He walked closer, and neither of us said a word.

It was beginning to register that John Ford was actually standing in front of me. Now, seeing him in person, all reason left my head, and for the moment, it seemed as simple as just being together.

John wore a T-shirt, jeans, and Converse sneakers. He was also wearing his glasses. He usually wore contacts around me, but his exhausted eyes showed why he'd needed to take them out. His expression was carefully devoid of any emotion. It was as if I'd been the one to surprise him at midnight at his hotel room. The only sign he was nervous was that his hands were shoved in his pockets.

I felt like a part of myself had just been handed back to me.

"Come into the light," I said, stepping closer to him and grabbing his hand from his pocket. Electricity traveled up my arm.

I led him into the bungalow, grateful that the room had just been cleaned—showing no obvious signs of Angus. Playing with fire, I pushed Angus and thoughts of how I was cheating—on our plan to stay apart for John's safety—to the dark recesses of my mind. On this beach, in the middle of the night, after weeks of not seeing each other, I couldn't resist him.

"You are so beautiful," I said. I felt I could now see him with a clarity I hadn't had before.

He shook his head. "You're staring."

I smiled. "It's hard not to."

"I feel the same way."

"What are you doing here?" I shifted my weight, tilting my head to one side. The space between us vibrated with energy and crazy attraction, each of us wondering if the other would make the first move.

"I wanted to see if you were okay."

It was the same lame excuse I'd given him when I'd shown up outside his bedroom door at dawn long after we'd broken up. What I'd really wanted then, even if I couldn't admit it to myself, was to make sure he was still a possibility.

Nothing had been rational about my decision to go to his house that night, hours before I was supposed to disappear to safety with my family. And yet . . . nothing ever felt as right as when John and I were together.

I broke the rules.

I dropped his hand and stepped forward, resting both my

arms on his shoulders. John laid his hands flat on my lower back, bringing me closer.

He lowered his head, and when we kissed, it was the first time it had ever felt desperate. I held his face, my hands threading through his silky dark hair, one of my legs standing between his.

He broke away, quickly whipping his shirt off before deepening the kiss.

My hands ran over his smooth back. "I missed you so much." I pushed him away so I could take off my clothes while he watched.

"You have no idea." He reached behind me, unhooking my bra expertly with two fingers. He kissed me hard but very gently lowered me to the bed.

I trusted John and let myself go, lying back, knowing how reckless we were being but too addicted to stop.

An hour later, I lay listening to the hypnotic crash of waves, loud inside the walls of the thin bungalow. "This feels like a dream," I said to myself, to the room in general.

John rolled over, sleepy-eyed. I should have let him rest for longer. He extended one arm to me. I lay back down, resting my head on his shoulder. A cool, California breeze came through the screens of the open windows. I pulled the sheet more firmly around me and pressed against him for warmth.

I found myself beginning to search for his thoughts. I wanted to know how happy he was, if he felt like I did.

"I thought you weren't doing that? No sixth sense," he said.

I raised my head and looked into his unfathomable eyes, my hair brushing his chest. *How could he always tell lately?* "It's only been now and again." I worried what his response would be and changed the subject. "We haven't talked about why you came or how you found me."

"Are you mad?" He smiled. "You didn't seem like it." John gently pushed my head back down to his shoulder.

"I just can't believe you're actually here."

"You know it was bullshit what you were saying about staying here." John let his hand glide up and down my bare back. "Isn't an advantage of you being here to find out what happened between a human being and a . . . ?" He said this lightly, but we both knew it wasn't a joke.

"If you met her, you would get it."

"No, I wouldn't. It's not okay that she won't tell you anything."

He was beginning to make me feel defensive.

"She seems to live on this higher plane. The past doesn't matter to her. She's let it go." And maybe I was too afraid to discover the truth of why my parents didn't work out. I also had empathy for Elizabeth. She was someone else who had been shattered by Novak.

"That's the equivalent of someone pretending something never happened. It doesn't work." He was referring to how I'd behaved when we'd broken up.

"I do know people who can do that. I grew up surrounded by them."

John rolled onto his back, breaking physical contact.

"We are efficient and cold," I reminded him, belatedly aware that I had unconsciously grouped myself with my family.

"You're not. Even when you try to be. You ended up amazing in spite of the family you had."

I'd survived because of my sister. "I'm not," I said automatically. But I smiled despite myself. Then, I ventured, "John? I don't think I'm cut out for college. I think I've been pretending all along, telling myself I can have things that I just can't."

"You haven't even tried." He abruptly sat up in the bed. I had to crane my neck to look at him, so I rose too. I grabbed my shirt from the floor, upset that the mood in the room had changed from dreamlike to harsh reality.

"I am a complete freak of nature. I do not fit in anywhere." In a way, it felt freeing to say it.

"Then I am too."

"No, you're not. I won't let you be," I said quickly.

John reached for his clothes. I watched as he turned and stood, swiftly putting on his jeans. It was something endearing about him—for having such a perfect body, he was surprisingly modest.

"My entire life, I've had people telling me what to do. I've gone along with it like a trained monkey." There was an edge to his voice I'd never heard.

"Are you talking about tennis?" I asked, surprised.

There was silence for a second. "Right when I was at my lowest point, you came along. Then later you tell me it's some kind of fate. I believe that. And that these things I can do are part of me that have always been there."

"What are you doing? What aren't you saying? Alex has told me more than you have."

John paused as if he was about to come forth. Then he reconsidered. "Nothing is going on," he said.

"No," I said simply.

"What do you mean, 'no'?"

"Being like me isn't who you're meant to be."

"How would you know, Julia?"

"So what you're saying is you're destined for something else? Something different than your brother and your family? Maybe something that feels great for a while but then gets you kidnapped? Disappeared?" I heard the sarcasm and hardness in my voice.

I thought that would have made him more angry, but he was serious when he asked, "If I can actually help people, why am I supposed to walk away from that?"

John didn't wait for my answer. He turned and walked barefoot into the small bathroom behind him, putting his shoulder against the warped door to close it.

The argument reminded me of why we'd had to separate for the summer. He would wear me down because I knew exactly how he felt. It was miserable. For a second, I pictured John trying to understand what seemed to be happening to him. Like the rest of us, at first he would feel like he was flying. Until he messed up.

I didn't know enough to help him or teach him with his particular talent. Angus and I had figured out some of our abilities, but there wasn't ever a good place to practice, or just let ourselves be. When I thought about John living in relative safety at the beach, I knew it would feel like a cage for him. He was just breaking free of his sheltered home life. Besides Angus was a fugitive and I was part of an FBI investigation. We were still trying to figure out how to live without the protection of the group.

I finished getting dressed and saw John's phone begin to vibrate on the side table. Alex's face lit the screen. It was two a.m. John needed to leave if he hadn't been caught already.

Pulling my hair back, I knew the dreaded good-bye was next. I'd promise to see him in less than a month and remind him to keep his head down—that next time I saw him, he'd be safe from Novak if what Angus said was true. I no longer believed that was our only threat. John was using, and he seemed addicted. I didn't know whether my presence was going to help or hurt him.

When I closed my eyes, I could feel a change coming. I realized that while living this calm life here at the beach, I'd let our problems fade in my head. They no longer played on my nerves, terrifying me every waking second. I'd grown lax.

The bathroom door burst open. John held out a black hoodie, larger than anything I'd wear. "Why is the toilet seat up? Whose is this?"

From the look on my face, John knew it wasn't mine.

I'd omitted Angus from every story, but I wasn't going to outright lie. But maybe at the end of the day, they were the same thing.

John gave me the dirtiest look. It was like he already knew.

"I thought about it, but it seemed crazy. It's Angus's, right?" John threw the sweatshirt to the floor, not wanting to touch it.

"I couldn't tell you I'd found him. You know that."

John was looking at me like he didn't know me. Then, he asked, "How long?"

I didn't know if I should come clean. It was true, the less John knew the better, but at this point, that was a bullshit excuse.

"Five weeks," I said.

"So about the time you said you wanted to separate for the entire summer?" The unerring focus of his eyes made me feel like I was in a spotlight.

I stayed where I was, leaving plenty of space between us, knowing perfectly well how horrible everything would sound. "He was the one who gave me the details about when my family would finally be gone. His father told him. That was around the time you started showing signs . . . I had to make a plan."

"He's been with you ever since we said good-bye?"

"We drove out here together." I heard myself digging my own grave.

"You traveled together? That's why I barely heard from you? And that's why you're having second thoughts?"

"I'm having second thoughts about trying to live like a normal person. Not about you. Not for one second."

"But here you are. You're cheating on me." John gestured around the room. "Sharing a room and a bed with him."

I could feel him looking at everything differently and said, "I know you know I would never, ever cheat on you. We shared hotel rooms. That's it. Here he sleeps on the floor." I knew it sounded like a lie. *God, it was even a lie because of that one night.* "He's my last connection. My only family I have in this entire world."

"You will always be cheating on me when he's around. He'll always win over me. Of course he would try to put me at a disadvantage, telling you I need to get rid of these abilities, I'm sure. I won't be able to compete with him, and you'll get bored. That's really what this summer has been about."

"I heard someone say my name." Angus's voice drawled

behind me from the doorway. The second he'd heard distress in my voice from afar, he'd made sure to show. He wanted this fight with John.

I didn't bother looking at Angus. I watched John's eyes snap to Angus, pure hatred on his face.

Angus sauntered closer, planting himself between John and me as if I needed help. "I think you need to leave," Angus said, possessively.

"Angus!" I said. "Go away."

"I'm leaving," John said and started toward me. His shoes were still by the side of the bed. Angus blocked him.

I knew what John was going to do the second before he shoved Angus hard out of the way.

"No!" I yelled, just as Angus grabbed the back of John's shirt.

John spun and punched Angus. Angus hit the rickety floor hard and took John down with him. He landed a fist in John's face so quickly, John had no way to see it coming.

"Angus! Stop." Angus knew I meant it, and he knew how badly he could hurt John. I felt him relent. But he got in one more shove to John's chest before standing up and backing away, acting grandly like he was only honoring my request. What I couldn't believe was that John had managed to hurt Angus. I could see by the way Angus kept an eye on John like a wary animal that Angus couldn't believe it either. He turned and spat on the bungalow floor.

What John had on Angus was more grace. He looked at me, swiped his shoes off the floor and walked out.

I shoved Angus, and he smirked, knowing he was going to catch so much shit from me later. He knew he'd won.

I ran, trying to keep up with John's long strides down the narrow strip of dry sand, shrunken from the incoming tide.

"John! Listen to me." I grabbed his shoulder. "We're the only Puris left."

"He uses that. And you let him."

"Don't leave."

John shook his head like I was unbelievable and began walking again.

"John! You know me. You know how I feel."

"We're done. We're too different."

"I thought that didn't matter to you."

"I'm talking about integrity."

Dammit. "He's not my boyfriend. He's my family," I shouted back. "You were the one who said have faith in us."

"No. I said to have faith in yourself."

He wasn't going to listen. Not right now. I watched him begin the long ascent up the stairs. It reminded me that there was something important I had to know.

"Wait. How did you find me? How did you find this place?"

"I could see it," John said over his shoulder.

Late AUGUST

JOHN

Alex was waiting for me in our hotel room in LA, and I made it back just before my mom knocked on our door. He took one look at my face and handled everything for me. Packed my stuff, looked under the hotel bed, chatted nonstop to my mom to keep her attention off of me.

I still have no idea how I got back to LA. I don't remember a single thing about that drive . . .

AUGUST

Chapter Twenty-Two

❧❧❧

I felt like I was in shock, unable to move, unable to process what had just happened. I remained in the same spot until morning, wide awake, perched on the side of the bed lying in wait for Angus. He never showed, but there were other unexpected visitors.

It began with a commotion on the beach, which was out of place in the early morning. Laughing, talking too loud, and giggling. Then, my name being called in a singsong, *"Julia! Julia!"*

Venturing outside of the bungalow and onto my deck, I looked down below onto a group of eight—six girls and two boys. They couldn't have been more than thirteen years old. They were being herded by Tana, the older woman with the braids who'd greeted me and Angus on our first morning. She was trying to shoo them out of the cove but was only driving them farther down the beach. They ran and laughed, a small, rowdy mob.

A girl with long blond hair wearing a royal-blue fleece drew up short when she saw me. Even from my distance I could see her holding a phone with my picture on it. She pointed and sprung up on her toes, excited. "There!" she shouted.

The others stopped and gazed up at me. They didn't do much more than jump up and down, stare, or start to giggle. One boy's phone came out to take my picture, capturing me wild-haired with eyes red from crying.

Farther down the beach, Emmanuel and Elizabeth, on a morning walk together, stopped to see what was going on. After a pause, Emmanuel began to swiftly approach the kids, Elizabeth just behind him. Typically it was only one or two people who wandered down onto the private beach, usually to walk a dog, and they were summarily redirected.

I skipped down the stairs two at a time. Already, more residents and guests were coming outside to see what the fuss was. Since I was the cause, I wanted to quickly quell the disruption before Emmanuel had to handle it. I did not want to be considered a nuisance to host.

Where had that recent photo come from?

When I came to stand in front of the group on the beach, they collectively backed up, as if they were surprised I was just a person like them, not a mirage on a movie screen.

Now that I faced them, I wasn't sure what to do.

Emboldened, one girl called, "Can we get a picture with you?" One of the others yelled out, "We love you!" And they all laughed.

I addressed the blond girl. "Can I see your phone?" She hesitated only slightly before handing it over. I flipped through an online photo series of me. In one, I was on my cell phone, hand on a hip, looking out at the horizon. I was wearing cut-offs and a concert T-shirt, tangled hair down my back, not unlike Elizabeth's. Another was a close-up of my face. From my warm, flirty smile and the downward cast of my eyes, it was clear I'd been talking to John. The photos had all been taken from inside Carrie's house, looking out into her front yard. Accompanying the photos was a brief column about where the Jaynes heiress was hiding. It divulged my exact location, naming the town and beach, and included quotes from locals about the suspicious, secretive community.

It was more than I could take at the moment.

I closed my eyes and pictured a ribbon wrapping around the motley crew, corralling them. Instantly, the group went from being dispersed and practically dancing to being drawn together into a tight, trapped pack by a compulsion they didn't understand. The teeming energy had instantly dried up and an abrupt silence overtook them. And then I pictured a great wave crashing onto the beach, reaching as far as the cliffs.

When I opened my eyes, I saw how scared I'd made them.

I mentally released them. The group hurried down the beach to the stairs to get out and as far away from the shore as possible.

Elizabeth and Emmanuel had drawn close, no doubt having experienced some of what the kids had. Their eyes were on me, observing me closely. Elizabeth whispered something in Emmanuel's ear.

Novak had the ability to change the energy of a room—I'd seen firsthand how Puris and outsiders hung on his every word. Me included. He made you feel what he wanted you to feel—it was like he could control the hive mind. Under pressure to do something, anything, to get rid of those kids, I'd just demonstrated the same ability.

When I saw the guarded looks on Elizabeth and Emmanuel's faces, I understood I had overreached. My newfound pride disappeared. There was a pure quality to Angus's levitation but something too powerful and ugly about mass manipulation.

A sprinkle of rain fell for the first time since I'd been at the cove. Angus had reappeared and was standing on the deck of our bungalow. I marched up the stairs, a defiant feeling flooding me with a strange sort of relief.

A minute later, Emmanuel and Elizabeth followed and stood across from us on the deck.

"Your friend left?" Emanuel asked in his deep voice.

"He did." I wouldn't apologize for John's intrusion even though an apology felt expected.

"It's time for you two to leave as well," Emmanuel said apologetically. I looked over at Angus.

"I'm sorry," Emmanuel said. "But we can't have this at the beach."

"Have what?" I asked.

"Violence," he pointed to Angus's split lip. "Drama. People we don't know arriving at all hours. Our livelihood depends on our reputation for quiet and discretion."

He sounded honest and slightly uncomfortable with the confrontation. I guessed this wasn't his idea. And it wasn't the true reason I was being kicked out. I'd reminded her too much of Novak.

"What did you do to those kids?" Elizabeth interjected.

I could see in her eyes that she'd already guessed. "I asked them to leave your beach." I shrugged, as if bored by the conversation. "When do you need us out by?"

"Today at noon," Elizabeth said, her gaze level.

I threatened both my parents' kingdoms—Novak's plans for his and the one of Elizabeth's new identity. I was a reminder of a past each of them wanted to forget. The funny thing was, I had never asked to be born.

"Thank you for having us. We'll be out by then," I said. I felt Angus's anger, wanting me to argue, to make them let us stay at a paradise not unlike the one Novak had preached about.

Elizabeth stood there, framed by the expanse of the cove behind her with her dark hair draped around her, white clothing flapping against her thin figure in the breeze and mist. She brushed her hair out of her eyes. For a moment, she looked like she was going to say more but stopped herself. Then she tried again. "The boy who was here . . . he's not one of you is he?"

"No," I said. "Why? Would you like to exchange more information?" I made a move toward her. She involuntarily stepped back.

For the briefest moment, she hesitated. Then she shook her head, indicating she had nothing further to say on the subject. That was what I'd thought. "I'll say good-bye at noon," she said and looked over at Emmanuel, ready for them to take their leave.

"Good-bye." I turned my back on them and walked inside the bungalow to the middle of the room. There was some satisfaction in losing hope, in knowing where things stood.

The screen door clapped shut, and Angus entered the room. I stared at John's glasses left behind on the small table.

"Can you believe that?" Angus started.

I didn't answer him.

"Will you at least look at me?"

I wasn't sure I could after what he'd done, but I forced myself. "Why did you do it?" He looked guilty, suddenly not meeting my eyes.

"You don't need him."

"That's not your call."

"It's the right thing to do," Angus said, surprising me. It wasn't what I'd expected him to say. Angus came closer. "I've never harassed you about the fact that you're sitting on the answer to all *their* prayers. That you're holding out on the group. I'm more loyal to you than them. That should tell you how much I believe in you. This summer, I wanted you to remember what it's like to be one of us before you throw it away completely."

He touched my shoulder with a pleading expression on his face that I'd never seen before. "Look, we could start something new out here. You were supposed to be a kind of queen and you're not. I was supposed to be a king. You and I have this power—more than anyone besides Novak. I was on the beach and I saw what you did with those kids. Julia, it's meant for something. Maybe there are others exactly like us. If your boyfriend hadn't shown up, if you hadn't made those calls to him up top and been recognized, we could have stayed here. I've never seen a better option." Angus searched my eyes, looking like a little boy, wanting me to join his fantasy. "It's the perfect time to let him go."

"But that's not what I want," I said, realizing finally that I didn't want to hide away from the world, even if there were risks.

In a soft voice, Angus said, "He could still go back to how things were before he met you. If you really want to save him, you can. This isn't going to go your way, Julia. I'm serious. They're going to find him unless you leave with me right now."

I went over to my bag and riffled through it, finding what I was looking for in a small zippered pocket. I shoved past Angus and out the door.

Elizabeth and Emmanuel's figures grew smaller as they walked down the beach. I wondered what they were saying to each other, if anything. I went in the opposite direction, veering into the grey water until it was up to my thighs. With all my strength, I took the necklace my family had left for me and threw it as far as I could out into the cold ocean.

"This is ridiculous."

"Come on. Let's go," I said in a monotone.

Angus looked disdainfully at the woman who'd shown up at noon on the dot with a broom and a bucket of spray bottles. He looked like he was on the verge of having a tantrum. It seemed so odd for him to let down his guard over being kicked off the beach.

The cleaning woman gave us the side eye.

"It's time to leave," I said more firmly.

We walked out in the clothes we'd arrived in almost three weeks ago.

Pausing one last time on the deck, we looked out at the beach. The water was only twenty feet in front of the bungalows. In the distance, off to the side, three peaked boulders loomed like guards.

"Elizabeth is different, and I wanted to figure it out," Angus said. "I know it's what Novak saw. You know what I mean?"

I realized I'd had maybe two actual conversations with her. She'd been as elusive with me as she was with her "guests." There was no pushing her further, even for John's sake. "We don't know her," I finally said.

"But we can read people, and there's something special about her. It's what draws these people to spend their money, just like people wanted to be near Novak. So what is it?"

I knew he was right but if I'd had the chance to find out more, I'd lost it. "She's a charlatan just like he is. Stealing people's money. It doesn't matter anymore."

"You're okay with never seeing her again?"

"This is actually easier. What if she had been full of tears and regrets and wanted me to be her long-lost daughter?"

"I don't know. At the end of the day, Novak was warmer."

It was true. He'd actually stepped up and raised me. And there had been moments when I knew he loved me, even if the rest of the Puris hadn't wanted him to take the genetic wild card in.

"She's alive. She's more than well. That's really all I needed to find out." I pushed away from the railing, heading down the wooden stairs.

We walked down the beach slowly. I wanted to be seen, for people to know that I was being kicked out. I saw how they looked hungrily at me and Angus—as Emmanuel had said, we were the only young people many of them had seen in years. Maybe she'd told her people I was related but not her daughter. Most likely she hadn't told them anything.

One of the blond men, Jerry, was jogging along the beach with a fishing pole, and Tana had her chalkboard and was hovering at the base of the dining hall. For the most part, the beach was quiet because of the high tide. There was no sign of Elizabeth and her good-bye.

Angus stood on the bottom step of the steep staircase to the road. "I'm going to leave this afternoon."

"Okay," I said, trying not to care despite my thin skin.

"I'm going to try to find them."

"What are you talking about?"

"I'm sick of this shit. If you won't be with me, I want to find our friends. I know where they are, and I'm going to get in, get my family back in. Maybe it is the best place. Maybe Liv will help."

"But you hate Novak. You hate him so much. Look at what you did to get away from him."

"I don't know anything anymore. This is too hard."

Maybe he hoped that if he threatened this, I'd change my mind and go with him to live off the grid. I couldn't tell if he meant what he said. I was still so angry with him after what he'd done with John, I wanted to get away from him in case this was a ploy to get in my head, to make me start to doubt. I didn't give him any reaction.

"What do you want?" I asked.

"I want my boys back. I want to be free." He looked out

at the cove. "For a second, I thought the future was here, with you."

After our road trip and the time at the cove, I'd noticed how happy he was when he was surrounded by nature. He began walking up the stairs, leaving his pipe dream behind.

Just as we reached the road, Emmanuel bounded up the treacherous stairs behind us like a mountain goat. I saw the flash of anticipation on Angus's face, like he was being saved at the last hour. But all Emmanuel did was hold out a leather-bound journal.

"We ask all guests to fill this out before they leave," he said, not out of breath in the least, his calves hard as rocks.

I opened the weathered, stained book and saw it was a guest book, the bookmark in place on a page not entirely filled yet. On a fresh line, I filled out "Julia Jaynes." Under comment, I wrote nothing. My hand hovered for a second over "address."

I guessed Emmanuel hadn't really cared about the guest book, that he'd wanted to make sure Elizabeth might have a way to get in touch, but in the end, I left the address blank. I didn't want the burden of wondering if she would decide to find me. I closed the journal and handed it back. Across the narrow street, Carrie sat on her porch swing, watching us.

"Thank you," I said, nodding.

"One more thing." Emmanuel studied me for a second as if trying to make up his mind. Then he whipped a manila envelope out from under his arm and handed it to me. "She told me to clean out her things way back when, but I didn't have the heart to throw that out. I'm sorry, I thought you being here would finally let a part of her rest." He pointed to the envelope and pivoted, starting his trek back down to the beach.

I held the envelope loosely with my fingertips, not wanting to touch it. For a second, I almost gave in to temptation and called after Emmanuel. I wanted to know what her tattoo meant, if my suspicions about 12-5 were correct.

Standing on the precipice above the beach, I remembered asking about my birthday when I was a child. I recalled sitting in front of a towering Novak and Victoria, Victoria holding Liv on one hip. I could still remember the strawberries Liv had been eating sitting on a plate on the glass tabletop.

I'd just asked when my birthday was, and a terrible silence had descended. I realized I'd done it again—I'd said something wrong but I didn't know what. Novak and Victoria had looked at one another. Victoria had silently left the room with Liv.

"November 28th," Novak had answered. I was only four but even I'd known he'd made it up on the spot.

"Hey," Angus said when we got to the beat-up car he'd driven us here in.

"What?"

"I'm sorry about Elizabeth," Angus said as he turned the key and the engine wheezed to life.

I ignored Carrie's wave. Pulling away from the cove, I closed my eyes and silently screamed. Birds surged from a tree in a chattering black burst.

"Don't be," I said. "She showed me you can reinvent yourself and forget all about the past."

JOHN

It was hard to believe we split up. I went to Kalamazoo. I wouldn't acknowledge what had happened in my head. I was in shock so that was the easiest thing to do. I couldn't handle that you'd lied and cheated on me.

If I was quiet off the court when I was with my family, I let everything out when I was on it. I did it out of spite. I didn't want you to take everything away from me. I wanted to keep what I could for myself—all that strength and heightened sensory everything. That physical outlet was the only thing that felt good. If I could keep it going, maybe in a fucked up way I could stay close to you.

Chapter Twenty-Three

I was sure I looked and smelled like a sea rat as I strode down the Rosewood driveway somewhere around midafternoon. All I was thinking of was getting back to my room, putting the sheets over my head, and staying there for days.

"Julia!"

I whipped my head around. Agent Kelly was wearing aviators and a light blue-and-white checked button-down and tan slacks. He camouflaged well with the other men milling at the entrance, waiting for their rides to make their post-lunch meetings.

"What are you doing here?"

"You wouldn't return my phone calls," Rafa said.

Other eyes were looking me up and down. While Rafa did not do the same, I knew he had already taken measure of my appearance. Now he moved between me and the bystanders, blocking their curious gazes.

My first thought was Angus. He should be miles away by now, having dropped me off in a parking lot ten minutes ago. After barely speaking on the drive, once we arrived in Menlo Park, he'd asked me one last time if I wanted to go with him. We hadn't had much of a good-bye. I refused to believe he would or could execute his plan to find the others. He was only baiting me, craving my attention, wanting me to say I'd stay with him.

A valet hopped out and tried to hand car keys to Rafa. "Can you hold it for me? Ten minutes?" he said to the young man.

"I need to call my lawyer."

"No, you don't actually. Come inside. This will only take one second." Somewhere along the way, a familiarity had grown between Agent Kelly and me. It was easier to get it over with. I chose the most public area, and we sat on sofas in the middle of the hotel.

"Why are you here?" I asked. "The phone couldn't have been that important, I assumed."

"I received word that the investigation is closed." Rafa let that set in.

"What do you mean? How?"

"My boss was informed by his boss who was informed by her boss. Your father has pulled some strings from wherever he is." Now I could see Agent Kelly's disgust.

"It's over?"

"It's over. I got called back to Texas."

"I didn't even know you were in California. Were you following me?"

"I was going to transfer here."

To watch me and wait to see if Novak contacted me.

He added, "You can still tell me what exactly happened to Kendra so I can tell the Ashleys."

I hesitated, then demurred once again, shaking my head like I had no idea what he was talking about. He looked at me like a parent expecting more from their child: disappointed.

I was free. I should have been amazed and happy, not ashamed. But I was ashamed about Kendra, ashamed of the power money wielded and how justice for the average person was an illusion.

"That cell phone you gave me," Rafa said.

I looked up, thinking about how Donna and Kathryn would have been all over me had they known I'd met with Agent Kelly and given him the phone. But that didn't even matter anymore.

"The cell phone belongs to a man named Hank Grady, who works for Donna Williams."

What he said took me a second to understand. I stared at three large pink-and-white seashells on the table. People passed around us in the hotel lobby.

"Donna hired that guy?" I asked, as if I were suddenly on the same side as Rafa.

"He reported weekly to Donna on your whereabouts."

And she reported to Novak, or most likely to some secret person on the chain below Novak.

"But I interviewed her for the job," I said, my throat suddenly dry at the realization that Novak still controlled me. My mind reeled, thinking back to meeting her for the first time. She had been my first friend besides John after my family had left. I hadn't even suspected.

"She pulled it off and got the job like your father wanted her to or maybe he was in contact with her once she took the job."

I felt like such a fool that I had thought it would be that easy to trust someone new who came into my life. Now I had to worry about Kathryn.

"Did this guy have photos of my boyfriend? Or was there communication about him?"

"Not very much."

"What do you mean?" I asked, my voice louder.

"There's a mention of you having dinner with a male your age but no photos were sent."

"Nothing else? No other mention?"

"No. They may have spoken in person though." Rafa sounded confused as to why I was so focused on this detail.

I was silent, still not quite absorbing what he'd said about Donna and busy redrawing the picture of her in my head. "She has all my financial dealings under her thumb," I said aloud.

Agent Kelly nodded and remained with me for a moment. When he stood, I didn't want him to go. I watched him walk out of the hotel lobby. I wasn't free at all. I'd just learned that Novak was unbeatable.

I knew John was flying to Michigan—to Kalamazoo for Nationals. That is, assuming he made it back to Southern California in time for his flight. It was the biggest tournament of the summer, the last tournament of John Ford's life played as a junior. The winner received a wild card entry into the US Open.

For part of the day, maybe he didn't answer because he was on the plane. But as the shadows grew long on the thick gold carpet of my suite and the sky turned pink, I realized he'd shut me out. The one thing that scared him the most when it came to me—his most jealous fear—was that I'd run away with Angus. And whether my intentions had been good or not, I had to acknowledge that I'd done exactly that.

I texted John throughout the day.

He's just family.

It's nothing more.

He had nowhere to go.

I didn't want you to get in any deeper, but I should have told you he was back.

I left a voice message only one time, my last try. "It's me. I love you."

It had taken about one minute to decide to move my money out of Donna's hands. She'd tried to call me, but I refused to communicate directly. Instead I faxed her forms, and the money was wired into my new Wells Fargo accounts. I didn't know what potential damage she'd done to any of my finances. I was scared even to trust someone new to help me look into it.

I didn't leave the room. I slept. Something resembling sleep. Sleep felt like the last safe place for me. If I hibernated long enough, I could will myself into a different existence. At one point, I imagined that if I slept long enough, when I woke up, this would all be a dream: the Puris, John, California, and the cove. What an amazing dream, a wild fantasy world set right in the real one. I'd wake up shaken but refreshed, ready to go off to college like a regular eighteen-year-old girl who ate dinner every night with her family.

Instead, I was a creature of unusual origins. And alone. I knew when I opened my eyes and lifted myself from the sweat-stained white sheets, my life would have to take a different direction.

When I had walked out of my father's office the night of Relocation, leaving my sister and everything I knew, I'd had faith. Something deep inside me told me this was my future. Now that seemed like a childish dream.

I pressed my face hard into the pillow. I could join Angus's family. Angus had said if I wanted to find them I should travel south and check into the Hotel Bel-Air. But their situation sounded frightening. Instead, I would roam the country and keep traveling to see more. I wanted to unravel my finances and see what good I could do with it. Maybe I could check in on John from afar, at least for a time.

As for my abilities, I'd thought I could tame them but they just continued to evolve. An unanswered question I would deal with alone. I couldn't stop, and I no longer wanted to.

I lifted the hair off my neck and recrossed my legs, the black spiked heel of my ankle boot swinging impatiently. It was my third day holding court in a corner of the lobby.

Without a clear plan, I'd lingered at the Rosewood. When the crushing loneliness had finally driven me from my hotel suite, I'd eavesdropped on the conversations taking place all around me. I tested how many I could keep track of at one time. My number was up to five. When I'd heard a start-up pitch, an idea struck me. I was bored and decided I wanted to play too.

First, I'd chatted up a pair of dejected men, boys really, not much older than myself. They'd had a few too many in the bar, and I got them talking about their idea, which had been freshly rejected by a venture capital firm across the street. To boost their confidence I'd planned on giving them seed money regardless, but their idea for a cellular agriculture technique was somewhat interesting. They were thrilled when I scrawled my illegible signature on checks issued from a company account that was part of my trust.

Almost instantly, I had conjured a fully formed alter ego. It reminded me of the old days with the Lost Kids—messing with people, having fun. But now I was smarter and a lot more decent. I was intuitive enough to sense good intentions, and I loved nothing more than denying greed. Condescension and arrogance were also nonstarters.

Petra Lipovski, my alter ego, was the agent for a philanthropist who wanted to give away her fortune. Petra wore jeans, someone's forgotten Pretenders T-shirt from the cove, and large Chanel sunglasses indoors. In my mind it was like a badass soundtrack accompanied her wherever she walked. Meeting requests came via assistants who would find me personally, and meetings took place from a specific armchair next to a southern-facing window. From the outset, arrangements were made to have each meeting catered by the hotel. As anticipated, enough money was spent that the staff never asked a single question. With hair dyed bottle-black again, sunglasses covering half of my face, and a vague Eastern European accent adopted for the occasion, I didn't worry about being recognized.

"Ms. Lipovski?"

A petite woman in a rumpled, out-of-fashion business suit approached. She quickly shook my hand. "I'm Kim Tran. Thank you for your consideration and agreeing to meet with me."

Kim was so nervous, I almost wanted to save her from selling her idea.

From the number of varied fingerprints on the glossy cover of the prospectus she handed me, I saw this idea had made the rounds. But I was impressed she'd gotten the meetings, and she launched into a surprisingly dynamic pitch. She had a fascinating idea for a solar-powered moped but required enormous capital investment. I was willing to take the risk, and I gave her more than she was asking for. When I told her the number, she lost her composure and hugged me. It was the only company where I took less ownership than was offered because I liked Kim so much.

Minutes after Kim left, two men in their forties appeared for their ten o'clock meeting brokered by an assistant who'd approached me the day before.

I didn't stand but leaned forward to shake their hands. One of them sat in the armchair across from me. The other briefly looked up from his phone to shake my hand and then went right back to his screen. He remained standing.

I waited.

Eventually, he looked up. "Where's your boss?" Just like that.

Clearly, the assistant hadn't properly explained the situation. "I'm the boss."

"We're on a schedule." He looked at his younger associate and made the move with his head that they needed to leave.

"Ms. Lipovski?" A woman in cream slacks and a pink short-sleeved sweater stopped in her tracks. "Mina Patel. I wanted to introduce myself."

I stood to shake her hand, and she continued on her way after handing me her card. The name Mina Patel clearly meant something because the asshole put his phone away.

"So—" began the man.

"Our meeting is canceled due to you being a classic douchebag," I said in the accent I was coming to love. "Go tell that to your boss." From behind my sunglasses, I squinted my eyes and fried the battery of his phone.

"I understand," he said and backed away, scared without knowing why.

Life was easy when you no longer cared what might happen to you.

The man wasn't the first to show disrespect. People who trusted that I was a decision-maker typically had ended up with a lot of money. The two ideas I'd heard about clean water took home the largest share.

See, Elizabeth? I'm not like my father.

The fact that Mina Patel had heard of me meant word was spreading and my time here was over. I was disappointed the fun and games would have to end and I was without a distraction. But it was time to face what was next.

I was conscious of today's date—Thursday, August 15th—and had decided not to entertain old dreams. I would let my scheduled college interview pass. When I returned to my room, I lay on my bed with my shoes on.

Don't do it, Julia. Don't look. It's time to move on.

But I felt around on the side table and grabbed for my

phone, preparing myself to know that once again John hadn't called. I shot upright in bed after seeing I finally had a text.

Call me if you go to the interview on Thursday. Until then, I don't want to talk.

JOHN

In the early rounds at Kalamazoo I had gone next level on some people. The first few days we were broken up, it was like I wanted to kill every opponent. They'll get over it one of these days. I don't know if I lost a single point to a few of these guys.

I had decided that we would never speak again. It was a crushing decision . . .

Chapter Twenty-Four

A mile of palm trees lined the corridor into the university in a dramatic statement.

No wonder John loved this place, I thought. I kept seeing California through his eyes—the oxford-blue sky and the perfect, temperate weather with its cool mornings and evenings.

As I approached the front entrance to the school, it was like entering the Emerald City. I walked past the Rodin sculpture I'd seen in the online video tour, the burghers so black and shiny and beginning to bake in the sun. Two tourists took photos of themselves in front of the sculpture.

The office for my interview was close to Memorial Chapel at the end of Palm Drive. I also recognized its gold-leaf tile, now glittering in the sunshine, from the video I'd watched.

The campus already felt busy, but I suspected it was a summer school–type busy. I liked the atmosphere as I walked under the arches and over bronze tiles marked with the year of every graduating class. I entered the building, approached the front desk, and ignored how cold my hands felt.

"Hello, I'm—"

If I ever said my name, she didn't hear it. The student—presumably that's what she was—stood up as if I were a very important guest even though we were roughly the same age. She wore jeans and a T-shirt, and I felt overly formal in the thin, long black sundress I'd picked out for the interview.

"Hello! Yes, we're ready for you. They want to start in Dr. Yu's office."

She showed me through the small reception area and into a much larger office. It was empty.

"You can wait in here. Let me know if you need anything."

She softly clicked the door shut behind me. I remained standing and walked over to the sunny windows behind the desk. Students swiftly passed by on their bikes. For the first time I really tried to picture myself at Stanford. It seemed impossible. I felt a hundred years old compared to the incoming freshmen.

I looked at my watch.

The door opened and a petite woman wearing wide-legged trousers and a light-blue blazer walked in.

"Hi, I'm Michelle Yu, Dean of Admissions." With her knowing look, I could tell she had heard all about me.

"I'm Julia Jaynes. Thank you for seeing me."

"Thank you for coming in person. I know it was a very odd request this late in the process. But my colleague, whom we want you to meet, wasn't available earlier in the summer."

If it was odd, I hadn't known it. I'd declined their offer of transportation and lodging, preferring of course to have control over my own arrangements. I'd simply been glad not to receive an immediate rejection.

"We wanted to talk to you a bit about your potential admission here, and it's obviously more complicated, given awareness of you on a national level." To her credit, she was all business and didn't dance around the fact that a manhunt for my father was world news.

Nervously, I smoothed my hands on the skirt of my dress, and I experienced my first glimmer of wanting to make a good impression. I glanced back out the window, and for a second I saw myself as one of the students I'd been watching.

"We wanted to talk to you about accommodations. It's sensitive so we needed to do it in person."

Suddenly wanting to convince them I was worth the trouble, in one rush I said, "I'm perfectly willing to change my name. I know you've had high-profile students here, and I read that they blended in. If I were accepted, I may need a small bit of security detail, but I also know you've had Secret Service here in the past."

Professor Yu smiled at my string of words, losing a little of her formality as if I'd reminded her I was just a kid sitting across from her.

"Did anyone offer you water?" she asked.

I shook my head.

"Let me get you one. Dr. Gottlieb is running behind." She smiled. "Make yourself comfortable." She gestured to the cluster of armchairs on the left side of the airy room and left the office.

More waiting. I plopped down into a velvet armchair, the jagged sadness over John stabbing my stomach again.

Automatically, I glanced down at the low, wood coffee table. Lying on top was one piece of paper that read "Letter of Intent" with my name on it. I half-smiled. So they wanted me.

Next to it was a folder. I leaned forward in the chair and moved it with one finger to see if I could read the label. The tab said, "Elizabeth Blackcomb."

I didn't hesitate. I'd had no idea she'd attended Stanford. I opened the folder, scanning the typewritten cover page of Elizabeth's Stanford application from 1991. Elizabeth's senior portrait from Sidwell Friends School was attached with a paper clip, showing me what she had looked like at my age. Her eyes were laughing and knowing at the same time. Her face looked so fresh, her cheeks fuller and pink.

I glanced up at the door, speed-reading through the application before anyone came back to the room. Quickly, I got an impression of a young Elizabeth. She had been an off-the-charts student—perfect grades, perfect scores, valedictorian—a popular girl who wrote a witty and scathing personal essay about being the only child of a four-star general and a psychiatrist. There was ballet. Community service. Leadership positions. Her letters of support from teachers all boringly echoed what her grades told me. Only one teacher's recommendation was a little more oblique and not altogether an endorsement:

> It goes without saying Elizabeth Blackcomb is an excellent student. When her plate is full, she is happy. When it's not, she grows frustrated, pushing boundaries, seeking more challenges, often testing her peers, parents, and teachers. Her learning

style is atypical. In my years of teaching, I've never seen someone so gifted in a way that strains what we believe to be possible. Elizabeth falls into the prodigy category.

Behind the application was a transcript of Elizabeth's grades from her first year at Stanford. Perfect. But then there was a record of complaints inserted into her file. One was a written request from Elizabeth's freshman roommate. The letter formally asked for a transfer to another dorm, citing intimidation. One letter came from a classics professor who wanted to bring to attention some unusual behavior from Elizabeth that the professor felt was putting other students on edge. Then there was a formal reprimand over a gambling pool run by Elizabeth.

After her freshman year, her transcript stopped recording grades, and every additional semester through her senior year was labeled "Institute for Progressive Learning." The records ended there.

Goosebumps raised on my arms. I closed the file the second before the door opened. Dr. Yu opened the door wider, and a tiny, older woman dressed in a linen pantsuit entered the room. I knew I'd never met her before, but she seemed familiar. She was far more wrinkled than the older people in my family, but she looked incredibly similar. Like she was one of them.

I half-stood and then had to sit again, in sheer disbelief at who I might be seeing. If I was right, I was looking at another Puri who existed outside of my family.

"Julia, this is Dr. Gottlieb."

"Hi Julia," she said, gazing at me. "I'm Miriam. I'm so glad you're here. You are not the easiest person to get in touch with."

I was surprised I could still use my voice. "You tried to get in touch with me?"

"Through letters and email, yes. I run the Institute for Progressive Learning here at Stanford, and I was the one pestering you to apply." Her eyes were warm. She looked truly pleased to meet me.

"Oh, I thought that went to everyone—that it was another opportunity available." I scooted as far back into my chair as I could, my heart pounding against the walls of my chest.

Dr. Gottlieb laughed. "No, it is definitely not offered to everyone. When your father was in the news and I saw your image, I connected you to Elizabeth." She gestured to the folder on the table. "I know a bit about your family history. Would you like to come walk with me and tour the Institute?"

I saw the security guard at the door and hesitated. Neither woman explained his presence.

Dr. Yu simply said, "I'll leave you two alone for a moment." The door closed behind her.

I didn't like being manipulated. And the security guard was scaring me. Part of me wanted to leave when Dr. Gottlieb took my hand. A warmth traveled through my veins up my arm. I knew it was intentional. It was something I'd only ever felt from Novak's touch until now.

"I could tell you were cold." She looked at my face, wanting to see me comprehend. The hair rose on the back of my neck.

"I'll have you back here in fifteen minutes, I promise you, but you're free to leave at any time."

I somehow knew this was the moment when I would find what Angus had been looking for. I'd stumbled on it, or maybe I'd been led to it.

We left the building. The security guard trailed us down the covered walkways.

"This way." Dr. Gottlieb scanned a key card and entered a building a short distance from the dean's office.

I hesitated a second before following. Dr. Gottlieb smiled, but I couldn't tell if it was with understanding or mirth at my skittishness. The security guard took up a post outside the building.

Immediately there was another door, and she used a code, the technology that controlled access a contrast to the classic architecture. She saw me watching every keystroke.

We walked down a long hall and stopped for Dr. Gottlieb to do an eye scan.

I looked up at the security cameras. *Who the hell was this woman?* I suddenly felt like a dead man walking, resigned to fate, and thought I'd been lucky to come as far as I had. Who might be waiting for me? The FBI? Another branch of government?

The next hallway was lined with windows that looked into a series of classrooms. Miriam knocked lightly on the glass. A girl with a chimp on her hip looked up. She came over to the door and unlocked it.

"Etta, how are you?" Dr. Gottlieb said. "I wanted to introduce Julia, a prospective student."

"Hello." The girl's glasses were falling down her face,

and the chimp reached up to push them back on her nose. I smiled despite myself. The chimp reached for me.

"It's okay, you can hold her if you like," Etta said.

Startled, I took the chimp in my arms and stared into her eyes. She put her hands on my face. Then she pushed away from me and reached back for Etta.

"Aww, she wanted to see if you could talk to her."

"Oh, should I have said something?"

"Oh, no. Not out loud."

"Silently?" I looked to Miriam, and she nodded. "You can talk to her?" I asked Etta.

"It's just this thing I can do."

Without telling them, I tried again. I held out a hand to the chimp, and she took it. We locked eyes once more. I could hear her heartbeat, and I began to sense her curiosity but nothing more. She shook my hand as if she wanted to comfort me because I couldn't do it.

When Etta took her back, she said, "She likes you."

Miriam gestured for me to follow her to another room down the hallway.

"I don't understand," I said, suddenly thinking this might all be a messed-up dream—a feeling John had expressed more than once. My teeth began to chatter. Miriam didn't answer.

Miriam placed her phone on a ledge in the hallway and then led me into the next room. She nodded to two older-looking students who were seated at a small table across from a young man who had his eyes closed.

"Ahmet?"

The young man looked up at us, confused. His pencil

hovered over a piece of graph paper with a meticulous, partially completed sketch of a swimming pool and an ivy-covered wall directly behind it.

"Ahmet, this is Julia."

He nodded and then silently went back to his work.

Miriam smiled and turned to me. "I shouldn't have interrupted. Here, let me show you." She led me back out into the hallway and the door fell closed behind us. She collected her phone, and after a moment, pulled up a video for me to see of a group of people seated next to a swimming pool with an ivy-covered wall behind it. Ahmet's drawing was exactly what the group was looking at.

"We're running a remote viewing project. We have a team at this location right now. Ahmet's not told where they are. They need to stay in one place until he's finished, which can take up to a few hours. We use the photo of the location to compare with what Ahmet sees and draws. So far we've had varying results. Let's go talk in my office."

As I walked with Miriam, fear ignited a strange urge to cry. "I don't understand what this is."

"It's a place to learn and to create. Students come, no strings attached, and explore their ideas. We have students from across the US, the Philippines, Malawi, India—all over. The hope is that their work will lead to achievements benefitting the common good. That's the official line for the Institute anyway. Other universities have them as well. Einstein came up with his theory of relativity at Princeton's. We all work to provide an environment that fosters breakthroughs and contributions to society."

"But how is what I just saw . . . ?"

Miriam opened a door to a corner office and entered after me. We were enclosed in a sun-filled room.

"How we differ is that this institute is devoted to exploring ways of learning and creating that aren't accepted yet. There is so much more difference out there than many people believe or want to know about. What we consider reality is only an agreed-upon reality. It's not the whole picture. We'll never know the whole picture, but we can keep looking for answers. Why don't you have a seat?"

Miriam settled behind an old-school metal-and-Formica desk that looked like it once belonged in a lab. "It's everywhere," she continued, "the person who does something extraordinary or masters something that's eluded the experts. After decades of working here, it's my belief that these talents can't just be written off as oddities. I think they're displays of people becoming increasingly sensitive to their environment, more empathic, more intuitive. Though the students here aren't exactly like you and me."

"Excuse me?" I remained standing in the shadow cast by a large oak outside the window.

"They aren't descendants of a people who made an evolutionary change. See, I'm descended from the Chachapuris as well."

I knew my job was to pretend I had no idea what she was talking about. That's what I'd been taught to do. But the problem was, I believed her. I'd recognized it the second she walked into Dr. Yu's office.

Miriam leaned into her chair and glanced at the ceiling. "I could always do the strangest things. I would go to school and bend silverware at lunch, showing off for anyone who wanted to see." She looked back at me. I was still standing across from her. "You can imagine how long that lasted before my parents told me to stop. My grandfather always said I could do these things because we were directly descended from Puris who were captured and forced to work the mines. In the Chachapuri lore, the fate of those who escaped had always remained a mystery. In the stories, they were still out there, maybe hiding but hopefully thriving—keeping our history and culture alive and continuing to develop our unique talents.

Miriam leaned forward again and folded her hands on her desk. "Apparently, I didn't do such a good job at hiding my quirks because the CIA recruited me when I went to college. They were looking for so-called psychics during the Cold War to interact with Soviet targets. The program was disbanded, but it landed me here as a teacher where these people from all different walks of life who had these odd but undeniable gifts surrounded me. We developed this independent institute for exploration, to see if any of our abilities could add up to anything that could be useful."

"Not even one is like you?"

"No. We search for them all over the world. They're unique, but they aren't altogether different the way you and I are. The students who are invited usually need help; they're struggling to make sense of their gifts and, for the most part, have learned to hide the extent of them. We've found that they can cultivate these abilities while their brains are still growing. Some people aren't ready, and we back off immediately. I think there are more people than we know who suppress these traits.

"I *do* think there are more of us out there. I have hope; I like to think Chachapuris find one another. As of today, I've met two in my lifetime."

She reached into her top drawer and then handed me a photo. I automatically took it and turned it over. I didn't say anything as I studied it. In the photo my mother looked so young, standing with a lanky man with black hair.

I looked up at Miriam. "Are you saying she's a descendant like you?"

"No, I think she is brilliant and an aberration, someone who was well on her way to exploring her gifts until she stopped. Your father is the other Chachapuri I've met."

I dropped the photo on the desk and had to pick it up again. The only thing that looked at all similar was his build. But from his stance in the photo, I knew it was Novak. Both he and Elizabeth seemed unaware that the photo was being taken. Looking at it more closely, I saw now that she was slightly leaning back against him, staring at something in the distance.

I was speechless. I looked up at Miriam.

"I didn't mean to shock you."

I noticed the framed family photos on a bookshelf behind her, including one of Miriam and kids who were probably her grandchildren.

"I brought Elizabeth into my program, and right away, she calmed down. She was still flashy and confident but she quit scaring other students. She stayed on as a graduate student in biology, but she mostly worked with me here, and at that point we were still government-funded. The FBI heard about some strange activity at the tech company Oracle regarding this incredible young man. The agency called me, as it still does when news of a questionable event makes its way up the food chain. I asked Elizabeth to investigate."

I remembered what Lati told me, the one time he'd ever spoken to me about my mother. "She worked there. You had her take a job? Like a spy?"

Miriam didn't look at me, and if she thought she'd done the wrong thing, she didn't admit it. "Elizabeth walked into something that blindsided us. We had no idea there was an actual group of people with similar talents. It was exciting because they were the only living example of a people who had made some sort of genetic change together as a group. At least the only one we know about."

"He told her this?"

"He opened up to her. About the group's identity and their semi-nomadic lives. When Elizabeth told me about the tribe I finally had proof my grandfather's stories were true. Your father told her about Relocation and how they were worried about sustaining their numbers. From the beginning, we knew they were planning to make a move soon."

Miriam tensed, which told me she was getting to an uncomfortable part of the story.

"Elizabeth kept getting in deeper. I think from the start, she knew she would follow him anywhere. She claimed just being around him seemed to enhance what she could do, that she was getting sharper and quicker at everything. At that point Elizabeth lied to me and said she'd already told him who she really was. That he was thinking about coming in to speak with us. She stopped checking in, but I kept dropping in on her. And then she couldn't hide that she was pregnant." Miriam stopped suddenly. "She would never tell me what happened between them at the end. If he left suddenly. If they made an agreement of some sort."

Elizabeth would never tell me either. "Did you ever meet him?"

"One time. The FBI was losing patience with the way we were running things. I was worried about your mother and that your father's group would disappear. I went to his office to see him. He played nice, never revealing a thing about himself or that he was surprised to find out who Elizabeth really was. If he felt betrayed, he hid it for months. Now I realize he was just waiting for you to be born. I don't know if he ever thought about my proposition to him and the Puris to come into the Institute . . . or maybe he got scared, told someone, and they convinced him otherwise."

"Maybe you shouldn't have interfered and she could have gone with him for Relocation."

"They never would have taken her."

"But Novak took me."

"Perhaps they didn't want to leave a trace of themselves behind or give Novak any reason to come back. I am so sorry, Julia. I should have known there was a possibility that we could lose you."

I quickly ran my fingertips under my eyes.

Miriam said gently, "I'm sure you were a way forward for them."

"No, they want to stay the same."

"You are special. You're the bridge between cultures. You're both. Once Novak and Elizabeth got together, they opened a door to take your group in a different direction. The fact that you're here in front of me is extraordinary."

"You want to study me."

"I want to offer you an opportunity to reach your full potential."

We looked at each other for a beat.

"Your group has eluded us for the past twenty years, and they are smart enough to probably continue to do so. But their numbers must be dwindling, and they must be making decisions from a place of insecurity."

"They don't feel insecurity."

Miriam sized me up for a second, seeing more of me than I wanted her to. She lowered her voice, as if she didn't want to offend me. "I don't know how you were raised, but I can guess that you felt a degree of shame about your difference. You're an outsider no matter where you go. That will never leave you. Every human being feels that: shame, self-doubt. But instead of being on your own and hiding your skills, here you can be fully integrated into a community. We can teach you how to coexist with others. You can safely explore and fail—just like the Puris were able to cultivate their gifts hundreds of years ago. One day you may want to teach or work with me to find other young people to bring into the Institute who think they need to hide their gifts to get by."

I hovered near the door.

Miriam continued, "Kids come here, and at first, we give them all the tools they need to master their skills. They build their confidence. But at the end of the day, those are just excellent tricks. Once our students learn the extent of their capabilities, we invite them to find a larger purpose. I know how lucky I am. If I hadn't found that, I would be hiding my gifts and battling the feeling that I'm not quite there yet, that there has to be something more. Something beyond just myself."

"Like what?" I asked flatly. The longer I stayed to listen, the more exposed and cornered I felt. I wanted to know I could in fact exit the building as Miriam had promised.

"For you, I think it's written in all stories about the Chachapuris. Their incredible empathy and their natural capacity to help. From what I saw with your father and what I feel now with you sitting before me, you have a physical effect on people. At best, I've seen it enhance the consciousness of those around them, inspire a feeling of interconnectedness. At its worst, it's used to take advantage of others' trust the way I suspect your father did later in life."

Miriam reluctantly stood, knowing she didn't have me for much longer. "We're at a crossroads. We've come so far, and now it seems as if we're going backward. Humans have an undeniable instinct toward self-destruction. Just a few greedy people can cause so much suffering. Here at the Institute we want to tip the scales on the side of progress. You are full of light and goodness; it's easy to tell. So was your father. But unlike him, you're just choosing your path."

My hand stilled on the door handle.

"Your other choice is to sit back and watch. Regardless, I need to warn you. If you remain on your own, you have to conceal your abilities. We'd love to talk to your friend too, eventually. It didn't take long to hear about what you and he did in Colorado. If you continue, unfortunately someone will end up stopping you."

She let that sink in. "We want to know about the Chachapuris before they're lost. I know it's a lot to think about. To come in and talk about your culture, expose who you really are."

I'd never dreamed I'd find a meaningful outlet for my abilities outside of my family. But this felt dangerous and like a betrayal.

"You having a life is not a betrayal."

Now I understood how upsetting it must have been to John when I read his mind without permission.

"Uncertainty is dangerous. But that's the case with every beginning. I'll back off now. We'll hold a spot until the start of school. If we don't meet again, best of luck, Julia."

I left, blown away, never bothering with Dr. Yu's office or her Letter of Intent.

JOHN

I thought I was getting better. I went from comatose to just feeling kind of dead inside. But it was a manageable dead. At least I was eating again.

I began to get a lot of attention at Kalamazoo, and I started having serious thoughts that it would make sense to go pro. I had fantasies about what it would be like to be a star. Have tons of money. Pay my parents back. I wanted you to read about me in the news.

It was a low point, for sure. I was pretty out of my mind. Winning was the only thing that felt good.

You gave me a card last year when we first started dating. You tucked it in the pocket of my tennis bag for me to find, and I left it there so that sometimes I could look at it before matches. You painted it yourself—a landscape of Lady Bird Lake and downtown Austin in the background. Remember? It must have taken you hours, or for you, maybe not hours, but you gave it time and care. It was so good. When I first saw it, I thought you'd bought it. Later you told me you liked to paint and how it was okay but not your best work.

Inside, you wrote stuff like: good luck, have fun on your trip, I'll see you when you get back.

I was so surprised that you'd made me something. At the time, we were barely dating. When you gave it to me, I realized you were into me. I was never going to throw it away.

In Kalamazoo, a water bottle leaked in my tennis bag. The card was ruined, all the watercolors blurred together. I tossed it right in the trash.

When that was gone, I was all out of proof that we'd ever been together.

AUGUST

Chapter Twenty-Five

❧❧❧

My one bag was packed. The room had been cleaned while I'd been at the interview. I could slip out today—now—and leave without checking out and no one would know for at least a day or so. I could take cash and go to the San Jose airport in a taxi, buy a ticket to Los Angeles, and get picked up by Angus. From there, I could fall off the map for another two weeks, at which point my family would be gone for good. Angus's family would presumably help me procure new identification.

So why wasn't I leaving?

Housekeeping had placed some of my overlooked items on the glass-topped bedside table. A hairbrush, a book. And that manila envelope Emmanuel had given me.

Don't. You've made your decision.

I wheeled the bag behind me. Whether it was fate or just the breeze, when I opened the door, the envelope slid with a whisper onto the carpeting.

A couple of guests wearing name tags walked down the

hall, and I quickly stepped back into my room, vacillating in the doorway.

Once I shut the heavy door, I picked up the envelope and opened it quickly, giving myself a sharp paper cut.

I slid out three pieces of paper.

One was my birth certificate. The card stock was thick. It read that my name was Julia Blackcomb. My mother was listed as Elizabeth Blackcomb. Caucasian. The father's name was left blank. My birthdate was December 5—I'd been right about her tattoo. I'd been born at three p.m. and weighed almost eight pounds. Elizabeth's signature was at the bottom.

There was something amazing about touching the eighteen-year-old birth certificate that had been in her hands just after I was born.

I looked at the two other pieces of paper. They were printed emails from an AOL account, wrinkled as if they had been read and reread a hundred times.

The first was dated early September. It said: *Don't be scared or worry what your parents will think. The three of us are going to live the most beautiful life. I've seen it. And I've seen her. She is going to be amazing, Elizabeth. I can figure this out. You are my life.*

The second said: *I cannot wait to meet her.*

That email was dated December 7.

I took a ride share all the way to the beach.

It was a clear day, and a surprisingly strong late after-noon sun glittered off the water. I took the beach stairs down quickly, the envelope in my hand.

The shore was quiet, but I knew where to go. I knew the schedule by heart. "Excuse me," I interrupted. I'd let myself into the dining hall and saw some familiar faces, including Emmanuel's, and a crop of new ones. New week, new guests.

Emmanuel saw the envelope in my hand and leapt to his feet. He made a gesture for me to follow him and guided me out of the dining hall and onto the deck, allowing the group to resume their last meditation of the day.

"Is she here?" I asked as Emmanuel softly slid the door shut behind us.

"She hasn't left in ten years," he joked. He put a hand on my back and smiled.

"I need to talk to her."

Instead of arguing like I'd expected, Emmanuel simply said, "Well, let's go find her."

He walked me to the bungalow at the very end, set apart from all the others. The sound of the ocean roared in my ears as I stood in the shadow of the quiet bungalow above me. For a moment, I paused, knowing this feeling and hating it. It was the same as when I'd wanted an audience with my father and knew the ask was unwelcome. But this ask was easier because it wasn't entirely for me.

Emmanuel let himself in first. Elizabeth's bungalow felt more like a home instead of a vacation destination. There was more furniture and lots of color. Music was playing at a low volume from speakers suspended in the corners of the room. The ceilings were low and the walls paneled with dark wood.

"Hello?" he called. From behind him, I had a partial view of Elizabeth walking out into the main room in nonwhite clothes. She was wearing shorts and an old T-shirt, as if she'd been caught without her costume. She stopped mid-step when she saw me, caught as off guard as when I'd first shown up at the beach.

She cleared her throat and snatched a long sweater from the back of a tapestry-covered chair. She put it on and wrapped it protectively around herself. "Emmanuel?"

I saw her look at the envelope in my hand.

"You always say we go through exactly what we're supposed to," Emmanuel said. "Just talk to her, Maya." Silence, and then Emmanuel finally asked, "Do you want me to stay?"

"No," Elizabeth said. "It's fine."

Emmanuel smiled and walked back out the door, leaving me alone with Elizabeth.

"I've tried not to need the story—about where I come from and what happened." I paused. "But I do. I just do. I'm desperate to keep us all safe. You must know what it feels like to be scared." I exhaled loudly. "I hate asking for help."

Elizabeth watched me, not saying a word. I expected her to say something guru-like and before I knew it, I'd find myself on the top of the cliff again and headed to Bel-Air.

"Let's get some air, okay?"

Elizabeth led me out, down to the beach. I wasn't sure if this was her consent.

It was low tide, and the water was calm, gently rolling in and out. We strolled a ways, both of us quiet, and just as I began to get frustrated, she said, "I haven't spoken about this in a long time." She stopped walking and looked at the water. "He was young. I was young. Twenty-two. I think he was the same age—he never told me. I met him at work, fell desperately in love, and got pregnant. Then he left with his family and he took you with him when you were five days old, I think. No, I know you were five days old."

"But what happened? Why did he leave? What were you doing at Stanford?"

Elizabeth gave a half laugh. "Miriam Gottlieb found you."

"I think I found her by accident. Now she's offered me something I don't know if I can take." Elizabeth just looked at me. "It could be a way for me to live. But I don't know if people like me can do that. Why didn't it work for you and my father?"

"Who was that boy who was here?" She narrowed her already narrow, sleepy-looking eyes.

"He's talented like you, and I don't know if being around me makes it stronger. Is that what happened to you? Was it too intense to stay together?"

Elizabeth looked up at the sky and took a deep breath. Then, her whole body seemed to relent, as if she couldn't say no any longer.

"I was part of this—thing—at Stanford, and I'd been sent to get a job in the same department of the tech company where he worked to check him out, to report on whether he was just another genius or if something more was going on.

"My first day I walked into the office, and there he was, sitting in a cubicle, an almost identical-looking friend in the cubicle next to him. I'll never forget meeting Chris for the first time. It was the strangest feeling I'd ever had. It was . . . there's no describing it. I felt electrified."

"What do you mean?"

Elizabeth smoothed her hair into a ponytail and then held it firmly, running her hand down its length. "I'd always been different—there were these odd, extra-sensory things I could do—and then all of the sudden I met him. It felt like I'd been calling out into nothingness my entire life and then he showed up, like he was my answer back. And around him, I kept feeling sharper and more alert."

Elizabeth kicked at some sand with her bare toe. It was like I was seeing beneath the Maya shield. She seemed so much softer and human, like the person I'd glimpsed when we'd first met eyes.

"Did he tell you who he was?" I asked.

"We worked together for only about two weeks before we were a couple. I knew he wasn't supposed to be seeing me, but we couldn't stay away from each other. His friend who also worked there was eerily like him. Being around Chris almost constantly, it was like he was changing me. Maybe that was why he opened up about who he really was and about the tribe. It was clear pretty quickly that his people considered him special. He was so excited that he thought he had found someone like them, from the outside. That they weren't alone."

"Were you telling Miriam everything you were learning?" It was hard to imagine Novak ever being so open and trusting. The Novak I knew was the opposite. Outsiders were to be either ignored or controlled. There was a wall between them and us.

"I was at the beginning," she said. "It felt like I had to because everything I was learning about him seemed unreal. Too marvelous, like this magical circus had suddenly appeared in my life. Miriam kept me tied to reality. Until I wanted to slip away into his." Her voice trailed off. "And then, like idiots, we slipped up, and I got pregnant."

Elizabeth intertwined her fingers and placed them on the crown of her head, leaning back into her hands. "I couldn't tell my parents because my father is very religious and would have disowned me. I flipped out, but Chris was so calm. He kept assuring me that he had these visions that he knew this was supposed to happen. He said it was what would finally make them all accept me and open up the tight circle."

"Did he want to get out of the circle?"

"He was restless. He was tired of the secrecy and the sameness."

"You met them?"

"Once. He took me to this Victorian mansion in San Francisco. I think because he was revered, he was too cocky in thinking he could convince them to accept me. They were not happy to meet me. I didn't get the sense that any outsiders had been let in before. I remember how they all looked alike. They just stared at me. And it was like walking into a room with so much white noise, I almost couldn't take it. I was hallucinating sounds and colors, and it was hard to keep track of what was reality. But it was also the most uplifting thing I'd ever felt. It made me want to be with them. Chris wanted me to show them these telekinetic things he'd taught me how to do, but I could barely stay coherent in their presence. It was humiliating. I think that was the beginning of Chris pulling away." She said the last part like she was explaining it to herself.

It was flowing, like the story had been right there, close to the surface, this whole time and needed to come out. Faint chimes drifted from the main bungalow, signaling the end of the meditation.

"So you were pregnant," I prompted, keeping all emotion out of my voice, not wanting to scare her off from telling me the crux of what I'd always wanted to know.

Elizabeth crossed her arms tightly around herself again. "So I was pregnant. I hid out near Half Moon Bay, avoiding work, avoiding my family by telling them I was at work, stonewalling Miriam by telling her I was working on Chris. His visits became more sporadic. He finally told me his group was leaving soon but that they wouldn't take me. He said he was going to stay behind with me, and he genuinely seemed happy. I should have told him about the FBI and about Miriam, but I held off, thinking I'd tell him after his family left, when there was no danger of him changing his mind."

We began walking again, angling down toward the water, to the wet, hard-packed sand.

"I had you by myself at the hospital," she said. "I was so angry when he didn't come. Days later, he finally showed at my apartment and told me he'd been busy negotiating with his family to bring us with them after all." She smiled at the memory, completely transported to that moment. "The three of us together . . . it felt like I was getting it all. I loved him so much, and we had this baby together. My future was right there. I was touching it."

Elizabeth moved her head to the side, as if she were trying to turn away from an emotion before it spilled out. I was so scared she was going to stop there.

She cleared her throat and more quickly said, "Then he told me he wanted to show you to his family. He said he could only take you at first though. I told him that was hard, I was nursing, but he convinced me. He said he'd be back soon, and I handed you off with my backpack filled with clothes and diapers. Then he said 'I'm coming back.' There was something in his eyes, like he was trying to tell me something, but I also think he meant what he said. At least he did right then.

"I waited and waited. And then I got scared. A day passed. I called him. I went to that Victorian house in San Francisco, but it was empty. After a week, I called Miriam and she told me that she'd gone to see him, thinking I'd told him everything. I knew then what he thought of me. And I knew it was over. You were gone."

"Why didn't you fight it? Try to find him."

"I wanted to. I would have. But they were ghosts. I knew no one would ever find them. So I told myself it was okay. That it was better for you to be raised in all that splendor. Be with your people. Maybe you would be safer if you were more like him. And he was convinced you were going to. He said you were going to be important to them. I thought I could start fresh.

"But this hole opened up inside of me." She started shaking her head, and I knew she wanted to cry. "I can't describe what it's like having your baby taken away from you and not knowing anything more. A part of me did die then."

I could tell how hard it was for her to ask the next question. "What did they tell you when you were growing up?"

We'd drifted down to the surf, and the shallow water lapped at our ankles.

I answered, "We weren't allowed to talk about the past. As a child I knew I had a different mother, but I thought maybe she was from the tribe and had done something bad and been left behind. It's so stupid now in hindsight. I should have known—look at me. But I had no idea why I was the way I was until this past year. Why I couldn't seem to conceal the parts of me that were different in the same way. Why I had darker hair and pale skin. I think I told myself it was an aberration, just like they happen in any group." I realized I could ask her. "Why do I have pale skin? What's my background?"

"Irish." She smiled.

"What happened to the traits he brought out in you?"

"I wasn't functioning very well for at least a couple of years. Maybe that was it. When I tried to use my abilities again, they were gone. It felt like a part of me that was supposed to happen never did."

"You never felt like it was dangerous, how he was changing you?"

"Are you worried about what you're doing to that boy?" she asked.

I nodded, looking behind me at a small group that walked past and waved.

"No," she said, "the opposite. It felt like a relief. Like I could finally realize everything I was capable of and go one step further. I felt a whole other layer of connection to the physical world, to other people. What I wouldn't wish on anyone is to have this heightened experience and then have it suddenly taken away. To open up a new world for them and then close off access."

"Do you regret it? Do you wish you had never met him?"

Elizabeth looked out at the water, resting her hand on her clavicle. "I was positive that was the future I was supposed to have. It didn't help that he kept saying he saw it, this life we were supposed to have together and what we would be able to do together as I grew stronger. He talked about how our daughter would be the next leader and integrate his people into our culture. I believed something went horribly wrong because I messed up by keeping secrets. Maybe that's true. Chris also had an equal part to play." Elizabeth gestured around her. "But this did grow out of that. And, I think I'd rather know what I do than to have never experienced it at all."

More people were clustered onto the beach now, and I prayed no one would interrupt us.

Elizabeth faced me. "I had to believe that with him, you could get that—that those people could give you an experience I couldn't. I'm scared to know the truth because obviously you chose to leave it."

"It was like that in some ways. I have a sister. She's gone with the rest now. But I loved her." I wondered what Liv would think of Elizabeth. "You know he kept tabs on you."

"Excuse me?"

"You bought this place from him. He was Edgewater Holdings."

"Are you serious?" Elizabeth looked around, as if he were watching us right now. "I had no idea. I never would have guessed . . . but I guess that's why . . ."

"Why what?"

"After leasing this place for so long, I bought it for so little money. The owners approached me and said it had been in the family for fifty years and they wanted it to go to the right person." She shook her head. "That was totally made up." Elizabeth suddenly seemed miles away.

"So—Miriam Gottlieb," I said. "She wants me to come in, go to Stanford, be myself." I knew her reaction would help me determine my future. If Elizabeth scoffed, I had to consider leaving town.

"Miriam." Elizabeth shook her head. "Miriam is amazing. I guess I just never forgave her. Out of all of us, Julia, she may be the best person to take care of you."

"I don't need someone to take care of me," I said, automatically.

"We all do." She laughed and glanced around, as if looking for Emmanuel.

"I should trust her?"

"I've made a life of not wanting anything because I couldn't have what I really wanted. But when I look at you, I think you should want something. When you walk away from something you want with your heart, I think a part of you dies. Yes, it's risky. But is it worth it?" She smiled—as wide as I'd ever seen. It was beautiful. "I think the answer is yes."

JOHN

I never thought I'd see you again. It was easier to think that. I kept thinking about you and your friends playing around with your abilities together and how nice that must have been. I was alone in this, but it felt right to quiet my mind on and off the court. My skills were expanding rapidly, and I was playing impossibly good matches. I was still healing myself and somehow I was going to find a way to heal other people. I was doing the improbable and the impossible. And in doing them, I realized I was becoming calmer.

You triggered this, but I was making it my own . . .

Chapter Twenty-Six

The man next to me on flight 2224 to Detroit stretched and put his elbow on the armrest, brushing against mine. On my first flight on a commercial airline, I tried to relax, to not let the close quarters and the scent of coffee and cleanser overwhelm me.

Welcome to my new world.

"Cross-check," I heard murmured over the PA system.

It was crazy to go to Michigan and see John earlier than the start of the semester, but I couldn't wait any longer if I was losing him.

I closed my eyes, the hope and fear inside me wanting release but I had to sit perfectly still for hours. Admittedly it was an exciting kind of fear. I was headed down the untraveled path Elizabeth and Novak had decided not to take. If John would still let us.

I sensed eyes on me and opened mine, warily meeting the curious pair belonging to a fashionable-looking girl across the aisle. I closed my eyes again, wondering if I'd been recognized. I wore a baseball hat of John's that I'd found at the bottom of my bag, and it still smelled slightly like him: a citrus-scented sunscreen mixed with sweat.

All through the airport, I'd hurried to make the direct flight to Detroit and for the first time all summer, I'd forgotten to worry about who might be watching. I'd used cash to pay for my ticket, but I'd used my full name and shown my ID to the ticket agent. I was on their manifest if anyone wanted to find me.

Donna was likely keeping tabs on me at the Rosewood, but I'd made arrangements. So as far as she knew, I was sitting back in my hotel room, running up my bill.

I shifted uncomfortably in my seat, trying to stretch out my legs. What was I going to say to John when I first saw him? I knew I should get in and out of Michigan and be back at the Rosewood as fast as possible. We weren't out of the woods yet, but we were so close, and nothing, not one suspicious thing had happened since the photographer incident back in June that would lead me to believe my family knew about John. Unless I'd missed something.

I couldn't relax. I pitched forward, searching through the airline magazines in the seat pocket. There wasn't anything that could hold my attention. I glanced at the paper my seatmate was holding, thinking I could read along without him knowing.

Unfortunately, it was the sports section instead of my preferred world news. Just as my attention drifted from the front page, out of the corner of my eye, in a bold headline was: John Ford.

I asked to borrow the paper and scoured the slim story on the front.

> Texas high school graduate, John Ford, attending Stanford in the fall, ranks number seventeen in junior tennis in his state. In the wake of his win at the Boys' National Clay Court Championships, he has gone on to the National Boys' Tennis Championships in Kalamazoo and skyrocketed into the semifinals, beating many of the nation's best players with near perfect games, wowing gathering crowds, and becoming the most talked about junior player in years.

It continued onto another page, accompanied by a photo. What John was doing would have made headlines regardless, but it was superficial good looks that would keep him there.

After four hours of sitting on the red-eye flight, dying a slow death, knowing at that moment I was unable to protect him, I hurried through the airport and tried to keep my patience as I waited for the car service that would take me the two hours west to Kalamazoo and Stowe Stadium.

Flags welcoming the USTA National Boys' Championships to Kalamazoo College's Stowe Stadium flew above me as I made my way to John. For the semis, he was playing on center court with stadium seating, much grander than the courts where I'd seen him play regional tournaments.

There was a media tower in the background and the air was muggy. Families milled about this epicenter of junior tennis. This tournament was the penultimate dream for the kids who had been playing since before they could remember.

Entering the stadium, I found the Ford family almost immediately. All four of them were gathered together, gazing down at center court. When they began to walk together, Alex had his head bent, trying to hear what Kathleen was saying to him. Taro and John walked behind them, Taro's hand on John's back. Alex turned his head and said something to John over his shoulder, making John smile.

I'd imagined running up to John the second I saw him, but now something held me back as I watched their family.

Right then I wanted to leave. I felt like I was from the wrong planet, that I was all wrong, that I wasn't worthy of John or his family. I remembered this feeling; it was how I'd felt around my family.

I decided I was never going to feel that way again.

The family splintered off into different directions, but Alex lagged behind, stopping to check his phone.

When I approached him, his reaction was the opposite of what I was expecting.

"You're here," Alex said with great relief. "I don't know what's going on, but something's going on. It's becoming obvious. I'm proud of him but . . ."

"Do you know where he's headed?"

"Locker room. He has a match in ten minutes. Maybe wait until after."

"I don't think it can wait."

Alex thought for a moment. "Yeah, go."

When I found the locker rooms, there was a gathering on the men's side, as if a VIP was about to exit at any moment.

"Allie?" I said, surprised to see a familiar face although

we had never officially met. I recognized her from the graduation party in June and because she had lived large in my mind that entire weekend until she'd left. "What are *you* doing here?"

She reared her head a bit at my question, taken aback at my rude tone.

"I've known John since kindergarten. My family came to see him play in the semis," she said evenly.

"No, I mean, what are you doing right outside the locker room door?"

"Wishing him luck." There were three other girls hovering at the edge of the locker room. John had fans. The others were now looking curiously at Allie and me.

"What are you doing in Michigan?" she asked. "I thought you and John broke up." She said this stonefaced.

Oh. In the background, the crowd on a nearby court gasped and then started clapping. Before I could think of how to respond to Allie, there was a bustle of activity at the entrance of the locker room. A silver-haired gentleman walked out, and then gestured broadly to the people behind him to tell them to proceed.

John emerged, head down, with a stride that said he was going to a job. Right away, I saw that John had that *thing* fully now—that star power.

Allie walked forward and approached John's official entourage. Then a man scooted in front of Allie, blocking her. A flash from his camera went off, surprising everyone.

"This is a private area," one of the tournament officials in a staff polo shirt barked at the small crowd.

John saw Allie and smiled his sexy, warm smile, happy

to see her. Then he saw me. A curtain immediately dropped over his expression.

"John!"

He paused briefly and then kept walking. The event organizers stared at me.

Allie muttered under her breath, "Leave him alone."

"John," I said louder, more insistently. Everyone in the small space stared at me.

John looked like he was going to ignore me, but then he paused and turned around, confusing his escorts. He walked the fifteen feet back to me.

"*What?*" he demanded, softly. "Why are you *here?*"

"I came here for you." Everyone heard me. John didn't say a word. "I got your text, but then you wouldn't answer my calls . . ." I drifted off, aware of our audience. It was weird to stand across from John and not touch him, but I knew he would flinch.

"What text?"

"The one that said you wanted to talk to me after I went to Stanford," I said impatiently, knowing we didn't have much time. I saw one of the escorts flick out his wrist and look at his gold watch.

"I didn't send that," John said blandly.

"What do you mean?" I asked, but I didn't have time to address it. "Look, nothing happened between me and him. So don't do this. Don't let this be a fuck-you to me. Please stop. What if you win this and go to the US Open? You're already drawing a lot more attention to yourself."

"No."

"It's not a joke," I said in a serious voice. I touched his

back, already lightly sweating beneath his white tennis shirt. "We agreed."

"You broke all our agreements," he said and walked away.

The standing ovation rode through the crowd like a wave, everyone around me rising when John stepped onto the court below. He was the story, the sweetheart from Austin, Texas, who'd decimated a handful of the nation's best juniors.

John didn't react to the crowd as he walked onto the court with his tennis bag slung over his shoulder. He set it down on a bench. Then, he did smile, and his vibe was modest, which ingratiated him even more to his audience. From the few matches I'd actually watched John play, he always seemed like this—relaxed. Back when I first read his mind, I'd realized what a mess of stress he was on the inside. I would have killed to know what he was thinking now. Angus was right, now I could sense that John had an energy, a kind of humming vibration; it was similar to the sensation I had this summer when Angus was near.

Match play commenced, and John was sleek, covering the court in seconds, making it look easy, like he'd been born for this. He seemed so free as he played. But I also felt like I didn't know him—the boy who'd been losing high school practice matches when I first met him about a year ago now wasn't losing a point.

John hit wide to his opponent—the number three junior in the country, an eighteen-year-old from Los Angeles with an almost identical build to John's—toying with him, hitting from his backhand to his forehand over and over again in a falsely reassuring, hypnotic rally, the tension becoming almost unbearable as we anticipated it ending any moment.

When John won the point, the crowd rose to its feet again, a catharsis after the collective holding of breath. But everyone kept holding their breath because John was on a streak.

I stayed seated for what felt like hours, tucked tightly in the stands, a huge distance from the scene that felt like an endless, unmasking spectacle. I had to do something before John won forty-eight straight points in the semis of the Nationals.

It was like the first time I saw him play in high school. I'd messed with his game, except, back then, I'd helped him win.

I focused my energy on the ball and did what I could to alter its path when John least expected it. His perfect second serve went out and he lost a point. The crowd was so disappointed.

John looked up and searched the stands for a moment, no doubt knowing what I'd just done.

It wasn't as if he hadn't been playing tennis almost his whole life. This was something he had worked and practiced for. I waffled. How could playing a game really be that dangerous? When John began to play again, I reluctantly stopped interfering. I couldn't do it anymore. I didn't want to take this away from him. I was also so tired of being controlled by fear.

I rose and excused myself, edging past annoyed tennis fans who craned to see around me. The match was just minutes from being over, and I needed to position myself so I could try to catch John on his way out.

The pathways were nearly empty as I walked through the maze back to the area where I thought John would reappear. People began to stream out of bleachers and fill in the walkways.

I thought I sensed John's energy and that was what was guiding me to him so I was confused that I seemed to be lost. When I finally found John near the locker room once more, his family had gotten to him first. Kathleen was holding his face and kissing his cheek and then Taro hugged both Kathleen and John at the same time. Alex stood back a bit. Trapped, John held his hand out to the side to Alex and the brothers managed to clasp hands for a second.

When Taro and Kathleen moved away from John, their faces showed how stunned they were.

"I don't know what to say about that match," Taro said. "That wasn't like any tennis I've seen you play."

"One more match and then the US Open," John said it like it was a done deal.

Taro paused and then, in a serious tone, said, "Just to be clear, taking this further has to be something *you* want."

I didn't want to approach the Fords, who at that moment felt more intimidating than the family I'd had. Probably because they were the family I wanted.

"Hi." I forced myself to interrupt.

"Julia," Taro nodded.

No one said anything for a long moment.

John just watched me squirm.

"You made it to Kalamazoo," Kathleen finally said.

The Fords were at the very least always polite.

"Do you mind if I speak with John?" The moment I said it, I knew they were annoyed that I was interfering during this historic moment for their family.

Kathleen looked at John, who didn't say no, just watched me passively like he didn't give a shit. Perhaps Kathleen didn't like seeing this behavior in her son because she said, "Go," nodding at John and me. "We'll see you in a few," she said to her golden child, and she and Taro headed toward the public area. Once they were out of sight, John walked into the locker room, leaving me and Alex standing alone.

"I need to take him out of here."

"What are you talking about?" Alex asked.

"You've seen it, Alex. At this rate he's going to win the US Open just to piss me off. Pretty soon it's going to become obvious that something's not right. Just tell your parents, he's with me. That's he's safe. He'll be at Stanford when he's supposed to be."

I expected a fight but Alex wavered. I could see how scared he was by the changes he saw in his brother. Then he said in the most forceful voice I'd ever heard him use, "Do not fuck with him, Julia. Help him." He turned his back and walked away, giving me his consent.

I rounded the corner into the men's locker room. It was quiet and luckily occupied by only a few junior players who took one look at me and left as fast as they could after I projected a sense of unease their way.

"What?" John said when he saw me. He was taking his time at the locker.

"Are you going to listen to me?"

He slammed the locker door. "Was everything you told me bullshit?" He searched my eyes, like maybe if he looked hard enough, he'd see something he'd missed.

"No! I would never lie to you unless it was to keep you safe."

He shook his head at that.

"You know me," I said. "Nothing happened between Angus and me. My God, at this point, he's like my brother. It was a risk traveling together, but I needed the help. I should have asked you. Not him."

"You're always going to need what he can give you, and you want him as himself."

I moved closer. "I want you as yourself. Look, this isn't worth it. Not being with you, getting in your way. When I just watched you play like that . . ."

I put my hand against his still-sweaty cheek. When he didn't jerk away, I reached my other hand to his face. Then John moved his head to evade me. I lowered my heels back to the ground but stayed close, resting my hands on his shoulders. He grabbed my wrists to remove them.

"I'm not going to be the asshole who gets lied to and cheated on by every girl he's ever with," he said, shaking his head.

"John, look at me!" He reluctantly lifted his gaze. His dark eyes remained cold. "I'm sorry, I should have been honest," I said, solemnly. "From here on out, whatever you want, that's fine."

John's eyes were still reserved, but he shifted, relaxing his stance like maybe he was starting to listen.

"I don't want to stop," he said point-blank.

I exhaled, excited that he was beginning to negotiate. "Don't. I'm not hiding anymore either. I'll help you as best I can with what little I know. Hopefully I'll learn more. In the very short term, we can go to Canada to lay low. Maybe rent a cabin in the middle of the woods. It's only a matter of days now. Please."

He was still holding my wrists. I was so close. I saw in his eyes the second he became aware of all the places where we were touching.

I heard some voices farther back in the locker room and automatically looked over John's shoulder.

John took the opportunity to extricate himself and walk away. "I need to think."

Shamelessly, I followed him.

John glanced over his shoulder, feeling me behind him, but he continued, ignoring me. I heard the talking again deep in the locker room, but this was my best shot until they kicked me out; I had to keep trying while I knew I might win.

He headed straight into the restroom area and to a urinal. Surprised, I quickly put on the brakes and ducked around the corner, back into the dressing area.

He was trying to lose me, but with my back against the tile wall, I called around the corner to him: "I need to tell you about Stanford. I tried to call you right after the interview like you asked, but you haven't answered any of my calls." I listened for a response. He didn't make a sound, but I could feel him standing still in the other room.

"I told you," he suddenly said. "I lost my phone. I left it at the cove." I heard him turn on the faucet, the shrill whine of the sink pipes reverberating in the wall behind my head.

"Then who texted me?"

"John?" My voice came out strangled, a primal, rising noise I'd never heard before.

As soon as he was done, I was taking him away from here.

As fast as humanly possible. I peered around the corner. The water was still running, and the towel John had been using lay on the floor.

But he was gone.

Maybe it was nothing. I didn't sense anything unusual. In fact, I couldn't sense anything at all. It was suddenly like the locker room was the most neutral place I'd ever been. I couldn't feel the heat of John's body in the room. I couldn't smell anything, hear anything, or sense anything moving.

I ran through the rest of the rooms in the small labyrinth, a high-pitched ringing in my ears. My eyes darted everywhere, half-expecting John to walk around the corner and ask what my problem was.

I returned to the bathroom and stood in the middle of the floor in front of the still-gushing faucet.

No one had walked past me, and there was only one exit.

I faced the bathroom stalls. Two doors were ajar, but a third was closed. I pushed it open and stepped partially in.

Then I looked up.

Like something not altogether human, a figure scrambled over the top of the stall and leapt. It happened in a millisecond, that thing crashing onto me, pinning me to the ground.

Smothered, I used my elbow and fought for an opening. I managed to pry myself partway out from under the body that felt immoveable.

"Come on. We don't fight, and I don't want to start now," the deep male voice said, trying to sound soothing.

Please.

If I didn't get out of this, John's life and my life were over.

In one burst, I got the body all the way off of me, climbed

to my feet, and kicked off the hand that tried to grab my ankle. Falling into the stall door, I staggered backward. Daniel, one of the thirty-year-olds from the family, faced me. If a Puri could look even more perfect than the rest, Daniel did. But he had a completely different skin color than before; he was so pale that blue veins were visible beneath his translucent skin.

My surprise cost me. Daniel lunged, his hand extended like a claw. In response, I flung the first thing I saw, telekinetically ripping a ceramic hand dryer off the wall. The dryer hit some kind of barrier and ricocheted back at me, smashing into the side of my head.

The entire world tipped on its side, and I couldn't hear. I lurched toward the exit. The moment I touched the handle of the door, the lock slid into place. My fingertips touched the door, and I exploded the lock. I opened the door and fell into the sunlight.

Suddenly I was grasped under the arms and lifted up into the air as if I were weightless.

I was abruptly dropped, hard, onto the ground and the side of my face smacked the cement. Daniel's sneakers hurried by my face just as a noisy group of witnesses rounded the corner.

I painfully rose to my feet. The people in front of me were blurry.

"Are you okay? It sounded like a crazed animal back here," a teenage boy said.

I realized I'd been the one making those sounds I'd been hearing.

"My boyfriend's been taken," I thought I heard myself

say. I still couldn't really see. I reeled to my right into a wide parking lot behind the facility, leaving chatter and debate about calling 911 behind me.

Dazed, I saw a fleet of three white Mercedes. I wasn't quite sure they were real.

A tall man ducked into the first car, and it began to drive away, the other two slowly beginning to follow, forming a procession.

In the last car, I saw Liv, but her long brown hair was now black hair. I was confused but then understood this must be a dream. Liv was twisted around, watching me through the rear window, her face growing smaller as the cars drove farther and farther away. I smiled and waved madly at her, swaying on my feet, knowing I would sit as soon as the good-byes were complete and the cars out of sight.

The three cars stopped one after the other. The scene felt like it was happening on a giant screen, which is why I didn't move a muscle when the tennis shoes swiftly approached. I held up a hand in welcome to Novak's friend, Nick, not understanding why he had a pillowcase in his hand.

When the pillowcase went over my head and I was tossed into a backseat, I still couldn't catch hold of a lucid moment. I couldn't remember what it was that was just out of my reach.

JOHN

For a brief moment at Kalamazoo, I had it all. I was still so upset with you, but I felt like we were going to be able to figure it out.

I believed you and I were meant to be together. I've always said I don't know why I went to Barton Springs that day I met you. It's funny to think about now—how drawn to you I was the second I saw you sauntering in that parking lot with your tall sister. Looking like you owned the world.

I knew what you said about me and your family might be right but I didn't want to admit it to myself, even as I was changing. Because, to be honest, I liked what was happening.

I'm sorry, Julia, for not listening to you. I'm sure you're not happy about being right. I know I'm not. I'm pretty scared.

I wouldn't take it back. Once I met you, that was when my life really began. Everything about me made sense.

No matter where this is leading, we had that time together.

It's crazy to say, but I think I should be dead by now. But I keep breathing, even with less and less oxygen.

When I accept that I'm underground, it gets hard to control my mind, so I'm just going to talk to you. I'm going to pretend you can hear me, okay?

Chapter Twenty-Seven

❧

I lifted my head, and someone gently pushed it back down. My face was damp inside the pillowcase, the air nearly used up. My body throbbed, my bruised cheek rested against a seat, and I could feel the vibrating of an engine. We were in the backseat of a car, I thought, before I went under, giving into the sweltering dark.

❧

My limbs were dead. I couldn't control them or help as I was lifted and tossed into the air, then caught and better positioned in someone's arms.

"Careful!" I heard Liv's distinctive, sweet voice. The grip on my arms gentled in response.

The person carrying me walked up a flight of hollow-sounding metal stairs.

The quality of the air changed, and I was dropped onto a seat in fetal position.

Soon the airplane lurched alive and began to taxi, lifting off quickly as if wanting to flee as fast as possible. The screech of wheels folded under the plane, and we were suddenly airborne.

I kept trying to swim to the surface, but the pain was so bad, I'd waver and sink. My barely suppressed panic seemed best avoided by staying in the darkness. There was a commotion in the back, the sound of tray tables being kicked.

"Jesus. How much more does he need? He's had enough to put down two horses. They metabolize it too fast."

Something clicked. In a burst of adrenaline, I was lucid. I sat up, clawing at the head covering.

"Whoa. Whoa. Hand me the syringe."

"Get Liv to talk to her. You don't need to give her any more. Liv?" A younger male voice called. I knew that voice.

"You better sit down right now," someone said scornfully. "You're only here because she wouldn't get on the plane without you. In fact, cover his head too," the man ordered just as a needle slammed jaggedly into my thigh. There was a wave, a rush, and then black.

Had it been hours or days?

The moment I came to for real, it was like being kicked high into the sky, hovering above ground, able to see with total clarity before crashing down to earth.

It was pitch-dark, and I was lying on a hard floor in a small space. The smell of natural gas was overpowering. And it was sweltering hot. When I rolled from my back to my side, the cage rattled.

My clothes were soaked with sweat. One leg still wouldn't move. I couldn't stop thinking that this was where I would die.

I'd tried so hard to hide John from Novak, and I'd almost made it. Or maybe Angus was right. They were always smarter, and they'd always beat me. It seemed laughable now that I'd tried to fight. If I'd known that all roads led back to Novak's visions, would I still have walked out of my childhood home that night? Who had I thought I was?

Where was John? I doubted I would see him again.

Maybe they would leave me here as punishment for hiding John. By first pretending Novak was mistaken about John and then by hiding him, it had been the same as deciding to let the species die away.

I tried to stretch my legs, but couldn't fully extend them. The elevator was too narrow. Claustrophobia began to rise up in my core. My thinking was quickly taking me to a place that would destroy me.

I lay my head on the hard floor, rattling the cage. It was so quiet.

John should have been by my side all summer. Not Angus. I had all of our time together in my memory. To keep my mind occupied, I thought about when John first told me he loved me and I'd been too scared to say it back.

It could have been seconds or hours later when I heard his voice.

I'm just going to silently talk to you for a while so I don't go crazy. I have to take my mind off what's going on. I hope you can hear me, but I don't want you to hear me because it would mean you're nearby. And I want you close, but I don't want you anywhere near this mess.

I tried to sit up. "John?" I called.

It was silent.

I realized John's voice was in my head. That meant he had to be near, letting me into his mind for the first time in months in the hope that I could hear him. But he couldn't hear me. I slowly leaned back against the bars, afraid to make a noise for fear I'd miss a word.

He told me everything that had happened to him while we were apart. I heard him start at the beginning of summer just after his graduation party and trace his way through tournaments, motel rooms, all the way up to Kalamazoo. He told me what he had been thinking and feeling even before we separated for the summer. And then how he'd developed his abilities.

I should have been there for him. I knew how tough it was like to go through that and do it alone.

If he was feeling what I was, that air was very difficult to come by, it was amazing that he was able to keep his thoughts to me so clear. And then abruptly there was nothing. At first I thought he fell asleep or maybe I fell asleep. But when I listened hard again, he was gone.

I'd lost all track of time. Periodically, the cage would unexpectedly lower. It moved in small increments, no doubt to terrorize me, slowly drawing me deeper into the black hole. It was disconcerting to have no idea how deep down I was. At one point I may have lost consciousness—it had been so long since I'd had water. The times I was alert, I'd try everything to mentally open the cage: to bend the bars, break apart the lock mechanism. I couldn't do it. Over time, my efforts grew weaker until I barely had the strength to open my eyes.

If I counted the passing minutes, I panicked. If I thought about whether it was night or day above, I couldn't breathe. When I thought about whether or not someone would come to get me, the space began to feel cramped, and I'd try and fail to stretch out my limbs. What undid me completely was thinking about John suffering. When I thought about them not giving John any water, I began kicking at the bars. It took every ounce of mental control to focus my thoughts and stay sane.

I was thinking about my mother and her beach community, listening to the rhythmic sound of the ocean in my mind when there was an abrupt, loud click, a whir, and white light suddenly flooded the space. My pupils dilated crazily, and I covered my eyes, waiting for them to adjust.

As they did, I realized the metal box I'd been in was actually an open-air elevator that had doubled as a cage—an adult-sized birdcage. I was in a mineshaft, and this elevator must have been used to transport goods, not people. Now the cage door was ajar. I heard a distant door open and the clicking of heels on cement.

"I need to check your vitals." Those were my stepmother's first words to me since I'd snuck out of her house thinking I would never see her again.

"I'm pretty disoriented," I said.

"It's the natural gases. And they also had to give you a huge dose of ketamine," Victoria said with remove. "Just stay still for right now."

She came closer. She was forced to touch me when she

held my wrist to take my pulse, but she dropped my arm the moment she was finished. I was surprised when she helped me to a seated position, leaning me against the bars of the cage. She handed me a canteen of water.

I couldn't stop drinking once I started.

"Not all at once or you may be sick," she said, annoyance in her voice.

"Is he okay?" I rasped.

"Shhhh," she said sharply. I realized she was listening for my heartbeat. Victoria wore fine clothing from Austin, which didn't seem to fit the reality of her new accommodations.

"If I'm this sick, he won't make it. You're a doctor," I said, implying some kind of ethical responsibility.

For a second, I didn't think Victoria would deign to answer me. Then, she said, "Novak is never wrong. You know that."

"I want to see my sister." The stark room tilted, and I felt an overwhelming surge. I threw up. All over Victoria.

She left without another word. Vomit pooled on the floor.

Throwing up had jolted me at least half awake and I had a moment of clarity. I needed to find John. I used all my strength to pull myself to standing, immediately falling to the ground, my legs not working yet. Using my elbows, I heaved myself out of the cage, my last connection to the world above. I made it as far as the concrete landing, but then fell again, my cheek resting on the gloriously cooler floor.

It was silent. A softly lit walkway with dirt floors and stone walls was before me. The construction was brand new, and the smell of gas was thick in the air. Straight ahead was a hallway. The door was open, and the hallway beckoned as if I were a welcome guest.

I must have passed out only to be awakened when someone prodded me.

"She's still out. They almost killed her," said a male voice I recognized.

"So do we still move her? Victoria said she was fine." It was a girl's voice, one I also recognized but couldn't place.

The male voice said, "I think so. Let's just do it. What's the worst thing that can happen?"

"She dies," the female voice said.

"Tell me where he is," I said. I strained to look up at the voices. It was Paul and Emma. One former Lost Kid and one of Novak's chosen ones who hadn't been told to suppress all abilities. I wondered if all divisions had finally collapsed.

"Is he dead?" I asked, scared to hear the answer.

"We can't say a word," Emma said. Standing just behind her, Paul shook his head ever so slightly, indicating that John was still alive. They were expressionless. Calm. I didn't know if they were happy or sad to be here.

"Tell me. Where is he? Please, Paul." But with Emma there, I knew he wouldn't. We'd been friends once, but mainly due to circumstances.

"Come on," Paul said. "Let's try it, Julia. Can you stand up?"

My legs wouldn't cooperate. "Can you help me up?"

"I don't really want to touch you right now," Emma said, willing herself not to breathe in the vomit stench.

Paul scooped me into his arms.

Emma led the way down the dark hallway, burrowed deep into the earth. The rock walls made it clear we were in a cave. Then Emma stopped in front of a steel-fronted elevator. She did nothing but stare at the panel and then the elevator began its crank of ascent. Paul adjusted me like I was a rag doll. I was so tired and resisted the temptation to put my head on his shoulder.

"You ready?" Paul asked me in a serious tone that made me wonder if this was going to hurt.

The elevator moved down slowly, as if I were a scuba diver going another few feet underwater.

"How is he?" I asked.

"Sick."

"Paul," Emma said.

"Tell me what's going on," I begged. "Please."

"You lost that privilege when you left," Emma said. "God, just let us get to the bottom. It's easier when you can forget we're underground," she said to Paul. I noticed she was sweating.

The doors opened onto a landing with hard-packed dirt floors and pebbled walls. The lighting was modern. It could have easily been confused with a boutique hotel or spa, not an underground compound. There was more space on this level. Halls were wider. We walked through a lamp-lit living room with two large white sofas on layered throw rugs and a large white orchid on a low coffee table. Expensive works of modern art that I knew Novak had anonymously bought and then stored now hung on the walls.

This floor felt different. My brain and body clicked into gear in a way that hadn't happened since my family left Austin.

You could feel the concentration of Puri presence here. But it had never been as palpable in my life.

"Oh thank God, I feel better," Emma said.

Of course she felt it too. It felt like my entire insides were growing warmer.

We proceeded down another hallway, but this one was different. It had one wall made of glass, giving me my first broad view out into the cave. Paul sped up, walking swiftly, but I saw enough.

The new Puri world was finally revealed.

The scene below looked like a strange, bustling town. The same symbol that had been carved on Kendra's body was painted on one wall. A lavish living room, not unlike the large one at my old family home, was the center of a labyrinth with multiple hallways branching off. The design was reminiscent of a luxury hotel located in the jungle, all of the touches meant to distract the senses from the fact that this was a mine. A waterfall poured down a rocky outcropping in one corner of the room. Likewise, there were living walls of succulents. It took me a moment to realize the lush, tropical plants weren't real. They were scenes plastered on the walls.

For the first time, I saw what it meant for the whole population to let down their guard. I hadn't seen my family in nine months, but so much had changed. You could now see energetic traces of light between them, a tangible sign that they were bound together as a group. No one used their hands. Water glasses gently slid forward. Chess pieces moved swiftly across the board untouched, both players sitting back in their chairs, eyes closed. There didn't seem to be any verbal communication. The adults stayed on the sofas, mostly in a meditative state.

But even from my vantage point, the energy felt like it was on steroids. It was like reaching the center of the maze I'd been feeling my way around in, lost, my entire life. This was what it had all been for. I couldn't help but feel the pull, to want to experience this self-sustaining space that Novak had been working on for years.

Instantly, I no longer needed to be held by Paul. "I can walk. What's down on that level?"

"That's the best part," Emma said. "That's where we live."

Paul kicked open a door to a utilitarian bedroom housing a cot, with a neatly folded stack of clothing at the end. A small bathroom was attached.

I knew I had to ask the question. "Are we sealed in?"

In the moment of silence, I imagined this being the place where I took my last breath.

"Not yet," Paul said. "We're waiting on *him* to acclimate to the heat and gases."

"So it's not over yet," I said, more to myself, feeling a sense of misplaced relief. Paul and Emma glanced at each other. "How sick is he?" Why had he stopped speaking to me?

"Last I heard, he was pretty sick. The ventilation is better where he is, but they need to get him down here with all of us quickly."

"Paul," Emma said, warning him to stop talking. What was the rush if their prized possession was at risk? There was something else going on. An outside threat.

"How long has it been since I got here?"

"Hours? Days? I'm not sure," Paul said. "Time is different down here. We don't care to keep track." Then he instructed me. "Shower. Stay here and try to sleep it off."

Emma made a move to leave. Paul lingered for one second. "Where have you been?" he asked.

It took me a moment to understand what he was asking. "All over. Colorado, Utah, San Francisco."

"That sounds nice," he said and then began to follow Emma.

"Where are we?"

"I have no idea. We were given the same thing you were—some kind of tranquilizer and hallucinogen. Something to calm us and help us get down so deep."

He walked to join Emma who stood waiting in the doorway.

"Paul!" I shouted, wanting more answers.

He looked over his shoulder at me, his beautiful blue eyes glowing, but his skin tone was that same sickly pale as Daniel's.

"Someone will come for you when Novak is ready," Emma said.

"Tell Liv I want to see her."

Paul clicked the door shut behind them.

AUGUST ... Sometime ...

JOHN

Chapter Twenty-Eight

Time did have a different quality here. Everything seemed slower, as if we were moving underwater.

I'd changed into the clean clothes that were provided—a borrowed slip dress that dragged on the floor since I was far shorter than every female in the family. I could walk up and down the corridor by my bedroom, but the hall where the elevator was located was now sealed off. I spent all of my time by the door to that hallway, listening for signs of John's arrival. I didn't eat the food that was mysteriously left for me once I set foot outside the room. I didn't sleep, waiting to catch the person delivering it. It was frightening to think I could be anywhere. On any continent.

It became evident immediately that I wasn't to have contact with anyone. That didn't stop me from waiting for my sister.

When a meal was delivered, it gave me a way to keep track of time. Three meals had been delivered, each the same—

a small plate of raw fruit and vegetables served on bone china. They went back untouched.

If the meals were any indication, three days had passed. I sat slumped with my ear against the wall near the elevator, listening for any movement outside the door. I was worn out from throwing myself against the door, trying to get to that large picture window I'd first seen when I'd left the elevator. It seemed as if the place was proofed against my abilities.

I wouldn't accept that John might have died. I would have—and thought I was—doing everything I could to keep John away from my family. Now I just wanted him to live.

My vigil was interrupted when I heard whispers of someone entering from the door at the opposite end of the hall, closer to my bedroom.

Jumping to my feet, I sprinted down the short hallway, knowing whoever had been picked to deliver the tray would sense me coming and slip out. I hadn't expected to see anyone when I rounded the corner, so it took a second to register.

Liv.

My sister appeared in the same long, black dress she wore the night my family left. Her hand was on the door, her back to me. There was a moment when she could have pretended she didn't know I was in the room and walked out. But she wavered.

Liv slowly faced me. Instead of regarding me with hatred, Liv looked at me with utter nothingness, like she didn't feel a thing. It was how we used to look at outsiders. But that was not just how we looked at them—that was how we truly felt about them.

Liv's blue eyes glowed, an aqua color against hair that had

been dyed black. As I took in the black hair, a bell rang. I sifted through the drugged dream state I'd been in, picking at pieces that may have been real. I remembered her presence at the tennis tournament, seeing her through the back window of the white Mercedes.

"Angus was with you. Wasn't he?" I blurted, remembering I'd heard his voice on the plane.

Traitor.

For a second I saw a flicker of annoyance break Liv's mask. I realized I hadn't even said hello.

I wanted to say, "*I never thought I'd see you again.*" I wanted to hug her. But my little sister was terrifying now. It was the way she was looking at me—the same way her mother did.

Just when I thought she would leave without saying a word, Liv suddenly spoke. "You *left* your family for him." She said it like it was the lowest act imaginable. She'd stumbled over the word family. What she had been about to say was "you left *me* for him."

"He's alive?" I moved closer to her. She didn't step back, but her whole body leaned away.

Liv clasped her hands behind her. "For months, I've wanted to ask you why you left. I thought it was for Angus, not for *him*. You convinced me you were embarrassed and he was nothing. You treated me like I was dumb that last night at the show when I told you you'd found him and that he was one of us."

"I didn't believe it! I thought it was crazy."

"You thought about yourself, not what that meant for me, not what that meant for an entire group of people. You made a conscious decision to let us die."

"How can one person save an entire species?"

"Novak says he will."

I leaned my head back and covered my face with my hands. When I lowered my hands, for the first time in my life, I hoped Liv saw every raw emotion on my face.

"John belongs with me out there."

"That's not how Novak sees it." Liv shook her head.

"What if I told you Novak's lying? You have no idea what he did to me, Liv."

Liv squinted her eyes ever so slightly. She'd been indoctrinated in this lifestyle, in these ideas, her whole life, just like I had. My sister hated me now. It was a joke to try to frame this as a choice between Novak and me. Still, I needed to find any crack I could because while chances were slim, she was my last hope for getting out.

"Did you know he kidnapped me as a baby? And that he tried to take away my abilities? And the boys'? That's why he separated our groups. He doesn't want anyone to be as powerful as him. Especially not me because that will mean I'm supposed to be the next leader. And I represent something different."

A type of small black insect I'd never seen above ground scampered over Liv's feet, and she hastily shook it off a pristine ballet flat.

"You knew I had power like Dad," I continued, my voice hoarse. "You even wanted me to be the one to bring John to him."

"Why didn't you?" she asked.

"Because I don't want this. Because I don't steal lives. We didn't used to be like this before Novak—kidnapping people."

"This isn't an abduction. This is a prophecy. We can offer him something he wouldn't have in his world. We have the ability to make him exceptional."

"What if there's a possibility we could do that out in the world? I've met people like us, Liv. He's not the only one."

Liv shook her head. "We're finally safe. I've seen what we can do as a group, and the world would see us as a threat. We're better, and we're able to truly explore it down here. Finally, there's nothing that can interfere."

"I'd rather live. I don't want to know at age eighteen that I'm in the same place where I'm going to die. We're really here because the group is scared. If you don't evolve, you die. That's what nature is telling us. But Novak wants to seal us away so we're his, perfectly preserved." My voice had grown panicky. "Help us get out, Liv."

"Why didn't you try to take me with you that night?"

I was so taken aback by the question, it took me a moment to answer. "Because you're one of them. I never thought you would consider going with me."

"By doing what he did in public, Angus made the choice to leave. And then you were next." Liv gestured with her hand as if Angus and I had flown off without a thought.

"How long have you been talking to Angus?" I asked. "How was he willing to come without his family?"

"Angus sees it differently than you. He's learned he wants to be here."

I remembered the glint in Liv's eye the last time I spoke to her in my bedroom on the day of Relocation. She had a look of determination I hadn't liked. Liv got what she wanted, and indeed, she had somehow managed to gather the people she loved close. Angus and I were back by her side, whether it was because she was stubborn or because she still cared.

"They were going to leave me behind, weren't they?" I asked with a rising realization. I remembered standing at the tennis complex, waving to Liv as the fleet of white Mercedes drove away. "But you made them stop for me. I'm not supposed to be here."

She didn't say a word. She just turned and left the room, leaving me alone again.

I'd told Liv too much, putting myself in danger. Since I'd left the family, I'd assumed I was safe from Novak as long as he never knew I had gifts equal to his. The last time I'd seen him, he'd believed I couldn't threaten his leadership, that he'd stifled my abilities by separating me from the other Puri kids for months.

So now Novak might know I'd found the person he'd been searching for.

I didn't imagine myself as this leader my father seemed to have felt the need to suppress. I'd always handed the reins to my sister, the heir apparent, when asked. I'd even protected them from the FBI, withholding the little I knew. I would have gladly left them alone in their life.

Except now I was being pushed.

I tried to calm my boiling blood. Every instinct urged me to break out and find John. But then I told myself that I'd lost to Novak already and that going forward, it was about picking up whatever pieces I could. John needed me down here. I didn't dare jeopardize that.

Whether it was intentional or not, Liv had left the corridor open. At first I was too tentative to go near the glass wall. It took me time to creep out, down the hallway, feeling exposed. That fear gave way to a high that seeped into my bloodstream as I looked through the glass wall in that drawing room. It was the perfect climate, every cell of my body coming together to make me just what I was supposed to be: a part of the group. I felt a seductive pull I'd never felt before, a languorous complacency.

I walked within ten feet of the window and began to observe below. If, *when*, John made it down, this would be his home.

Novak had always bragged, hinting at paradise. From what I had seen so far, this was his masterpiece.

The living room was filled with white sofas with straight lines and priceless kilim rugs in decorative patterns. The ceiling of the main gathering space was high, giving way to offshoots with much lower ceilings that must lead to other sections of what was beginning to take shape in my mind as a giant beehive. One grand glass chandelier was hung at my level to dangle as the centerpiece of the great salon. The people below were gathered according to the old groups I remembered. Victoria's father, mother, and others of their generation sat at one end of the great room near the waterfall. Victoria and Novak's peers were in the middle, taking up several sofas with Victoria seated at the center. At first, there was no evidence of the kids. Almost beyond my line of vision, I saw them along the perimeter of the giant room.

The separation between the two groups of kids—the Lost Kids and Novak's chosen ones—appeared to have dissolved.

Paul and George walked next to each other, shoulders almost brushing. The Lost Kids had retained their sleeves of tattoos, but otherwise they looked nearly identical to the other half of the kids, as if the entire group were morphing to become more and more alike, pulling each other into a homogeneous center. Their hair was still light brown, but the gold streaks were gone and their skin was nearly translucent now.

To stop my mind from spinning, from looking for any possible escape route, each new day I focused below. I studied the structure of the room, the twelve arteries that presumably led to living quarters and the food source. Different members of the group carried in silver trays laden with produce, and crystal pitchers of water were set on every side table. Novak had bragged that his paradise would be self-sustaining.

As I observed, I began to recognize that the days of my former friends had a pattern.

When the kids weren't playing games, reading books or listening to music, they walked a giant circle around the perimeter. They did this for many of their waking hours—only the younger people. They walked until the lights dimmed and everyone stood, streaming to different exits, leaving the center of the hive. They returned after a number of hours and resumed the same activities. Wondering if it was normal, I no longer slept and I didn't feel the need.

It could have been for exercise, but I wondered if maybe, just maybe, the walking was a coping mechanism. Something devised to stay sane in their prison yard. That would mean there was discontent.

After a while, Angus appeared. He was the first to look up to the glass, staring at me piercingly. Had they all seen me this whole time? If they had, they'd ignored me completely. I held Angus's look and sent back waves of hatred. He looked away. John was my soulmate, but Angus had been my best friend. These last weeks, from Austin to California, I thought he stayed by my side because we were each other's solace.

All of our old friends surrounded him like he was a king. He'd reestablished his place already. I wanted to ask him if he was happy. Of everyone, Angus had seemed the most open to living on the outside. Even more than me. The hope that began to enter my brain was put out before I could entertain it. Even if he tried, Angus couldn't go up against Novak. We were under Novak's microscope now.

Chapter Twenty-Nine

"It's time," a voice said as my door opened.

I rolled over to face him, my nemesis in Austin who had tried to corner John that night before Relocation.

I'd felt a presence coming, and I was ready—for whatever was to come. Because George didn't know how right his two words were; it was time to end this torture and know what lay in store. The best possible scenario was watching John from afar as he tried to forget his old life and adapt to this new one. Most probably with my sister.

George seemed to hesitate.

"What?" I asked, rising from my cot.

He didn't look well. His skin had the pale cast like the others, but there was also a grave look in his eyes.

"You want to leave," I said.

The words left my mouth and traveled to the ears of the number-one rule follower of all of us kids. George had never had a reason not to follow the rules—he'd inherited the best of everything. In a group of perfection, he was the tallest, one of the strongest, the boy the girls had always wanted. He had always been a favorite of Novak's.

I thought I saw a flicker of hope, but then, probably paranoid, George directed his gaze toward the observation window and seemed to close in on himself.

The last time I'd seen George, the night he tried to subdue John and bring him back to Novak on Liv's advice, he'd been pissed at me for messing up his plans to be a hero. I'd sworn that John was just a normal person, which I'd fully believed at the time. Now, I'd expected George to lord it over me that John had been apprehended and I'd been caught in a lie.

"We outnumber him," I said, fishing.

"Shhhh," was all George said in response. Then, "He said this would be paradise. What do you think?"

"It's a tomb."

"I can't hear that." George actually put his hands over his ears. I understood what he meant. Once you thought of it as a tomb, it would be easy to lose your mind.

"I have to take you to him," George said. "Come on."

I walked behind him back through the narrow hallways to the elevator Emma and Paul had brought me here in. How many days had it been? How much longer until John's parents realized he wasn't coming back?

The area grew less polished as we neared the elevator, bits of debris and fallen rocks on the floor. I looked up at the wooden support beams crisscrossing the ceiling as if it were a hasty patchwork job on a problem area.

I stood next to George as we waited for the elevator. He

didn't look at me when he spoke quickly, in shorthand, "Liv never told him about the bar that night, how we suspected back then. Play dumb. Let Novak think Angus just discovered him."

At that moment I was surprised and grateful for Liv's loyalty. "How did Angus get back in?" I asked.

"Liv said Novak has people watching your mother. When they saw your boyfriend show up, they approached Angus, and he made a deal in order to come back."

All of those trip wires I hadn't seen—Donna, spies watching the cove, and then, my best friend. I remembered a change in Angus's behavior when we drove away from the beach that last time. I hadn't really believed it when he'd said he wanted to be with the group. Now my heart couldn't fathom the depth of his betrayal.

The elevator arrived. George stepped into the spacious enclosure. I hesitated for a moment. George held out his hand in an act of kindness that I wouldn't have expected. I took it and squeezed hard as we descended one floor deeper into the heart of the mountain.

The doors opened. I was now in the salon I'd been watching, in the same room as my family. In unison, everyone looked at me, suddenly frozen. Then they turned back to what they were doing.

George kept me on the periphery instead of walking through the middle area where the older members of the group were. Wilted orchids decorated the side tables. The vents at the seams between the wall and the ceiling that made up what looked like a shoddy ventilation system were another reminder that this was an artificial environment, a bunker for hiding. They hadn't gone back to their roots nor was this living in nature.

From her perch on a leather bench, Victoria scrutinized me, eagle-eyed. The gazes pulled me to look at them, but I couldn't connect with any of my former friends. I was too intent on calibrating my walk so I could come face-to-face with Angus.

George led me to an exit and just before I reached it, Angus's progression around the outskirts of the room landed him, perfectly timed, right in front of me. He wore a grey T-shirt and loose olive-green cargo pants. He looked strong and healthy in comparison to the Puris who had been living underground for months. He had said he wanted to be back with his boys, and apparently it suited him. He looked at me long and hard as we passed.

It took all I had not to lunge for him. I had really believed he loved me, and I hope my harsh stare told him as much.

We exited the great room into a dark passage, leaving behind the fishbowl of Puris—so many and all so beautiful, you could almost no longer tell the difference between them.

The air felt even closer and thicker. George walked me through room after room of a substantial palace. We passed pods of living areas as we traveled down the hallways. Instead of mimicking corridors that looked as though they belonged in an upscale home, the halls were rough-hewn rock tunnels, as if the job had been rushed to completion. The passage became more difficult to walk through, tighter, the ground uneven in places with sharp rocks cutting through the earth. We passed a large window beyond which I could see an expanse of hydroponic vegetables growing under lamps.

"We're here," George said, halting outside the only double doors I had seen. The smooth doors coated with glossy white paint were a sharp contrast to the rock walls streaked with orange veins. "I'm supposed to leave you here," he said, gesturing for me to go ahead.

George slipped away behind me, beginning the long winding path back through the narrow tunnels. The lights along the sides of the tunnel flickered, putting me in pitch-black momentarily, like I was buried alive. With an outstretched hand, I found the peaks and valleys of the rough stone wall, orienting myself until the light came back.

In my heart, I knew I would have always been looking over my shoulder, wondering when I was going to find myself in this exact spot, when Novak was going to punish me for my hubris in thinking I could make a life for myself.

I placed my hand on the stainless steel lever of one of the glossy white doors. I was back to needing permission, and it did me no favors if I revealed my hand before Novak told me what abilities he knew I had. Novak was the jailer with the keys to John. I pushed, opening the door to my father's rooms.

The suite was smaller than I would have expected—almost cozy with low ceilings and dim light cast by two glass wall sconces framing a sparsely filled bookshelf. Carpets in hues of red were piled on the ground as well as oversized cushions, similar to the ones used for meditation at Elizabeth's beach. I'd expected a series of rooms where Novak and Victoria and probably my sister dwelled—much smaller than the mansion where we'd lived together but just as interesting and well appointed. Instead, I entered into a den, right off a hallway.

A man sat on one of the cushions on the floor, cross-legged. He was in the center of a ring of chairs. Two simple flower arrangements were placed on matching glass side tables nearby. He wore jeans, no shoes, and a long sleeve T-shirt. He didn't stand when I opened the door. His head was bowed, but when he lifted it, I was nailed in place by his gaze.

Novak regarded me, his prodigal daughter, with familiar eyes that blazed. But the rest of his facial appearance had drastically changed. I would have assumed he'd had plastic surgery had I not seen the photo in Miriam's office—the one taken of him with Elizabeth. Like in that photo, his hair was darker, his face more chiseled. Was this what he really looked like? Had he been his real self with Elizabeth? He was far less beautiful than he had been during the years I lived with him. Then he had looked like a sun god with his glowing tan, appearing half his age. Seeing him like this, the only Puri who looked drastically different, I wondered why the other adults were holding on to their Austin visages before I realized they didn't have to change their looks; they never left the cave.

"You recognize your father?" Novak said, his voice retaining its soothing quality.

"I saw a picture of you when you looked like this. From before I was born." My voice faltered. My knees knocked together. Staring at his new face but into the same eyes was terrifying.

There was something that passed over his features at my mention of a photo. I saw it—Novak looked like he wanted to ask me a question but thought better of it. For almost twenty years, he may have kept tabs on her, but he didn't know what she was really thinking. But now I knew.

"When did you understand who he was?" Novak asked. Like an animal, Novak leapt and had his feet under him so quickly that I took a startled step back.

"Understand?" I asked.

"About the boy? It was in my office, correct? That night you left."

I knew complete subservience was my only path to stay in this dwelling with John. I had to let Novak win.

"It happened slowly. I didn't really know until just a couple of months ago. And then I had no way of letting you know."

He didn't buy it. "What was it I said that night that made you leave instead of telling me the truth?" Novak walked closer, intimidating me with his proximity. He didn't look like my father, and the trace of him that had acted like it was gone. I was smart enough to know I was dead to him. I'd left him. It didn't send a good signal to the rest of the group.

"I just didn't want to go," I said.

"No one could figure out why in the world you would ever choose to leave. We all thought it was young love—you chasing after Angus. I was sad to lose you. You were my first-born."

His sweet breath fanned my cheek. "But then you stayed in Austin. Longer than I would have thought. I knew you were smart enough to evade the authorities and stage your own Relocation. I left you the money to do it properly and hints that your advisor could arrange it. So when you walked back into your mother's life, I was surprised. I had assumed you were finally sick of the attention and had gone underground. I didn't know you would have any interest in finding Elizabeth."

Why had he always had someone watching my mother?

"I was informed Angus was with you. And then I heard about this boy who showed up looking for you. I was curious. You always wanted to be one of us so badly, I didn't know you would have a romantic involvement with someone outside."

"But you did," I said, immediately wishing I'd kept my mouth shut.

"With someone special. That's what made me want to take a closer look."

"Angus helped you?"

"I had my helper make contact with Angus. I knew he and his family would do anything to be back here."

"Does Angus know you won't let his father back in?" I kept my eyes on Novak's shadow on the carpet, a garishly long silhouette.

Novak didn't answer until I glanced back up at him. He smiled, "You're a smart girl. I'm sure he's figured it out by now. Why are you shivering?"

I shook my head, indicating I didn't know why. Nothing should be bothering me. I was with my own father after all. If I were smart, I'd be expressing relief that I was here after a long, disappointing journey apart from the group.

"So when did you know? Did you read his mind, Julia? I need to know who he is. Just one of the few who try to be like us or is he the one I want?"

He wanted to know if the wrong child had carried out his vision after he'd spent years preparing Liv.

If I told him, he'd know I had abilities he didn't want me to have. If I kept it to myself, it would make a difference in how John was treated. As much as I hated it, I knew John was the one Novak had been seeing in his visions and he would be cared for accordingly. If Novak thought he was just another struggling outsider who was a moth drawn to the flame, who had some special abilities but would ultimately break, John would be treated like Kendra had been—disposable.

It was an easy decision.

"I did," I answered. "I read his mind."

Novak closed his eyes, and I could see relief ease his stance. He was going to deliver on his promise, the pursuit of which had weakened his power, had at times made him look like a fool. It had been the one thing that made his leadership vulnerable. Since he'd introduced my mother to the group and she'd been rejected, he had been trying to redeem his reputation.

Novak opened his eyes, brought his fingers together in a steeple, and placed them to his lips for a long moment, seeing me anew, not happy about the other part of what this meant.

"When?"

"At Barton Springs, the day we were arrested."

"Why didn't you say anything?" Novak's voice was low—kind even.

I kept my eyes on his lips and his bony right shoulder. "I didn't want to get in trouble. You said not to do one thing out of the ordinary after we were arrested. All I wanted was to be part of Relocation. But then I walked into that school and he was in my first class."

"Of course he was. Fate," Novak said, almost to himself.

I could see him calculating, now knowing how dangerous it was for me to be down in the cave. It was fate that we'd found John, but it was also fate that I was here, his successor.

The room was far too hot despite the fans strategically placed in the four corners of the close room, the ventilation inefficient in the most important room in the cave. The ambient noise of the fans thundered in my ears.

Novak approached. He reached his long fingers to touch my cheek and lifted my face with his thumb. I tried to relax even though everything in my body wanted to push him away. If I'd thought it difficult to force myself to fit in before—with my family, with outsiders—I knew this had to be the performance of my life. That's what it would take if I wanted to remain near John. I had to go back to who I used to be.

"Why were you with him?" Novak asked.

"I fell in love with him," I said.

"Ah," my father said. "That wasn't supposed to happen."

I knew better than to beg Novak to let John go. "I can make his transition easier. The way you did for my mother. Gentle instead of forced. I can help you."

Novak ignored that. The lights flickered again, putting us in pitch-black for a brief moment. "I heard about your actions when they approached you, you fighting back like that. You can do other things beside read his mind?"

I cleared my throat and shook out my hands, trying to draw out all emotion from my voice. "Not much. I can move things with my mind. But so can everyone else." In other words, I am not a threat. I'm a good girl.

Novak moved away. "I want to thank you. Thank you for bringing him to us. You executed the plan laid out for you. That's exactly why I sent you to that school. You were able to retrieve him for us when the rest of the group needed to take shelter. For that, we thank you."

This was the cover story. This was what he was going to tell everyone out there who wondered why I had been with John when they'd caught up to him.

I nodded, indicating my consent. I would never breathe a word of a different version. In exchange, I took it that I could stay.

"Can I ask a question?" I asked politely.

"Yes?"

"He's only one person. I don't understand why he means so much."

Novak put his hands in his pockets. "He's the proof. He's the beginning. He's only the first." He said this like I was an idiot.

"But, I thought—"

"I have my ways. I'll keep looking above."

"What about everyone else?"

"They'll be secured down here. I'll assume the risk. I'll be the one to draw them in."

He'd lied to them. Even if John and I had made it to Stanford, Novak would have still been at large. With an eye on me. I imagined an odd tug of war between Miriam and Novak, building competitor societies. I knew who I trusted more. If it hadn't been obvious to me before, it was now. If I ever had the chance to get out, I would throw my lot in with Miriam, who wanted to help me become who I was meant to be.

Novak brushed past me. "We need to get moving."

"Why down here? I mean you could have done something similar above."

"It's no longer safe out there. In a few short years, the

world will be a different place. You don't need to be like me to see it. The cracks are apparent now."

"If you've seen what's going to happen, why can't you do something? That's your gift. Outsmarting every system." I hated my father now, but I hadn't lost my little-girl notion that he could do anything. If he could be so reckless in Austin while not getting caught, I knew he was invincible and slippery, a fish that could swim out of any situation.

"I'm sick of people hunting me and my loved ones."

Of course there was the not-so-distant history of our people being slaughtered for their differences. Still, Elizabeth had said he'd wanted more. He'd been interested in figuring out how to live a real life instead of a shadow one. What had changed him so completely to lead to this? Maybe she had—when it seemed as though someone he trusted and loved had been hunting him.

"Elizabeth would have done anything to go to Austin with you," I said. "It's like she's been trying to recreate the state she was in when she was with you." Novak should know he had steered the course of his life based on false information about Elizabeth's character.

"She was a liar," he said. "She wanted to entrap me and the entire family."

I'd never before seen the look I was seeing in Novak's eyes. It was a wavering somewhere between interest and having long ago put something to bed—*telling* himself he'd put it to bed.

"She told me she was ready to forget her parents, change her identity, everything." It felt like I was talking about two strangers. Not the people who were once a couple and became my parents. "I know she was the first to show you that there are other people like us. They haven't made it as far, but they will. The difference is they'll be living their lives out there. If you'd stayed with her, you would be twenty years ahead of this—you'd be integrated into society instead of trying to keep the group frozen in time. You said it in Austin; this is just a beautiful coffin."

"No, this is enlightenment."

"But there doesn't seem to be any purpose." That drew his ire.

"The way you feel is purposeless? I somehow doubt that. You feel better than you've ever felt, am I wrong? Here you can use every advantage you have. The full expression of your powers."

"Why do you still have her watched?"

"It's time to go," Novak said, in one motion pushing me aside and opening the door.

I'd overstepped, unable to help myself. The course of Elizabeth's life and mine had been altered because Novak had made a snap judgment about her intentions. I felt strangely lighter knowing Novak had all of the information even if it was too late.

"Where are we going?" I asked as Novak led me through passage after passage.

"Do you want to see him?" Novak asked.

I paused, unsure if Novak was being sincere. "Please," I said with gratitude.

"He's in the zone you came from," Novak said, striding ahead of me down the tunnel. Maybe Novak was tempted to take me up on my offer to guide John through the transition.

I couldn't imagine Novak would have left Elizabeth alone for one second in those first days if she'd been allowed to cross the boundary and live in Puri territory.

"He's okay?"

Please tell me.

"I'll show you," Novak said with a forward thrust of his chin.

My heart rate increased as Novak's pace seemed to slow, his sharp shoulder blades jutting beneath his shirt. He strolled with a leisurely pace through the tunnels, as if he were taunting me, dragging out the endless walk through the thick air.

Novak bounded up a steep rock staircase, taking four steps at a time with the same uncanny animal grace I'd seen in the den.

It was a back way to where I'd been kept. I recognized the corridor of my quarters. Novak halted in front of a closed door with a small window.

"You can look through here," Novak said.

He wasn't going to let me in?

I stood on tiptoes and peered through the small square, my exhale spreading a fog over the glass. From inside, my sister immediately looked up and made eye contact. She sat next to a cot beside John's long body. He was lying on his side and had his eyes closed. Four fans were positioned right near the cot to cool him down. I physically ached, needing to get inside the room and be next to him. My eyes met Liv's, asking her what was going on. From what Novak had said, I'd imagined John had been awake and aware, the Puri energy seeping into his veins, making this experience a dream. The white room was more hospital-like than the one I'd been in, and I saw an IV hooked into his arm and an oxygen tank next to the bed, showing the foresight and confidence Novak had had that John would one day be in this room.

He faced the wall but suddenly shifted, moving to his back and placing his forearm to his forehead, a gesture I'd seen dozens of times when I'd watched him sleep in my bed back home in Austin.

I pushed myself higher on my toes to get a better view, ignoring Liv's burning stare.

What?

When she knew I wouldn't look at her again, I felt her stare fall away. Then I saw her lean forward, hair cascading, grazing John as she whispered into his ear. My fingertips whitened as they bit into the sides of the windowpane.

Look at me, look up. I reached down for the door handle and tried it. It was locked, but I began to pull harder and harder, jiggling the door in its frame, about to use my mind to open the door.

"No, no," Novak said, sensing it and pulling me away, his fingers like talons hooking around my upper arm.

Look up! I'm here.

"Julia, it's time," Novak said, knowing what he was doing to me. It was an ominous sign that he wasn't going to forgive or forget.

Liv was watchful as I rested my forehead against the window. I hoped she was sorry. I looked at John for one long second, wondering when I would see him next, knowing nothing was in my control.

Novak pulled me away.

My thoughts were on John as I followed Novak down the short stone staircase. We were in one of the veins that led to the center. I didn't care where we were going. I only cared about when I could go to that room again. We came to a stop in front of a frosted glass panel. When Novak waved his hand over a silver plate next to the doorway, the door slid open seamlessly. I took one step through and found myself back in the main room.

The small waterfall made a delicate trickling sound down one wall. Only about half of the people were present, mostly the kids, but the others were trickling in, indicating where they were in the cycle I'd observed. In this room, the group could finally let their guard down and do the one thing we'd had to be most careful of always—gather all together without fear. I couldn't distinguish between the hum of energy coming from the people and the ambient noise of the underground installation.

Heads turned just slightly as I passed, following Novak toward the kids and the circle they walked. Whether it was deliberate or not, he cut right between Angus and Paul. I lowered my eyes to their bare feet, seeing the edge of a familiar tattoo, the fray at the cuffs on Paul's jeans. I had a flashback of the boys at their Austin hangout, jumping the sheer cliffs into deep water below while howling with glee. They slowed their pace and deferentially let us cut through.

Angus was right there in front of me, but I knew it wouldn't do me any good to rehash every moment I'd spent with him, looking for signs I'd missed. It had happened and it was over; I'd look up and I'd still be in this place. The sooner I stopped resisting, the easier life in the mine would be.

But I couldn't help it. I caught his eye.

I expected a crowing look or his dead-eyed stare. Instead, Angus gave me a penetrating look. Then he tilted his head as if he were stretching; he looked at the ceiling and slightly toward the corner of the room. His gaze fixed on the floor again, before slightly shifting to the other corner behind his right shoulder. I returned my own eyes forward again, leaving Angus behind me, but now I looked at the room differently—not as a haven but as an engineered biosphere. The only thing in every corner was the ventilation grates that allowed us to breathe.

For a second, I entertained the idea that he was inciting a rebellion. But quickly I shrugged away that dream. Novak loomed so large, almost like a different creature, ruling over everyone below him. Over time, the group had relinquished more and more power to him and now he was in a position to do as he pleased to us.

I'd been following Novak unquestioningly, my limbs alternately wooden and fluid, two halves of myself battling over whether to keep obeying. I tried to stop thinking altogether and let the vibration of the room fill me, cure me of fighting. As if he felt me trying to join the group's wavelength, Novak glanced at me over his shoulder, his disconcertingly different face jarring me again. Immediately, the bliss washing over me burned at the edges, crumpling, eating closer and closer to my center. I felt terrible. He was the one making me feel this way, not allowing me to share in the group's energy. He was informing me he had yet another way of owning my life.

I quickly looked away to avoid his direct blue stare. But the dread didn't go away.

"This way," Novak said in a civil voice, as if he were giving me a home tour.

Someone was watching me, staring hard at my back, wanting me to turn around. I glanced over my shoulder.

Angus was trying to warn me. When I faced forward, opaque panes of glass parted before me, revealing two sets of elevators. The steel doors of both were closed.

Then I knew where Novak was leading me.

"It's time for you to leave, Julia."

I stopped, shaking my head. "No."

"You know you can't stay." Novak hit a button, calling for the elevator and looking above, hinting at his impatience for it to arrive. He wanted me to leave while there were fewer witnesses, half the group still not present.

"No," I said louder, horrified. I felt it—it broke those in the room out of their headspace. The room suddenly seemed much smaller. The kids stopped their walk. Those entering the room entered onto a scene. Others came out of their various states of meditation, alerted to what was taking place.

This isn't how it's supposed to end. It can't.

"Go," Novak said, like he was talking to a stray dog. There was a pause. Then, as if he were unable to resist, he said softly, "Tell your mother what you saw here."

Surprised, I looked up at him. There was a well of anger and retribution in his eyes, so thinly veiling his real feelings for her. He wanted me to tell her what he'd built. What a king he was and what she'd lost out on.

I realized that because of his one weakness—my mother—he'd let emotion override better judgment. Instead of removing me as soon as he found out Liv had brought me down, he'd allowed me to see the space. And by doing so, he'd taken a giant risk by bringing me into the same room with the rest of the family. Now that Novak knew who I was, what I had inside of me, he needed me out. He'd known my potential since I was a little girl. He'd just thought he had destroyed it.

I needed to get as far from the elevators as possible. Novak was four steps above me in the vestibule in front of the elevators. I walked backward, stumbling on the end of a throw rug, but still edging into the center of the room. I didn't expect anyone to help me, but it made me angry when the closest members of the group backed away, creating a large circle of space around me wherever I walked. The pariah.

Helpless anger kept neatly stored for eighteen years flowed out of me, born from the unfairness I'd accepted and made a life around. I focused on one of the vents Angus had wanted me to see, making a big show of it, making sure everyone saw where I was directing my attention. I'd always been made to hide my intelligence and any resemblances to my father from these people. It felt satisfying now to crumple one of the metal vents, making it fuse into itself in front of this audience.

A swell of anxiety ran through the room, now filled to almost maximum capacity. I wasn't supposed to be able to do that. It wasn't part of the story Novak had told them about who was chosen and who was not. Like Angus had once said, I wasn't the right daughter.

Here I am, Novak.

I looked at his still frighteningly impassive face. I'd been avoiding showing myself to him since he took me to his office and exiled me from the group. I'd once listened to him and trusted him. Then, I'd lost him as a hero and spent months hiding from him. What did I have to lose now? No matter what I did, he still found a way to kill my spirit.

Then, with no warning, someone pushed my back, propelling me forward. But no one was touching me. Novak was dragging me toward him, toward the elevator.

Fighting against it, I whipped my body around, dragging my feet, able to resist the backward motion. I couldn't end up in that elevator. Once I was inside, that was it; I wouldn't see John again.

Angrily, I squeezed my eyes shut. With my eyes closed, I could actually see the white energy in which Novak had enclosed me. I imagined myself exploding it, bursting it into fragments. With a jolt, I stopped moving. I opened my eyes. The group was looking at me from all corners of the room with the dawning realization that I'd just overpowered Novak.

Sensing movement behind the window above our heads, in concert, all eyes flitted upward.

Liv had appeared on the floor above, behind the wall of glass where I'd been quarantined. I didn't quite believe my eyes at first when I saw John join my sister's side. They looked like a royal couple regarding their subjects below. I watched John's face as he saw all the Puris together for the first time, in a safe space but trapped nonetheless.

My mother and Kendra and others had come before John, but immediately, it was clear to our group that he was different from other outsiders. He was breathing in dangerous gases he shouldn't be able to withstand. Not only that, he had the same visible traces of light around him as the other Puris, connecting him to them. And connecting him to me.

This was Novak's perfect moment. He had proof, finally,

that his visions were correct. After eighteen years of being doubted, Novak was showing the group that others like us existed.

John's eyes searched the room, looking for me. At least he would see me one last time. I wondered if there were a way I could let him know that I hadn't wanted Angus or the family I'd left behind. I wanted him.

"Novak's right," I said, raising my palms upward. "There are others like us. But they aren't hiding in a cave." I looked at my former friends, at Paul, George, Ellis. "Do you really want to spend the rest of your lives here?"

I saw a pillar supporting the artificial ceiling above the elevator vestibule and I mentally kicked it in frustration. Cracks spidered down the column. Novak's fear was just perceptible when I did that. This place was fragile.

In that preternatural way he could move, Novak was at my side in the blink of an eye. His face contorted as he grabbed my hair and began dragging me to the elevator.

"Novak!" I heard Victoria's voice bark.

My hair was being ripped from my scalp, but I watched Angus run from the perimeter of the room like it was happening in slow motion. He was suddenly upon us, lunging at Novak, knocking him as far back as the elevator dais. Novak crashed at the foot of the stairs, Angus on top of him.

Angus started choking Novak. "Go!" he screamed behind him. The Lost Kids began streaming toward us, dashing for the elevators. To my surprise, most of the kids in the family joined the wave, not just the Lost Kids.

Novak flung Angus off of him like he weighed nothing. And then he stood, unfazed, facing the living room full of his people. He placed himself in front of the elevators, blocking them.

I'd landed on the floor, and dazed, I looked up at Liv. Both of her hands were planted on the glass, and then she was screaming, beating the glass with her palms. Then she swiftly disappeared from sight. From my perspective, I couldn't see John, and I quickly rose to my feet.

To my surprise, members of the group, young and old, began to plant themselves between me and Novak, keeping me to the side of the room.

I stood and looked up, but I was directly under the overhang now, which blocked me from seeing John.

"Novak," Victor said. The former leader walked forward, two other elders from the group right behind him. "You're acting like an animal. We came here to get away from people's base insecurities and violent tendencies. If they want to go, let them go."

"No," my father said simply.

I felt the air changing. This had never been a forced situation. To be in the group had been the ultimate privilege. Why the insistence? Why couldn't he just let those who didn't want his protection go?

I understood it. Novak needed to believe that almost two decades ago, he'd chosen the correct fork in the road. Because if he hadn't, he'd given up so much.

Victor looked at Novak. "I said, let them go."

"Law enforcement is close," Novak said calmly, as if this decided the matter. And for everyone in the room, I was sure it would.

Novak turned to a silver panel next to the elevator on the

right. In his palm he held a silver key fob. He tapped it once to the panel and immediately there was a small explosion inside the elevator, curls of black smoke unfurling from under the elevator doors. Apparently, the elevators were too strong for him to destroy with a thought.

I felt it—the ripple of panic run through the group. Safety or not, in taking away our exit, Novak was sealing us into a tomb. No one would ever know where we were. The world would carry on above as if we'd never existed.

Novak calmly crossed to the panel to the last remaining elevator. Angus was closer and placed himself in front of it. I saw the terror in Angus's eyes, imagining what it would be like to be buried for the duration of his life after all.

His look triggered something in me. I ran through the group to the elevator. I pried open the doors and turned to face the entire room, holding the doors at the threshold.

Novak slowly pivoted to face me.

"You've always known it's me," I said to him, my voice hoarse, but I was oddly calm. "You've been keeping me down to make sure this didn't happen. But what are the odds that I would be standing here at this moment? I'm supposed to take us in a different direction. That's what you were supposed to do eighteen years ago."

Novak just watched me, studiously relaxed, like a cat watching his prey exhaust itself. But those closest saw the tightness of his jaw.

I didn't move a muscle or take my eyes off of Novak, but I kept silently saying to John, *I'm sorry, I'm sorry for everything.*

No one moved, waiting for Novak to dispose of me either in front of them or once I was shoved in the elevator and behind closed doors where no one would see the act take place. It was clear he'd become capable of either option. Even the large group of kids stood still. No one tried overpowering Novak. The room was silent save for the sounds of the water and the whirring of fans.

Liv ran into the room, breathless, making her way to the center. "It's always been her. She's the one in Novak's visions—the next leader," Liv said quickly. "Not me."

I realized I wanted them to know the truth whether or not they believed it. What had been the point of subservience to Novak, to all of them? So they would call me one of their own? I no longer needed them—or anyone—to tell me who I was. I knew.

Then I realized I was holding everyone's fate in my hands. By standing here, I was stopping Novak from sealing away the Puris, securing their way of life.

If law enforcement was close, it was over. After all these years, the Puris could be caught.

I suddenly felt overwhelmed by that decision. It was too much power. I almost turned to Angus for help but instead, I looked up.

John hadn't moved from the window. I knew I shouldn't take my eyes off of Novak, but I couldn't look away. Why was John so calm? Then I understood he was trying to tell me something, but I couldn't read his mind. Novak had purposely kept that from happening, keeping us separated by glass.

Abruptly, Angus belted out a frustrated scream. The glass wall suddenly came apart in one large curtain, falling below and shattering into a million pieces.

I glanced at Angus, amazed, before I whipped my head back to John. Then, in place of John's beautiful, familiar face, I saw a flash of an avalanche of rocks and dirt exploding into the section of the room where the kids were currently standing.

John had shown me the future. I took it as a warning to stand down when John showed me a different image, communicating with me for maybe one last time.

The image of myself from John's perspective flashed across my mind. I was lying on my side in my bedroom at the W, lights from the gold necklace playing over my face, surrounding me like diamonds. For a second, I was there again, in a moment that felt like a hundred years ago.

This is still who you are, he'd said, warning me.

All the noise in my head faded to the background. I understood I had to trust myself even though I didn't know where it would lead. I also had to trust that John could handle himself.

I faced Novak, doing the thing I'd been avoiding since one year ago, what I'd always been most scared to do. When I looked into his crystal-blue eyes, it was a relief to finally face him as the real me.

"All Elizabeth wanted was to be with you," I said. "None of this was supposed to happen."

I didn't release his gaze. Then, for the first time, I could see someone else's mind beside John's. As if he let his guard down in his surprise, Novak's mind displayed itself to me.

He was angry. He was also angry with himself, thinking he should have been alert to this possibility. I experienced his memory of my mother, buried deep. I got the sensation that she scared Novak. It was the same thing that scared him about me as well—that he hadn't seen me clearly. Surrounding that was a deep love for both Elizabeth and me and also his shame for having this weakness.

There was his ego, his unwavering certainty of his leadership and also the weight of responsibility for so many people. There was a stubborn need for control but also a boyish fear of Relocation and never wanting to experience another one again. I saw a glimpse of the one that haunted him the most—the one when he was still young, taking me with them, wondering when Elizabeth would realize we weren't coming back. Then Novak was inscrutable again.

It was the first time I ever knew him.

"It's over," I said. One way or another it was. Paradise changed completely when you knew you were a captive.

Victoria had come to stand by his side. Gently, she touched his shoulder.

Suddenly, Novak moved away from her and stalked toward one of the tunnels. The one closest to the kids. Confused, we all watched him go.

Move, I suddenly thought. *Move!* I mentally screamed to the Lost Kids before I started screaming it out loud. Like John had tossed me a baseball with the image of the explosion, I mentally tossed it to Angus, to the Lost Kids, praying they could catch it and hear me the way the group had once before.

Then I saw Novak touch his fob to another silver panel before he entered a tunnel. Seconds later, metal plates ground down from the ceiling, at every point of the star, covering each passageway. The movement of the plates disturbed the foundation, unsettling a large section of ceiling. The kids had just cleared the mound of debris, but a new onslaught of gas rushed in.

Novak sealed only himself in, destroying his paradise for the rest of us.

Chapter Thirty

The elevator shook. Packed in tight with eight others, I kept thinking it was too good to be true. Something else bad would happen. One hand trembled during the endless transition to the top. The other gripped John's hand so tightly I could feel the bones of his fingers.

When the doors opened, I didn't know where I would find myself or who might be waiting for us. It didn't matter. All I cared about was getting out. Judging by how fast the elevator made it to the top, we hadn't been nearly as deep as we'd been led to believe. No doubt, the tranquilizers and hallucinogens Novak used on everyone helped create that illusion.

Suddenly, there was fresh, cold air. I stepped out into it, letting it surround me.

No one else was there. We quickly sent the elevator back down.

It was night. I led us out into the moonlight.

"Are you okay?" I asked.

"No," he said.

John let go of my hand and walked a short distance away, taking in his surroundings.

I immediately wanted his hand back in mine.

There had been silent screams in my head when I thought that Novak had sealed the passageway where John was located, trapping him on the other side. That momentary terror would haunt my nightmares for the rest of my life. I wouldn't have put it past Novak to take one last shot at revenge.

John had met me in the stone stairwell where I'd run to find him. Without a word, he grabbed my hand and led me to the elevator. The group let him leave first. He was Novak's great hope, but a lot of things had just gone wrong. We had an outsider in our midst with natural gas flooding the space and he needed to get out. It was the first kind gesture I'd ever seen from the group toward an outsider. I still didn't understand how he hadn't seemed afraid.

It wasn't the time to talk. It felt like we had to take one step at a time; to make sure we quickly put a distance between this nightmare and ourselves.

It was taking an interminable amount of time, waiting for the entire group. The remaining elevator could only take groups of eight, packed more tightly than was comfortable, gas leaking in increasing volumes. The cave had been built in a hub-and-spoke design and Novak had just rendered the hub useless while making sure the spokes were sealed. He'd remain untouchable for the rest of his life.

The group who came out with us had been quiet but unable to stand still and wait, jittery to get out of open sight.

"Where are we?" I heard Paul ask George.

"It looks like Colorado," he replied.

"I thought we'd be across the world."

I saw the Aspen trees and felt the dry, mountain air. Novak stayed so close to home. He was crazy. And brilliant.

Angus had reached the top, Victor by his side. Angus spoke as he walked up to me, gesturing to our surroundings. "Remember when we passed through Colorado? I kept waiting for you to feel it too—that we were close. And then we got that warning in the restaurant. About being sick of our kind?"

Victor snapped his head to look at Angus. "That wasn't us," Victor said, confused. "We came from Austin, directly to the mouth of the cave."

"What do you mean, that wasn't you?" Angus said to Victor. Then he put his hands on his hips, eyes gleaming, looking like he was about to say *I told you so.* "There's another group out there."

I reared back and punched Angus as hard as I could. He jolted backward but stayed on his feet, fingering his jaw and looking at me while the numbers of the group continued to grow around us.

"You asshole," I said. John came to stand next to me, across from Angus.

"I knew you had it in you," Angus smiled. "I just had to get you down there."

"Don't tell me you planned that," I said, my voice cracking. I wanted to smack the self-satisfied look off his face again. I'd seen how scared he was. "Finding John for them was the deal you made to stay down there and get your family in. You led them to Kalamazoo."

Angus looked at me like he was explaining something gently to a two-year-old. "They saw him at the cove. They were even going through his phone. It was going to happen. I had to control the situation and make sure you somehow got down there too."

"That was almost it—all of you down there, me up here."

"Once I saw where they were living, I knew I needed to get them out. We needed you to do it." Angus moved closer to me. "Growing up, I wanted to be the next leader. Then I thought you and I would make a new world like the one at the cove. When that didn't work, I thought, okay, I'll beg to get my family back in. I'll try to believe in Novak. But you saw it down there. It was complete BS. And then I realized what I'm meant to do."

"What's that, Angus?"

"I'm meant to lead the kids home."

I looked over at Liv who slowly approached, listening to our conversation.

"Where's home?" I asked Angus, shaking my head.

"It's where you are."

When the group was entirely present, a natural segmentation occurred—the teens grouped together, the older adults separate.

I glanced at John, his eyes large as he regarded us all, no more glass barrier between us. Out of the cave, there was a general sense of the Puris snapping out of it. Nothing felt surreal anymore. If anything, the opposite was true—everything felt hyperreal.

Victor approached me, having never spoken to me directly before. "We're going to do what we're best at—we'll keep moving."

"But how are you going to just disappear?" I asked Victor. As far as I knew they had only the clothes on their backs.

"We always find a way," he said. "But we need to go. Now."

"I'm not running anymore," I warned. "I want to have one life instead of starting over and over again."

"Good luck to you then." Victor started to walk away. A large group of adults filed after him, no one thanking me, no one saying good-bye. They were calm, but their posture and utter silence indicated that they were on high alert and they were scared.

"I don't know, Julia," Angus said. "The general population wants to believe it's a single-species world."

"So you're going with the rest?" I asked, accusation in my voice. I felt John stiffen.

"We could find that group. They're out there. I know it." Angus motioned with his head, away from John.

John stood at my shoulder, his body language defensive. After all we'd been through, he was waiting to see if I would choose my family over him now that I had a second chance. John had always been scared I'd regretted my decision before.

"I can't," I said. It didn't come out strong though. More like a whisper.

"What about the FBI?"

"It's a risk. But most of us haven't done anything, and it seems we aren't as different as we think. I think it's worth it.

For us kids, at least. We have our whole lives ahead of us, and we might get a chance to start over."

Victoria soundlessly approached, laying an elegant hand on Liv's back. A light seemed to have gone out of Victoria. She'd just lost her husband, but she still had her daughter.

Victoria nodded to me. I didn't know if it was a thank-you, but it wasn't angry or accusing. It was almost like I was suddenly her equal. For better or worse, me, Victoria, and Liv had lost the most—our closest family member.

The adults were growing impatient.

"Come," I heard Victoria murmur to Liv. I steeled myself for the good-bye to my sister. The first had been horrible, and now I had to relive it. I had no idea what we would say to each other. She had helped take everything away from me, but then she had wanted to give it all back, desperately. In that moment, she'd wanted to return years of what she'd taken.

Liv looked from her mother, to me, to Angus. I was aware of all the kids watching what move she would make.

In a thousand years, I would never have guessed she would hesitate. I suddenly wanted to ask her, *Who do you want to be? The best parts of yourself—warm, giving, kind?*

Instead I said, "Thank you. Thank you for helping me." It had been a practice my whole life; I had never asked Liv to choose me. Now she needed to make up her mind—it had always been her battle to fight.

"We have to go. If we're caught, they may not let us stay together," her mother said, real fear in her eyes.

Liv looked from her mother to me. Under the night sky, I felt Victoria's energy pulling Liv toward her.

"What do you want to do?" Victoria stepped forward and put her hands on Liv's cheeks. Liv pulled her mother's hands away and held them in her own. The two stood almost nose-to-nose.

"I want to go with Julia," she said, drawing out the words, apology dripping from each one of them.

I wasn't sure I'd heard right. Then Liv said, "He always talked about our potential, all the amazing things we were going to do. Then I was brought here and that was gone." She turned to me. "You started something down there, and now you can't stop. Like you said, you're supposed to bring us into the world."

It was a lot of responsibility. But I knew Liv was right.

"Come on. Are you sure?" Angus asked, even though he'd always known my answer. "Oh, God. Fine. We're going with Julia." He took a giant step away from the group and began to walk over to me.

"Really?" I said.

"What?" John's voice was nasty. It made me want to smile that one thing was back to normal. Then John's body relaxed when at the same time, we saw Angus surreptitiously touch Liv's hand as he passed her.

I watched first my friends, the former Lost Kids—Paul, Ellis, Sebastian, Cyrus, Rob, Roger—and then all of the kids reach out to their parents who squeezed them tight in a never-let-go hold. But then, the parents slowly relented, helpless, and one by one, the kids walked to where I was standing on uneven, rocky ground until there were two sides: those running and those staying. It became cleanly divided between those under and those over the age of twenty.

Liv held her mother close, and they stood for a long moment. They whispered to each other, and then Liv pulled back. They held hands until their fingers had to part, Victoria walking in the opposite direction, not looking back.

We were all silent, watching the older group walk away until they disappeared from sight into the dark mountain terrain. It had all come to an end—the end of a way of life and of staying together.

Now we were solely a group of seventeen kids, almost entirely made up of the last generation of Puris, taking a gamble to have a bigger life.

"Where to?" Angus asked.

The wind was whipping up, the sky beginning to lighten. "I have an idea—I'll need to talk to her first."

Angus laughed and nodded in agreement, knowing who I meant.

At the exact same second, we all heard the helicopter in the distance.

Chapter Thirty-One

The engines roared, and the plane tore down the runway until it seamlessly took flight. I closed my eyes to avoid the stares, waiting and waiting until I could get up to change seats and finally talk to John.

We'd arrived at the airport in separate groups, dropped off by unmarked white vans. After Rafa and his pilot had located us in the mountains, I had a moment of panic. As they landed, I remembered looking around at the sixteen of us Puris, out in the open, so vulnerable. I couldn't believe I'd put all of us right back into a powerless position.

Rafa approached me by myself.

"You're here," I'd said to him, confused. He had been so disgusted when he said the investigation was closed that I'd believed him.

"I decided not to listen. I flew back to Texas and reopened the case."

"Then you kept following me?" I asked, incredulous, feeling the visceral panic and uncertainty of the group rising like a curtain of steam behind me.

"Yes. And then I lost you."

"What are you going to do with us?"

"I have always told you, your father is the only one who's committed crimes as far as we know. We aren't interested in the rest of you except for what you can tell us about him. But now you need to show me where he is."

When the SWAT team arrived shortly after Rafa, it had been almost as scary as what we'd just been through underground. Novak's words about what the government would do to us rang in our ears. I didn't want to let go of John's hand, but we were quickly separated. After a medic provided water and a blanket, Rafa led me to a vehicle where we waited for hours while the SWAT team explored what they could of the mine. From the radio Rafa used, I overheard that the elevator no longer worked and exploration was contained to just the opening of the mine. Rafa questioned me relentlessly, wanting me to retrace every inch of what I could remember about the space below. He thrust a pencil and a piece of paper at me and made no comment about my shaking hand as I sketched as best I could. When I was done, Rafa held out the paper, and I had the feeling he wondered if I'd made up what I'd elaborately sketched. It looked like a fantasy, the scope unbelievable. How could such a large, self-contained world exist just below us?

According to Rafa, he had been sweeping the area for the past five days. That was how long we'd been gone. Five days. It was hard to comprehend that there was a real, quantifiable number attached to an event that felt more unreal by the moment.

I'd overheard that they would be getting an evidence response team based out of Denver to begin drilling into the mountain. Rafa wouldn't believe me that Novak was no longer a threat, no matter how I explained that he was trapped.

After I'd served my purpose at the site, I was transported to a nondescript office in a strip mall with an empty parking lot where, thankfully, I was reunited with John and the others. Before I could speak to anyone, I was taken into an office where Liv was being interviewed by Rafa.

After harassing me for several months, once he finally caught me with the group, what he was most interested in finding out, in addition to Novak's location, was what had happened to Kendra.

"She was electrocuted when she jumped over my father's fence. Then they buried her," Liv told him point-blank.

I was so relieved Rafa finally knew for Kendra's family's sake. There was no reason to protect Novak now. He couldn't come out from the shadows and punish anyone for telling the truth.

Agent Kelly had wanted to know one additional thing. "Who are you?"

When we both remained mute, Agent Kelly had said, "Look, I know there's been interest in your group that's ebbed and flowed over the years, but just because you may look and act differently, we can't put you under surveillance. At this moment we're only concerned with your father. So as long as you are law-abiding citizens, you're safe."

It was a relief too when I decided to say, "I can only tell

you what we know. We originally come from Peru, but that's over a hundred years ago now. We can do some extrasensory things, but then, so can other people."

Agent Kelly looked nonplussed, like he didn't believe in that kind of thing.

After everyone was individually interviewed about Novak's whereabouts, Rafa said we were free to go. There was no other choice but to trust his word and his integrity. In order to release us, they needed the guarantee of a guardian for the members of the group who were under eighteen. I'd told him where we wanted to go and somehow he had made it happen. He arranged transportation to the Denver airport and our plane travel. Time would tell whether they forced us to disband, but for now, they allowed us to leave together.

The car I'd traveled in had been the last to leave for the airport. John had already been seated on the plane by the time I arrived, just as they were closing the gate. When I'd walked down the aisle past him to my assigned seat, I saw he had dark circles under his eyes from lack of sleep.

When the fasten seat belt sign mercifully went off, I jumped out of my seat and carefully made my way back up the aisle.

"Can I trade seats with you?" I asked. Paul looked at me, and wordlessly I handed him my boarding pass. There were curious onlookers. *What had I expected?* The pack of us walked aboard the airliner wearing an assortment of clothes from a Denver Odd Lots store. No one could have missed the incredibly beautiful and nearly identical looks of most of the kids. Not to mention the kids' saucer-like blue eyes, openly watching all of the outsiders surrounding them.

The last time we had been out in public in a group this size had been at Barton Springs. And this was a much tighter space, and we were right up close to other people. Maybe it would get easier and my instincts to separate and hide everyone would begin to relax. But for now, the trip was still interminable. Liv didn't help matters when she easily caught a carry-on from an overhead compartment that fell hard in the flattened palm of one hand. Passengers in the vicinity had already had their eyes glued to her before that happened.

"Hey," I said. John opened his eyes when I took the seat next to him, treading not so gingerly over Angus on the aisle seat. I was sure that was part of the reason John was closing his eyes. Of all the rows, they had to be seated together.

It was incredible that Angus was with us instead of remaining detained, in danger of being locked away. In the millisecond I allowed myself to meet Angus's eyes in John's vicinity, I saw the glinting satisfaction. All I could think was that he must have traded information in exchange for his freedom at the moment. From random bits of information Angus had sometimes dropped since he resurfaced, it was clear his father, once my father's best friend, had told Angus all he knew about the Puris' future plans and the way the money was hidden and flowed. Lati must have known it was Angus's insurance to trade if the FBI caught up to him. It would remain to be seen if this was the end of Angus's legal troubles. But I guess Rafa felt confident enough that Angus could be found and wouldn't run again.

"Hi." John shifted and fidgeted, moving the shade up, glancing at the cushions of white clouds before sliding the shade loudly back down in place again. We hadn't been able to talk alone yet.

"What did they say to you?" John asked, facing me.

"It was mostly sketching the mine. Then when I got to the office, Officer Kelly from Austin took me to a back room and questioned me, alone and with Liv. What about you?" I asked.

"Same—where I thought we'd come from. They took statements separately from everyone while the rest of us waited in a conference room. Then they talked to the whole group about helping them get some identification."

That was another good sign that Rafa meant what he said, that we were free to go.

"They must be trying to find the others," I said. There hadn't been any mention of tracking the adults. Seemingly, they'd managed to disappear. Victor was right—it was what they were good at.

"Are they going to keep searching for your father?" John asked.

"I'm sure. They at least want to see where we were. I told them they didn't need to worry about Novak anymore. But I guess they want to see for themselves. Rafa—Officer Kelly— is nonstop until he gets what he wants," I said, annoyed, but it was also kind of funny.

"Once I explained who I was, they handed me a phone and I called my parents," John continued.

I sucked in my breath but didn't say a word. I wanted to touch John, but I was aware of Angus. John's tone and body language were neutral, as if he were still in self-preservation mode, and frustratingly, I couldn't read him. I didn't want to approach too quickly, unsure of how he was feeling about me, about what he'd seen.

"I was berated for about half an hour by my mom," John whispered, not wanting Angus to hear our conversation. Which was in vain of course, since Angus could hear every word, though he pretended to be sleeping.

"They thought I got cold feet about being on the national stage and ran off with you. That's what Alex told them."

I couldn't help it and started to laugh. "I thought there would be a nationwide manhunt for you."

John ran his fingers through his hair and looked at me with exhausted eyes. "Not at all. It gets better. My coach said I had an injury so I'd save face. So it was all a non-story. Except for people feeling sorry for me for getting so close." John shook his head. "My mom is going to meet me at a hotel near Stanford. Tuesday is move-in day."

"Your family must hate me. You must hate me," I hadn't meant to push it, but I was dying inside waiting to see where we stood.

"Why would you say that?" John said more loudly, his voice gravelly and annoyed. I could feel Angus's smile next to me.

"Why do you think?" I said, very softly. "Look what almost happened to you."

"It wasn't your fault. I didn't listen to you." John leaned forward in his seat to shoot Angus a dirty look. Angus was now openly smirking, though his eyes were still closed.

"How did you know what to do—at that moment?"

John understood exactly what I was referring to. His dark eyes held mine. "Haven't you ever had a premonition?"

Then I realized he was repeating my own words back to

me. Last year he'd asked me how I'd known to save Liv from drowning that first day he met me and I'd responded simply that I'd had a premonition.

The intercom interrupted us with an announcement.

"Were you scared?" I asked when the noise cut off.

"I've never been that scared in my life, and I'll do anything to never be that scared again." John pulled the shade up again to distract from the weight of his words.

"Where does that leave us?"

John turned his head to look at me so hard I wanted to squirm. There was a long pause. "You are the love of my life," he said, staring into my eyes. His look held a mixture of assurance and annoyance. "Are you really going to question that?"

"Noooo," I said, backing off and smiling. This was our real first moment of being together free and clear. I knew he could see on my face how ecstatic I was that he was still sure.

"*You're* sure?" John asked, taking me by surprise. He twirled his grandmother's bracelet on my wrist.

"Of course. How can you even ask that?"

"It's still happening. It's going to keep happening, and I'm not going to stop it."

"Can I ask you for a favor?" I asked.

"What?" John asked warily.

"Just go slow, be cautious," I said. "Let me check out this Institute for Progressive Learning and see if we're really free."

Both John and Angus asked at the exact same time, "What Institute?"

It seemed a long time ago that I'd come out of that interview, and I realized I'd never been able to tell John. And Angus—he'd been long gone. Or so I'd thought.

As beverages were served and both boys restlessly shifted in the narrow seats, I outlined the basics, making them read between the lines for much of it, given the excessive interest all around us.

I expected Angus to start mocking me, telling me I was an idiot to trust Miriam, but instead he shrugged his shoulders. "It's a start," he said and then he got up swiftly from his aisle seat and walked to the back of the plane, presumably to find his friends, maybe to tell them what I'd just said, though he was acting unimpressed. He was feeling competitive, I realized. It made me want to laugh again.

"So you're actually going to go to Stanford," John said.

"Yep."

"I never really believed it. Am I forcing you into it?"

"No, it's something I really want."

"Where are you going to live?" he asked, reluctance in his voice.

"I won't stay at the cove, okay? But I will visit."

John nodded, appeased that I wouldn't be living near Angus if Elizabeth let him stay.

"Stanford offered me accommodations," I said, "which is a joke, so I'll just live at the Rosewood, the hotel where I was staying."

"Can I make a deal with you?" John grabbed the back of his sweatshirt collar and pulled it over his head before settling back into his seat.

"What?" Now I was wary.

"Take those accommodations, Julia. Start over. Don't hide in a hotel suite. It's not life."

I was already shaking my head. "What if—"

"Try it."

"What do I get in return?" I asked, joking. The plane suddenly shook, riveting from side to side with turbulence.

Without a word, John reached for my hand. "I'll be more careful. I don't understand it, and sometimes I don't know what I'm doing, but I'll try to be more careful."

"And if I say no? Are you suddenly going to be showing off? Global tennis star?"

"No." John shook his head. "There are so many other things I'd rather do."

"Can I think about it?"

John saw my worry and nodded.

Without Angus there, I relaxed, no longer attuned to their dynamic. I hooked my foot behind John's ankle and turned my back on the row across the aisle. John lifted the armrest, removing the separation between us, and met me halfway. For the first time in what felt like forever, we kissed, his hand cradling my cheek, my arm winding around his neck, his lips so soft on mine.

John pulled away first. When I opened my eyes, he was looking at me closely. After a pause, he asked, "Could you hear my thoughts underground?"

I gave a nod, expecting him to instantly make light of everything he'd told me. "Thank you for letting me in like that," I said. "I loved being there."

John looked like he was quickly sorting back through all his thoughts to me. Then he nodded like he was accepting something.

Maybe I'll let you stay.

Chapter Thirty-Two

"Here she comes." Angus knocked into my shoulder with his and gestured subtly behind him with his head.

Elizabeth, dressed in her oversize sweater and leather flip-flops, appeared at the top of the stairs, her dramatic dark hair tied back. She took the last five steps to see me off, transporting her into the civilization that resided right above the cove.

"Do you want me to come with you?" she asked, surprising me. Pulling her sweater closed, she looked all around. If what Emmanuel had said was true, this was the first time Elizabeth had left the cove in over ten years.

"No," I said quickly. "Stay with them." I moved to face the beach below. If I squinted, I liked to think I could see figures playing in the surf.

I looked back to my family. The sight of my mother and my sister standing next to each other was such a strange one. Liv had followed Elizabeth up, even though we'd said good-bye ten minutes earlier. I stood with the small bag of things

I'd left at the beach, waiting for my rideshare to take me to college.

"Thank you, again," I said formally to my own mother. I hadn't asked if it was okay. It had to be okay. This was the best place for the kids to rest up and the first stop in their re-entry.

"It's fine." Elizabeth brushed it off. Fifteen kids displaced a lot of income. But there was something different about her when she'd greeted us the night before, a gentleness and a light in her eyes, like renewed excitement, like a part of her had come back to life.

Whether Elizabeth liked it or not, she was a temporary mother figure. Like *Peter Pan*'s Wendy with her very own lost boys—and girls. The day she had let me and Angus in, after keeping young people off the beach for years, she'd begun to reopen the gates.

My rideshare pulled up across the narrow street.

I looked out at the shimmering ocean one last time, then picked up my bag where it sat amid the blackberry vines growing up from the sand and gravel.

"Bye," I said to Angus. "Make sure they behave themselves, okay? You behave yourself."

"You know me. Nothing to worry about," he said jokingly. But at my look, his eyes grew serious, and we had a moment of shared understanding.

Then Angus smiled. "You're like an explorer," he said lightly. "Come back and tell us what you find. Tell us when we can come too."

I watched Liv, who was staring at her feet, looking lost.

"I'll be back," I told her for the millionth time.

She nodded her understanding, but she pursed her lips,

wanting to hold emotion inside. We had a long way to go before we felt at ease with each other, but we knew we had saved each other's lives. Our bond had survived Novak's ideals, her mother's jealousy, our own resentments.

"Thank you again, Elizabeth," I said, looking over my shoulder at my ride, ready to say a quick, painless good-bye.

When I was met with silence, I glanced at Elizabeth. She stood utterly still, making eye contact with someone across the street. I whipped around. All I saw was a beat-up yellow car pull away from the curb and the barest glimpse of a profile before it was gone. I wasn't sure if it had been a man or a woman driving.

"Someone you know?" I asked.

"No, no. I don't think so," Elizabeth said quickly.

I felt my driver's impatience behind me.

My last smile was forced. I turned and left them behind me, getting into the car with a stranger who had no idea he was delivering me to the next chapter of my life. I didn't look back.

The drive was clear as we sped down 280, sandwiched between rolling brown hills, passing the Crystal Springs reservoir. For the first twenty minutes, I pretended I wasn't going anywhere special. I allowed myself twenty minutes until I let myself worry. The twenty minutes went fast.

My heart began pounding when the driver took the exit that said Sand Hill Road and merged onto the wide road with its expansive view, heading downhill. I saw my former home, the Rosewood, pass outside my window. It took everything I had to not tell the driver to go back when the car swung a right onto Alameda, leading us directly into campus by way of the back roads bordered by oak trees, palm trees, and pine.

The driver double-parked under a eucalyptus tree and wordlessly got out, rounding the car to retrieve my one small bag from the trunk. After all of those riches, I'd arrived at college with almost nothing. The situation could be remedied, but I'd come to realize how little I needed.

It was still early in the day. Outside the car window, I could see banners of welcome hanging from buildings, students teeming down the street with their parents, carrying and wheeling belongings. I heard strains of greetings and introductions.

I opened the heavy car door and forced myself to get out, stepping onto dirt and pine needles. Bikes zoomed by, proving there was a rhythm to daily life here I didn't understand yet but would eventually learn if I was willing.

I took my belongings from the driver and thanked him. Then, carefully, I picked my way across the road, wondering if I looked as conspicuously alone and clueless as I felt.

I approached my new living space in Roble Hall, a Beaux Arts–style historic building with vines creeping over the façade. Suddenly, I couldn't imagine myself ever going through with this.

I instantly knew someone was watching me. I looked around and saw him. John, leaning nonchalantly against the pillar by the front door under the letter "B" spelling out Roble across the residence hall.

I couldn't believe he'd come.

"I thought you had practice?" I said, trying to act normal, which was impossible with the huge smile on my face.

"I have fifteen minutes. I had to see for myself if you'd actually show."

"I promised," I said. John and I looked at each other steadily. It had seemed like an impossible promise.

"Dr. Gottlieb just introduced herself to me."

Across the narrow street, an older woman with a head-scarf tied neatly under her chin stood next to a light-blue bike sporting a metal basket. *Miriam.* I nodded to her. With formality, she nodded back. She climbed on her bicycle and kicked off, standing on the pedals to gather momentum before blending in to the crowd.

"Hey. Sorry, I'm late." John's mom surprised me when she walked up to join us. "It is impossible to park."

"You have to go already?" I looked to John, assuming his mother had come to take him to his first practice.

"I thought I could help you move in," Kathleen volunteered.

I straightened, surprised. "You don't have to."

"I want to." She seemed to mean it.

John knew how much it meant to me that Kathleen had shown up to greet me. She understood that I didn't have someone like her in my life. Someone motherly. I nodded, not trusting my voice.

"Honey, why don't you walk Julia inside? I just have to call Dad, then I'll meet you up there. What's the room number?"

John stayed close, but I felt completely alone as I yanked open the door to the residence hall.

"Your room should be midway down," John said. He walked next to me, moving behind me to make way for a passing student. The boy nodded briefly in acknowledgment, brushing past us. I turned my head to watch Ahmet go down the hall in the other direction.

"Do you know him?" John asked.

"I met him on my first visit," I said, smiling slightly.

John stopped at a single door on the left side of the hallway. "This is it."

I realized neither of us knew whether to knock or just let ourselves in. I could feel more than one person on the other side.

John tried the handle of the door, and it gave. To my surprise, he backed away. The unspoken gesture meant, "you go first." I put my palm on the wood door and opened it fully.

There was a girl with long, brown hair, wearing a hoodie, sitting on a freshly made twin bed, sandwiched between two parents who were talking softly to her. The woman had her arm around her daughter. Both parents stood when I entered.

I walked into the little room.

"Hi," I said, extending my hand.

All three of them looked at me expectantly, the room bathed in sprinkles of light.

"I'm Julia Jaynes."

Acknowledgments

To my talented and thoughtful editor, Monica Perez, thank you so much for being on board with my vision for this series and for making the books better.

Donna Spurlock and the entire team at Charlesbridge, your time and effort spent championing this story is so appreciated.

Many, many thanks also to my agent, Kerry Sparks, at Levine Greenberg Rostan.

Once again, Amanda Ward, I am so grateful for your editorial feedback and guidance.

For advice, research, and help along the way, thanks go to: Megan Frederick, May Cobb, Debby Wolfinsohn, Vivian Raksakulthai, Chris Dammert, Vanessa Verzandvoort, Jennifer Freel, Matt Gravelle, Crispa Aeschbach Jachmann, Susan Hewlitt, Maureen Carlson, Dini Snow, Elizabeth Kramer, Nancy McDonald, Kjersti McCormick, and David Weisenberg.

My mother, Kathleen Weisenberg, gets a special shout-out for giving me a crazy amount of love and support, not to mention considerable help with child care.

I couldn't have written this book without my husband, Jeff Gothard. Thank you for being a great editor and for reading the book in all its different iterations. Writing is a solo journey, but you made me feel so much less alone.

Astrid and Margot, thanks again for being patient. And for insisting on a dog named Spirit. Trixie will be in the next book, I promise.